P9-DWS-688

A Cowboy at Heart

CALGARY PUBLIC LIBRARY

APR - - 2013

A Cowboy at Heart

LORI COPELAND
VIRGINIA SMITH

HARVEST HOUSE PUBLISHERS
EUGENE, OREGON

Scripture verses are taken from the

- Holy Bible, New International Version®, NIV®. Copyright © 1973, 1978, 1984, 2011, by Biblica, Inc.™ Used by permission of Zondervan. All rights reserved worldwide. www.zondervan.com
- King James Version of the Bible
- Die Bibel, Die heilige Schrift, nach der Übersetzung Martin Luthers, in der revidierten Fassung von 1912 (The Bible: The Holy Scriptures, as translated by Martin Luther in the revised edition of 1912)

Cover by Left Coast Design, Portland, Oregon

Cover photos © Chris Garborg; Shutterstock / Eduard Kyllynskyy, Iakov Kalinin, dwcreations

Published in association with the Books & Such Literary Agency, 52 Mission Circle, Suite 122, PMB 170, Santa Rosa, CA 95409-5370, www.booksandsuch.biz.

This is a work of fiction. Names, characters, places, and incidents are products of the author's imagination or are used fictitiously. Any resemblance to actual persons, living or dead, or to events or locales, is entirely coincidental.

A COWBOY AT HEART
Copyright © 2013 by Copeland, Inc. and Virginia Smith
Published by Harvest House Publishers
Eugene, Oregon 97402
www.harvesthousepublishers.com

Library of Congress Cataloging-in-Publication Data
Copeland, Lori.
  A cowboy at heart / Lori Copeland and Virginia Smith.
      p. cm.
  ISBN 978-0-7369-5341-2 (pbk.)
  ISBN 978-0-7369-5342-9 (eBook)
  1. Amish—Fiction. I. Smith, Virginia. II. Title.
  PS3553.O6336C69 2013
  813'.54—dc23

                                                                    2012036282

All rights reserved. No part of this publication may be reproduced, stored in a retrieval system, or transmitted in any form or by any means—electronic, mechanical, digital, photocopy, recording, or any other—except for brief quotations in printed reviews, without the prior permission of the publisher.

Printed in the United States of America

13 14 15 16 17 18 19 20 21 / LB-JH / 10 9 8 7 6 5 4 3 2 1

Hide your face from my sins and blot out all my iniquity.

Create in me a pure heart, O God,

and renew a steadfast spirit within me.

PSALM 51:9-10

ACKNOWLEDGMENTS

A huge thank-you to Ronda Wells, MD, for advising us on the treatment of gunshot wounds in the 1880s, and to Cayenne DaBell for proofreading our German phrases. We also truly appreciate the support and professional expertise of our agent, Wendy Lawton; our editor, Kim Moore; and the entire team at Harvest House who worked so hard to get this story from our heads into your hands.

ONE

Apple Grove, Kansas
May 1886

The first fingers of sunlight danced across the tips of tender wheat plants that had poked through the rich Kansas soil only two weeks before. Jonas Switzer stood on the western border of the field, his face to the rising sun, and marveled once again at this evidence of the Almighty's provision. Last fall he had sown this wheat into ground prepared to accept it, and throughout the long winter months it laid dormant with no visible sign of the planting. But now it rose from its earthy bed to bask in the warmth of the sun.

Jonas knelt to inspect a single plant barely taller than his finger. Though he was not normally given to poetic comparisons, something about the crisp morning air and the smell of the soil turned his thoughts toward symbolic expression. His life was much like the single grain of wheat from which this plant had sprung. How many times had he felt dried and shriveled, a tiny kernel buried in a barren field? When his beloved wife passed eighteen years ago, something died inside him. If not for the blessing of his daughters he would have sunk into the earth and disappeared forever, his life smothered by a grief he thought he might never throw off. But as they grew, the joy they gave him showered his parched world. He learned to trust that somewhere above the trench in which he was buried, sunshine warmed the earth and rains fell to nourish it.

Then they left the Amish. Jonas closed his eyes against a wave of sorrow. First his Emma and then his Rebecca had chosen to build their lives outside the faith in which they were raised.

It is their right. Their choice.

That he knew, but still his heart grieved that the children he loved had not found the same contentment in the Plain ways he clung to. That his grandchildren were being raised in a lifestyle foreign to his.

"Pride it is that makes you think yours is the only way. At least they are Christian. Gott sei Dank!"

His mother's voice rang in his head, and a smile tugged at his lips. Her attitude toward the Plain way of life had been forever skewed by the few years she had spent with her *Englisch* husband. And yet he did thank *Gott* that his children and their husbands professed a Christian faith, though Bishop Miller would argue that their way was not enough because they did not separate themselves completely from a sinful world.

Jonas stood with a sigh. All he knew was that his daughters were happy and they lived their *Englisch* lives in service to the Almighty and to their families. They had showered his life once again with blessings, with fine, strong sons-in-law and happy, smiling grandchildren. With a full heart he formed a silent prayer of gratitude for Emma and Luke's two, Lucas and Rachel, and for the baby Rebecca and Colin were expecting, who would be born before summer's end.

His gaze swept the sun-bathed field. A breeze rustled the fledgling plants, creating waves that swept from one end of the field to another. He was but one small plant, but at least he had broken free of the soil and could feel the warmth of sunlight once again.

A movement in the distance caught his attention. Beyond the wheatfield he spied a pair of horses standing on the slight rise that separated this field from the wide creek that watered his small herd of cattle and goats. Wild horses, perhaps? Squinting, he stretched his gaze. Were those saddle pommels on their backs? Not wild, then. But where were their riders? With a glance toward the house in the opposite direction, where *Mader* no doubt waited for him with a hearty breakfast, he headed toward the horses.

When he was halfway around the wheatfield, something else came into focus. What was that post sticking up from the ground? Yesterday there had been no post. He scanned the area around his farm, alarm tickling his stomach when he realized there were many posts, strung out as far as he could see. And was that a *wire* strung between them? His eyes were not so good today. Sound drifted to him from the location of the horses. Men's deep voices.

Slapping a hand on the top of his straw hat to keep it on his head, Jonas hurried toward the horses at a trot.

As he neared the rise, men came into view... *Englisch* men, four of them in their buttoned shirts and snug trousers held up by leather belts cinched around their waists. They worked at some activity. It took Jonas only a moment to identify what they were doing. Two of them were digging while the other two wrestled a large roll of barbed wire off a wagon. The wagon's bed was filled with sturdy wooden posts.

He could hardly believe his eyes. These men were building a fence. On *his* property!

Jonas stood on the top of the rise, watching them work with his hands hanging uselessly at his sides. Someone had made a grave mistake, one that must be corrected.

One of the men with the wire caught sight of him and straightened. "Woodard, we got company."

Woodard stopped digging and looked up. He planted his shovel in the soil and hooked a palm across the handle, staring at Jonas with a measuring look. "Howdy."

The man managed to turn the word into a threat. Jonas kept his face impassive, but an alarm rang inside his ears. The four *Englischers* wore menacing scowls, and their rough appearance hinted at a familiarity with violence. An ugly scar ran down Woodard's unshaven face from cheekbone to chin.

"Pardon me." Jonas spoke in the same soft manner he would use to greet any stranger. "There has been a mistake. This fence is misplaced."

Woodard held Jonas's gaze while he turned his head to spit. "No mistake. This here fence belongs to Mr. Andrew Littlefield. Heard of him?"

The name meant nothing to Jonas. He shook his head.

"Whew, doggie," said his digging partner. "Them Amish really are backward, ain't they?"

The others chuckled. Jonas gave no outward sign that the insult had affected him, though inside his nerves stretched taut.

A man who would insult another would be quick to injure as well.

A smirk twisted Woodard's features. "Mr. Littlefield's a powerful man in these parts. He's your neighbor to the north. Moved up here from Texas to start him a ranch a while back. Gonna bring a herd of Texas Longhorns up from Amarillo."

"We will make him welcome."

"Welcome him, will you?" Woodard barked a harsh laugh, and the other men joined in. "Well, I'll tell you right now that the best welcome you can offer him is to get your livestock off of his land."

Jonas looked in the direction in which the man jerked his head. A little to the east, beyond the thorny hedge he'd planted to border the wheatfield, a few of his cattle were making their way toward the creek for a drink.

"Pardon, please, but it is my farm the cows are on."

"Now, that's where you're wrong." Woodard pushed his oblong *Englisch* hat back on his head with a finger. "See this fence?" He pointed out the length of wire that stretched to the west as far as Jonas could see. "This here's Mr. Littlefield's property. He's filed a homestead claim to this land. The boys and me been working all night to get this fence in place."

"But this is my farm, my home." Jonas waved both hands to encompass the land that surrounded them.

"Yeah? I don't see no sign." He glanced at his companions. "You fellas see a sign?"

With their smirking gazes fixed on Jonas, they shook their heads. "Not a one."

"Well, there you go." Woodard's smile did nothing to veil his scorn. "Looks to me like this fence is the only thing marking the boundary." He waved to the area behind him, including the creek. "That means this part belongs to Mr. Littlefield. And that part," he gestured toward the wheatfield and house behind Jonas, "must be yorn."

A flicker erupted in the back of Jonas's brain. Did they mean to take his farm, his home? The area on his side of the barbed wire was a fraction of his property. What, then, of the field beyond the creek, the one he and Big Ed had plowed only a few days ago in preparation for planting corn? What of the pasture where his cattle and goats grazed? Angry heat suffused his face, but he took care to pitch his voice so that none of the anger might escape.

"The land belongs to me. Almost twenty years have I lived here. A trench I dug all around, as I was told to do."

Woodard's eyes narrowed to mere slits. He tossed his shovel aside and closed the distance between them with a menacing stride, stopping only when he was close enough that Jonas could smell the rank odor of his breath. The others also moved. They went to the wagon and each picked up a rifle before coming to stand behind their leader.

"I don't think you heard me, Amish man," Woodard said, his voice as low as Jonas's. "This property belongs to Mr. Andrew Littlefield. If you want to go on breathing, you'll keep to your side of that fence."

A cold lump of fear cooled Jonas's burning anger. The message was clear. If he or his livestock crossed that fence, they would be shot.

Injustice churned like acid in his stomach. It was because he was Amish that these men did this. They knew he would not retaliate.

They are right.

Did Jesus not forbid His followers all revenge and resistance? *He has thereby commanded them not to return evil for evil, nor railing for railing.* The words rose from deep inside, placed there by years of repetition of the Confession that all Amish professed. Though his sinful self would love to rail against these rough men, he could not.

Maintaining his silence was the only way Jonas could keep his anger in check. Without a reply, he turned away from Woodard and began the trek around the wheatfield and back to his house. Behind him, derisive laughter rose from four throats into the morning sky. Jonas kept his head up, though his back burned from the weight of their scornful stares.

I will not rail against them. I will not dishonor the faith to which I have pledged my life.

The laughter stopped, and soon he heard the sound of shovels carving into fresh soil.

But neither will I give up my home. I will stand my ground, but peacefully, with my friends at my side.

He lengthened his stride, a sense of purpose giving him fresh energy. He would hook Big Ed up to the buggy and go to his Amish brothers for help.

⁂

"Ow, stop! It hurts, Katie."

Katie Miller looked calmly into a pair of reproachful blue eyes belonging to her young sister-in-law. "The bandage must come off, Hannah, else how can I see if the wound is healing properly? Hold still. I will be gentle."

Eight-year-old Hannah studied her with a measuring look, as though deciding whether or not to trust her. Finally, with a brief nod, she placed her bandaged hand again into Katie's waiting one. She turned her head away, face screwed up and eyes shut tight, her muscles tense. Seated next to Hannah at the sturdy kitchen table, Ella Miller held her daughter's uninjured hand, worry lines carving crevasses in the smooth forehead beneath her prayer *kapp*.

And well she might worry. The injury to Hannah's hand had not been serious until infection set in. By the time they sent for Katie, it had swollen to twice normal size, and angry red lines stretched halfway up the child's arm.

Katie unwound layers of cotton bandages, a half-formed prayer for the girl running through her mind. When she pulled the last strip gently away from the wound, she let out a pent-up breath.

"*Das ist gut*," she told *Mader* Miller.

A relieved smile washed the worry from the woman's face. "See you there, Hannah. The smelly salve that angered you so has worked."

Katie pressed the skin around the wound with a gentle finger. Thank goodness the swelling was greatly reduced from two days ago, and the red lines had all but disappeared. "Wiggle your thumb and finger."

The girl did, and Katie breathed a prayer of thanksgiving.

"By the good Lord's grace, she will recover fully," she announced, and then she turned a serious look on Hannah. "But you must be more careful when playing around your papa's plow. You could have lost your hand, and then where would you be?"

A dimple appeared in one peachy cheek. "I would not have to milk cows."

"*Ach*, what a girl!" *Mader* Miller swatted at Hannah with a tea towel. "Indeed you would, but twice as long it would take you. In fact, you can return to your chore tomorrow and see how you like working as a one-handed dairymaid."

Scowling, Hannah slumped in her chair and remained silent while Katie cleaned the wound and slathered it with a layer of ointment. When a fresh bandage had been put in place, the little girl tested the tightness by gingerly clenching her hand into a loose fist.

Satisfied with the result, she bobbed her head. "*Danki*, Katie." She looked shyly up. "Maybe if I hurt my other hand you will come more often. I miss you."

The words twisted Katie's heart. Since she'd returned to her parents' home four months ago, she had only seen her family-by-marriage a few times outside of the district's twice-monthly church services. But though she loved them, there were too many reminders here. She and Samuel had lived in this house during the five years of their marriage. At this very table they had sat side by side for meals with Hannah and *Mader* and *Fader* Miller. In the room at the top of the stairs, they had slept as husband and wife. A sense of grief threatened to overwhelm her.

She shook it off and tugged playfully at one of the laces dangling from Hannah's *kapp*. "If you do, next time I shall make the ointment doubly smelly just to plague you."

Hannah wrinkled her nose, and Katie tweaked it.

"Off with you, now." *Mader* Miller snatched a basket off of the counter and pressed it into Hannah's hands. "The hens have waited long enough for their breakfast, and the eggs need to be gathered."

When the child had skipped out the door, the older woman

set a mug of coffee on the table in front of Katie. "It is good to see you, daughter. Too long has it been since you visited."

Unable to meet her mother-in-law's eyes, Katie stared at the steam rising from the mug. "I know. I am sorry."

Silence fell. Katie glanced up to see *Mader* Miller's unfocused gaze fixed on something visible only to her. A sad smile tugged at one corner of her mouth. With a rush of guilt, Katie realized she wasn't the only one whose memories of Samuel wedged like thorns in her heart.

She broke the silence with a whisper. "I miss him."

Mader Miller nodded. "As do I." Her eyes focused on the window. "And so does John."

At the mention of *Fader* Miller, an uncomfortable knot formed in Katie's stomach. Though she and *Mader* Miller had grieved Samuel's passing as only a wife and mother could, their grief combined could not touch that of his father's. In the span of a few months, Katie had watched the man go from mourning to near-obsession with his son's death. A mournful cloud hovered over him, and instead of dispersing with time, it grew darker and denser and more distressful for those around him. Though he continued to administer his duties as bishop to the Amish community of Apple Grove, grief had made him rigid. Because he found no comfort for his pain, how could he give comfort to the families who looked to him for leadership? The community of Apple Grove sympathized with the devastating loss of a son, but they whispered that their bishop should attempt to put the tragedy behind him instead of wallowing in his grief. Thus would he advise others, but he seemed unable to heed his own advice. At home every conversation centered on Samuel until finally, unable to bear the constant reminder of her loss, Katie had moved back to her parents' home. There she had been able to begin to let go of the pain of Samuel's death, and more and more remembered the joy of his life.

Until today. Coming back here tinged all her memories with pain.

Mader Miller reached across the table and laid a hand on her arm. The touch was brief, only a moment, but Katie drew strength from the contact.

"Life is not meant to be lived in sorrow. You are young, daughter. One day the Lord will guide you into happier times."

Katie looked up into eyes glazed with tears. Much time these past months had been spent asking the Lord what the future held in store for her. Surely love such as she and Samuel had shared came only once in a lifetime. Had the Lord not given her a task to occupy her lonely days? She had begun to learn the ways of doctoring and birthing, and through that had discovered the deep satisfaction of tending to those whose hurts were physical and therefore easier to heal. And yet...

She squeezed her eyes shut. Was she to always remain a widow, forever denied love and happiness until she quit this world for the next?

Mader Miller's hand pulled away. Katie opened her eyes to see her staring through the window. "A visitor has come."

"This early?" Katie twisted around to look through the glass. An Amish buggy approached, clouds of dust from the road rising beneath the wheels.

The buggy rolled past the house and continued toward the barn.

"That is Jonas Switzer." The older woman rose. "I will put on more coffee and warm some rolls. Go, daughter, and invite him in when he has finished his business with the bishop."

Obediently, Katie rose and headed toward the door.

The morning sun still hung low on the horizon, its brilliant rays shafting through the leaves of the apple trees that bordered the Millers' yard. Mr. Switzer's buggy had come to a stop, and *Fader* Miller emerged from the barn. He stood erect, waiting for Mr. Switzer to climb down from the bench and stand before him. Mr. Switzer began to talk, calmly at first. Then he waved his arms, churning the air around him. Clearly something had upset the normally unruffled man.

I hope Emma and Rebecca are well.

Jonas's daughters had been Katie's friends since childhood. Though she rarely saw them now that they had both left the Amish and lived almost two hours' ride away, Katie stayed informed through their grandmother.

She slowed her approach, unwilling to eavesdrop on the men's conversation. But Mr. Switzer was so upset that his voice rose and fell, and she couldn't help but overhear a few snatches.

"...weapons...fence...*shoot* me on my own land!"

Oh, dear. Someone had shot at him?

Because *Fader* Miller faced her way, she heard his answer more clearly.

"You must go to this Mr. Littlefield and explain to him the mistake. Perhaps he will listen and respond honorably."

Katie stopped several yards away and politely turned her back, though she could still hear.

"You will go with me? I fear to go alone will result in violence."

A stern note crept into the bishop's voice. "You threaten violence?"

"From me, no. From them? They are *Englisch*. Their honor is different from ours. If two of us go—"

"If two go, they will see a threat. If one man calls upon his neighbor to discuss a shared problem, it is a friendly visit. Have Marta bake a *snitz* pie."

Jonas's voice grew loud. "You would send me to the home of an *Englisch* man with rifles armed with a *pie?*"

Katie winced. Mr. Switzer must be distraught indeed to raise his voice to the bishop. She would never have the nerve.

Fader Miller's reply was low, alarmingly so. She couldn't make out the words, but the tone was one that would have set her knees to shaking if it had been directed at her. The sound of retreating footsteps followed.

Katie turned in time to see the bishop disappear into the barn, his back rigid. Mr. Switzer stared after him, shoulders slumped and arms hanging at his sides. Moving cautiously, she stepped toward him, and he turned at her approach. A struggle lay plain on his creased brow and troubled eyes.

She bobbed a quick curtsey. "*Mader* Miller says won't you come in for coffee and warm rolls?"

For a moment she thought he must not have heard her. He stared at her without answering. Then he set his jaw.

"*Danki*, no. I must go."

She stepped back and watched him climb into his buggy. Seated, he picked up the reins and then stopped. He looked at her as though seeing her for the first time. "Katie Miller. A favor you would do for me?"

"*Ja.* If I can."

"Take a message to my house. Tell my *mader* I have gone to Rebecca and Emma, and will return after the noon meal." He tossed a glance toward the barn, and his chin jutted forward. "I go to see my son-in-law, the *Englisch* sheriff."

Without waiting for an answer, he flicked the reins. Katie stepped back as his buggy rolled forward. She almost called after him, "Give my greetings to Emma and Rebecca," but somehow she doubted he would remember.

TWO

"Uncle Jesse, can I help? Please?"

Jesse Montgomery paused in his task of running a curry-comb over his horse and made a show of cocking his head to eye the dark-haired boy standing beside him. Four-year-old Lucas hopped from one foot to another, his expression eager.

"Well, I don't know." Jesse pushed back his hat and scratched his head. "You're not tall enough to reach Rex's back, and he's a might touchy about having his legs groomed. When you have another foot or so of height on you, I'll be glad for the help."

The child's smile faded, his expression serious. He heaved a sigh and then disappeared in the direction of the barn. Chuckling, Jesse continued running the brush in a circular motion across the horse's shoulder, working his way past the withers and onto Rex's back. Little Lucas had taken a shine to him in the past year since he'd come to help out on the farm of the boy's father, Jesse's old buddy Luke Carson.

Jesse paused in the act of flicking a chunk of dried dirt out of Rex's chestnut hair. Who was he kidding? He didn't come here to help out. He came to *dry* out. Luke and his wife, Emma, had been kind enough to take him in a year ago, even though he'd been nothing but a shaking, shivering bag of bones with booze flowing through his veins instead of blood. If they hadn't been willing to help him, he'd probably be dead by now.

He glanced toward the vegetable garden where Emma knelt among a row of tomato plants, taking shelter from the sun beneath a huge floppy hat that Luke made fun of in the playful manner of a loving husband who adored his wife. She could have refused to let Jesse stay. After all, she had two impressionable children to think about. Instead, she and Luke had not hesitated to take him in and make him a part of their lives. He switched his gaze to the blanket where little Rachel played in a patch of shade from a leafy oak tree. In a way, the kids had made it easier to leave the whiskey behind. Even in his worst state he cherished their innocence, and he longed to recapture some of that innocence in his own life.

Longed in vain. He'd wrecked any chance he might have had to build a wholesome life. Women like Emma and her sister, Rebecca, chose strong men for their husbands, upstanding men with goals and determination and strength of character. Not broken-down old cowpokes like him.

He gazed across a wide field to the little white church that stood surrounded on three sides by corn. On the fourth side was the sprawling house that was home to Preacher Colin Maddox, his wife, Rebecca, and four orphaned boys with sadder eyes than any child should possess. He'd helped build the orphanage with his own hands, the first decent thing he'd done in years. Jesse's brush paused over Rex's back as a sense of helpless frustration washed over him. Those boys had found a home with Colin and Rebecca and were slowly recovering from the trauma of a devastating past. If only he could manage to do the same.

A sound behind him drew his attention away from gloomy thoughts. Lucas exited the barn backward, dragging a sturdy wooden stool across the grass.

"Will this make me tall enough, Uncle Jesse?"

Jesse hid a grin at the boy's anxious expression. He made a show of examining the stool that he used for milking. "You know what? I think it might. Hop up there and give it a try."

Lucas's anxiety turned to instant excitement as he climbed up. Rex turned his head to watch as Jesse instructed the child in the proper use of the brush on his back.

"Run it in circles first to loosen the dirt beneath the hair, and then you can brush it away. But be gentle. Like this." He demonstrated.

The boy watched closely and then took the brush. "I can do it." Jesse hid a grin as he watched the child work, and then he gave an approving nod. "Good job. You're hired."

A movement in the distance snagged his gaze. A horse and buggy made its way down the main road coming from Hays City and turned between the cornfields down the narrow lane that led to the church. He shielded his eyes with a hand. Hard to tell at this distance, but that looked like Big Ed pulling Jonas Switzer's buggy.

Emma had seen as well. She came out of the garden, scooped up baby Rachel, and headed toward them.

"What is Papa doing here in the middle of the morning?" Concern etched lines in her forehead. "I hope nothing's happened to *Maummi*."

"I'll go." He took the currycomb away from a disappointed Lucas. "You want to help me saddle him?"

A smile lit the child's face. "Sure!"

When the task was finished, Jesse swung up onto Rex's back and looked down at Emma and the children.

"Two rings if everything's okay." Emma hitched Rachel up on her hip. "Three if we need to come."

Jesse nodded. The two houses were close enough to each other to see, and the sisters got together several times a week to cook, sew, or enjoy a cup of tea. But when the church bell was installed a few months ago, they had worked out a message system. Every morning Rebecca assigned one of the boys the task of ringing the bell twice, which sent a cheery good morning to Emma and told her things were well at the Maddox house. Three rings meant something was wrong, and Emma and Luke would hurriedly hitch up their wagon for a quick trip down the lane to see where they could lend aid. The system worked well. Only once had the bell rung three times, when the baby in Rebecca's womb had remained still for a full day and a panicked mother-to-be needed her sister's advice.

"And if it's nothing serious," Emma continued, "tell Papa I will have coffee and biscuits ready for him when he leaves there."

Jesse nudged Rex forward and took off. Across the eastern field he spied another horse and rider heading toward the Maddox homestead on an intersect course with his. Luke had ridden out not long ago to inspect the seedling corn and had apparently spotted Jonas's buggy too.

They arrived at the church together to find Jonas talking with more animation than Jesse had ever seen the Amish man display.

"*All* the way around." Jonas swung his arm wide as Jesse and Luke dismounted. "A fence! On my land. And I am to be *shot* if I cross."

He acknowledged their arrival with a glance from troubled dark eyes, which then focused again on Colin.

"They just up and strung a fence without a word?" Colin pushed back his hat and frowned.

"Who did?" asked Luke.

"*Englisch* men." Jonas's troubled expression deepened. "Rough *Englisch* men with guns."

Rebecca emerged from the house, her hands cupped around the bottom of her round belly, and crossed the distance with a quick step to where they stood. Though her face wore an expression of concern, Jesse admired the way her hair shone in the sunlight. Even heavy with child, she was a lovely young woman. A wave of regret passed over him. If only he'd quit drinking years before, she could have been his wife and the baby his child. She'd crossed the length of Kansas to search for him, and she had found nothing but a wasted hull of a man.

He pushed the thought aside. What she'd found on that journey was Colin Maddox, her true mate. The Lord had worked that out for the best. Never was a couple more suited for each other than Colin and Rebecca.

She hurried toward the little group standing before the church. "Papa, what is wrong? Is *Maummi* unwell?"

The fact that Jonas did not answer his daughter with a welcoming smile spoke to the depth of his emotions. He nodded in her direction, "*Ja, ja.* She is well. But my land is overrun by *Englischers.*"

Jesse remembered his instructions. "Emma's waiting for news."

Rebecca glanced across the distance, where Emma could be seen standing in front of her house, staring that way. Though she was too far away for her features to be discerned, her stance was as tense as a bird dog fixed on a bevy of quail.

Rebecca turned to one of the boys who hovered in the doorway of the house. "Butch, would you please ring the bell twice?"

Butch, whose face never lost its slightly worried expression, took off for the church at a run. A moment later the toll of a bell filled the air. Emma waved and then turned to disappear into her house.

"All right now, let's get to the bottom of this." Colin assumed the role of questioner. "Jonas, you say you got up this morning and found out that these men had strung up a fence across your property. What did they have to say for themselves?"

"That my land is not mine but belongs to an *Englischer* named Mr. Littlefield." He wrung his hands. "It is almost twenty years since we came from Ohio, my Caroline and I, with the Amish to establish Apple Grove. John Miller, Eli Schrock, Melvin Byler, Jacob Helmuth, and others. We rode the land together and picked out our farms." His chest swelled. "I chose the one farthest west, the most western Amish farm in the whole country. A good land, with plenteous water and rich soil for farming." His shoulders drooped. "How can this Littlefield say it is no longer mine?"

Luke's jaw became rocklike. "He can't. I've heard about this sort of thing. A rich man comes along and decides he wants to lay claim to a particular piece of land, no matter if it's already been claimed."

Outrage stiffened Jesse's spine. "They can't get away with that! There's a law against that sort of thing."

They all looked at Colin, who had been a sheriff for several years before he hung up his badge and hung out his shingle as a preacher. His hesitant expression did little to quell the sense of unease growing in Jesse. "I'm not sure what the law says about this. We all know land is plentiful in the West. All a man has to do is claim his hundred and sixty acres. That's what we've done here." His gaze swept the land around them and shifted toward Luke's spread as well. "I've heard about folks putting up fences to mark off their claims, but I never heard of someone fencing someone else's claim."

"Amish do not know about laws and such. We hold ourselves separate from the *Englisch* world." Jonas appeared to remember something. "He has cows from Texas he will bring to Kansas."

"Littlefield?" Luke's gaze strayed to the sky. "I heard tell of a Littlefield over near Coleman who had a good-sized herd. Can't say I remember anything about him, though." He exchanged a look with Jesse and then Colin. "This could be a real problem, gentlemen."

Jesse nodded as understanding dawned. The days of the open trail were drawing to a close. As men laid claim to Western lands, the fences they erected served as barriers, closing off access for the great cattle drives that had provided occupation for Jesse and Luke and hundreds of roving cowboys like them. It was nearly impossible these days to move a decent-sized herd any distance. Men such as this Littlefield had effectively put Jesse out of business and left him searching for work with skills no longer useful.

Colin nodded. "Jonas's spread has that creek running through it. Perfect for pasturing a herd of cattle."

"Especially because of the ridge off to the west." Luke's lips tightened. "Jonas, your northern field is prime cattle land."

"But that is my cornfield," Jonas protested.

Luke spoke softly. "I've run cattle for quite a few rich men, and most of 'em wouldn't give two shakes of a rattler's tail about your corn."

"They're doing this because he's Amish." There had been a time when Jesse had little regard for the Amish, but that was before he knew any personally. There was no way he would ever be able to live the Plain life they espoused, but he'd come to respect Jonas's quiet integrity. The idea that someone would try to take advantage of his friend lit a fire in him. "They think he won't put up a fuss."

Jonas didn't meet his eye, but he stared at the ground before his feet with creases on his forehead. "Bishop Miller said a *snitz* pie might make Mr. Littlefield remove his fence."

"Pie!" Jesse snorted. The idea was so ludicrous that all the men laughed. Even Rebecca chuckled. But the misery deepened on Jonas's face.

"It is the Amish way to resist conflict."

Incredulous, Jesse stared at him. "You can't mean you'd let that man take over your home? Throw you off your own land?"

"I can do nothing." The note of helplessness in his friend's voice stirred Jesse's ire. Then Jonas raised his head and fixed his gaze on Colin. "But you are an *Englisch* sheriff. If you talk to this Littlefield, he will listen to you."

Talk. Jesse turned his head to spit on the grass. Though he'd never met the man, he already knew the measure of this Little-field. Hadn't Jesse run cattle right along with Luke? Some of those owners had more money than they could shake a stick at, but they would cheat a working man out of fifty cents if he wasn't watchful.

Colin spoke in a soft voice. "Jonas, I'm not a sheriff anymore. I'm a preacher and a farmer." Jonas's shoulders slumped, and Colin went on. "But I'm also your son-in-law. I'm not going to let this happen to you."

Beside him, Luke straightened. "Me, neither. We'll go talk to Littlefield with you."

Frustration tightened Jesse's hands into fists. Luke and Colin were fine men, upstanding men, and he respected them both. But they tended to think the best of people and treated folks accord-ingly. Talk? If Littlefield had sent his men out armed with rifles against an Amish farmer, he wasn't prepared to listen to talk. What was needed was a show of force. The tyrant needed to know he was dealing with more than a peace-loving Amish man.

And nobody was better equipped to make a show of force than Jesse.

He stepped forward into the center of the circle. "I'll go."

Colin and Luke opened their mouths, but a look of hope rose on Jonas's face.

Jesse held up a hand to silence them. "You both have families here, obligations. I have a feeling this is going to take more than a brief visit. Besides, Luke and Emma could use a little privacy. I'll go with Jonas and hang around his house for a while—if that's okay with you, Jonas?"

The look he exchanged with Luke and Colin told him they agreed. If Littlefield wasn't open to reason, he was likely to do more than put up a fence next time. The presence of a non-Amish man who wouldn't hesitate to defend himself and his friends might cause the ruthless land grabber to think twice before acting.

Colin nodded slowly. "Sounds good to me."

Luke's expression held a little more reserve. "You're sure you can handle this without losing your temper?"

Jesse deserved that. Having ridden the trail with him for years, Luke knew more than most that Jesse was known as a hothead. Not much had changed—except the drinking. He mustered a confident smile. "I'm just going to talk to the man and explain how it is in language he can understand."

Luke frowned. "If you think you can handle it."

"No problem."

Colin nodded. "He's the best one among us for the job."

Jesse grinned. "I'll get my things."

And I won't be taking any Amish pie along with me, either.

⁘

"*Maummi* Switzer, I wish you would sit in the shade and rest." Katie tried to instill the right balance of concern and ease in her voice as she watched the old woman wrestle with a stubborn weed that threatened one of her tomato plants. "I will pull these weeds for you."

"Too many for a girl to handle alone." The old woman waved across the huge garden. "And I've left them too long." She looked up. "But I thank ye kindly for lending a hand. *So ist's ja besser zwei als eins; denn sie genießen doch ihrer Arbeit wohl.*"

Katie bit back a sigh. *Maummi* Switzer was well known

throughout Apple Grove for her ready store of proverbs. This one came straight from *die Bibel,* and how could she argue with that? Yes, the labor of two did yield more results than one, but if one of the laborers was a worried elderly woman with a weak heart, the risks were not worth the yield. Perhaps a dose of her own medicine would convince her.

"*Ein Unkraut ist nicht mehr als eine Blume in Verkleidung.*" *A weed is no more than a flower in disguise.* Katie's *mader* had quoted that saying to *Fader* in the week just past. True, she had been referring to a rowdy goat that had been terrorizing the rest of the small herd they kept, but it seemed appropriate to the moment.

Or not.

Maummi Switzer straightened and pressed a fist into the small of her back, her mouth a hard line. "Did our dear Lord not say *Das Unkraut sind die Kinder der Bosheit?*" *The weeds are the children of the wicked one.*

Did the Lord say that? Katie couldn't immediately think where in *die Bible* the quote appeared, but she knew better than to do battle with a master of proverbs. She conceded the point with a nod and lowered her eyes to her task of uprooting one of the wicked children that had begun to reach toward a righteous tomato plant. But she kept a covert watch on the elderly woman, who took the opportunity to stretch her back and stare toward the empty road.

Katie followed her gaze. What was taking Jonas so long? The noon meal had come and gone hours past, and there was still no sign of his return. This morning when Katie performed the favor he'd asked of her, to deliver the message to his *mader,* the woman she had called *Maummi* Switzer since she and Emma had become friends as girls, she'd been alarmed at *Maummi* Switzer's pale skin and the slight tremor in her hands when she heard the news. She'd ridden her cart home to tell her own *mader* she would spend the day with the elderly woman, at least until Jonas returned.

Not that she could do much for a failing heart. Though she was becoming adept at binding wounds and nursing fevers, the most she could do for internal ailments was prepare a hawthorn berry tea and pray it calmed her patient. Still, *Maummi* Switzer was a well-loved member of the Amish community of Apple Grove, and the thought of leaving her alone to worry and fret over her son's unusual behavior was unthinkable.

Katie didn't doubt for a minute that the older woman's worries were justified. She stretched her gaze across the wheat field, where the ominous thick wire sliced across the landscape. From the snatches of conversation she'd overheard, she surmised the nature of Jonas's errand. Someone had threatened his land and Bishop Miller had refused help. Therefore, Jonas had turned to his *Englisch* son-in-law.

Katie's fingers tightened around a fledgling weed, and she ripped it out of the soft earth with a savage gesture. How could *Fader* Miller refuse to help Jonas in the face of violent men? It was his job, his responsibility as bishop, to shepherd God's flock here in Apple Grove. A shepherd did not leave his sheep to face the wolves alone, did he? Had *Fader* Miller's grief over Samuel become so bitter that it overshadowed his God-given duty?

A flush warmed her cheeks at the rebellious thought. Who was she to question God's anointed leader? *Forgive me, Almighty One.* She looked again at the ugly line, the *Englisch* fence that stretched from east to west across the neatly plowed field. *And please bless Jonas with a peaceful solution.*

"There!"

Maummi Switzer's shout drew her attention from her prayer. She looked in the direction the gnarled finger pointed. An Amish buggy top the hill. Jonas had finally returned home, and he was not alone. Beside the buggy trotted a horse, with a man astride the animal's back in the manner of *Englischers*. A light-colored oblong hat rested on his head, and his trousers were the color of baked bread instead of black, as was proper for an Amish man.

The old woman shielded her eyes with a hand. "Who rides with him? Is it Emma's Luke or Rebecca's Colin?" Excitement lightened her voice. "Are there others in the buggy with Jonas?"

Had Rebecca or Emma returned with their father for a visit? A pleasant thought, but as the travelers neared, Katie could make out a single black-clad figure seated on the buggy's bench. "No," she told the woman gently. "Jonas rides alone."

Maummi Switzer's shoulders slumped, but then she brightened. "No matter. We will offer refreshment to the men to wash the dust of the road from their throats. Come, child, and fetch for me lemonade from the cellar."

Katie gathered the folds of her black skirt tightly around her legs so as not to brush against the plants unnecessarily and followed *Maummi* Switzer out of the garden. Thank goodness for the invitation to help. She didn't want to appear too eager to hear the news lest she be mistaken for a gossip, but her curiosity had been piqued, and she couldn't bear the thought of leaving before discovering the details.

The men arrived as they neared the Switzers' front porch.

"Neither of my girls' *Englisch* husbands," *Maummi* Switzer mumbled more to herself than to Katie. "'Tis the cowboy."

Katie stepped up on the porch to stand beside *Maummi* Switzer and watch their approach. A worried frown sat heavily on Jonas's forehead, and the gestures with which he halted Big Ed and climbed down from the buggy's bench were stiff. She turned her gaze toward the horse and its rider.

Jesse Montgomery sat easy in the saddle, his movements as he reined his mount toward a shady spot beneath thickly leaved tree branches seeming to be at one with the animal. With no discernible movement on the reins in his hand, he brought the horse to a stop and swung his leg over. He hopped to the ground with the grace of one who had done it hundreds of times before, and crossed the grass toward the house with a smile on his face.

"Afternoon, ma'am," he said to *Maummi* Switzer. "You're as pretty as ever. Been too long since you've been out for a visit."

"The road runs both ways." Though a scowl accompanied the comment, Katie detected a note of warmth in the often peevish voice. If *Maummi* permitted him to call her "pretty," she must favor the man.

"Yes, ma'am, it does." He approached the porch and stood looking up at her from the shade of his brim. "If Luke wouldn't keep me so busy planting and tending that sorry bunch of cattle he calls a herd, I'd have more time for visits." His gaze slid sideways to connect with Katie's, and he snatched the hat off his head. "Pleasure to see you again, Miz Miller."

During the moment in which their eyes met, warmth crept upward toward Katie's cheeks. Jesse's rugged good looks and charming manners had always tended to unnerve her on the few occasions when she'd made the two-hour trip for a friendly visit with Emma, her best friend from childhood. Not that Amish men weren't equally charming, but something about the half grin that hovered around Jesse's mouth when he looked at her made her feel special, as though he had a secret he would only share with her.

But he was *Englisch,* so certainly that half grin was inappropriate and her feelings sinful.

She lowered her gaze to the boards at her feet. "A pleasant afternoon to you, Mr. Montgomery."

"Call me Jesse." He made the same request every time. Was it her imagination, or had his tone warmed slightly when he spoke to her?

Jonas hurried toward them, anxiety etched on his face. "You have seen the fence?" He directed the question toward his mother, but he included Katie with a glance.

Maummi Switzer nodded. "*Ja.* We have seen." She took a step toward her son. "What does it mean, Jonas?"

"A man wants our land. An *Englisch* man. He says we must stay here, on this side, or he will shoot us."

"*Shoot us? Gott helfe uns!*" *Maummi* Switzer slapped a hand to her chest and staggered on her feet.

Alarmed, Katie stepped to the old woman's side and slipped an arm around her waist to support her. Her body felt frail, and she leaned heavily against the younger woman.

Jesse shook his head. "Now, ma'am, don't you lose any sleep over this. I'm here to help. Your land is safe."

The frail body relaxed a fraction within the circle of Katie's arms. "You will protect us?"

"Yes, ma'am. You can count on it. I'll need a place to stretch out my bedroll for a few days and maybe a meal or two."

Jesse was planning to stay here, on the Switzer farm? Relief bloomed inside Katie's chest. His presence would certainly deter ruthless *Englisch* men bent on disrupting the peace of their Plain lives. Though ruggedly handsome, he carried a formidable manner—no doubt acquired from years of wild living. Such stories Emma told about Jesse's rowdy days on the cattle trail! The man standing before her was as different from her peace-loving Samuel as a dove from one of the grey hawks that glided overhead searching for helpless prey on the ground. Samuel had been the perfect Amish man, her ideal mate from the time they tromped together across the fields to the schoolhouse, their lunch pails swinging from their hands. And yet, in a secret part of her heart, she was fascinated by Jesse. What made a man choose to live a wild life, as he had done?

With a start she realized she'd been staring at him as her thoughts wandered, and he had become aware of her regard. His private smile deepened and carved the hint of a dimple in one cheek. Blushing, she busied herself with brushing a speck of garden soil from her skirt.

"You will stay here with us?" *Maummi* Switzer's voice was bright with enthusiasm.

"If you'd be so kind, Miz Switzer. I promise not to be too much trouble." His grin was exactly the same as a young boy promising to eat his vegetables *after* he finished a piece of pie and cream. When that grin turned toward her, a pleasant tickle started deep in Katie's stomach.

"*Ach!* What help will you be? Trouble follows close wherever you go." Though *Maummi* Switzer pasted on a scowl, Katie noted that her voice contradicted her words. "You will sleep in the back upstairs room, where you can watch the fields through the window." To Katie she said, "Come, child. You can fetch for me the lemonade while I begin the evening meal."

Katie turned to follow the old woman into the house, but not without a final look toward Jesse Montgomery.

THREE

Jesse stood at the window of his new quarters and watched Katie's cart disappear over a rise in the road. She was a fine-looking girl, with gleaming dark hair mostly hidden beneath that white bonnet thing all Amish women wore. The sun had kissed the smooth skin of her cheeks and scattered a charming spray of freckles across her nose. He'd seen her once or twice over at Emma and Luke's place and found her attractive, though a touch on the quiet side. He'd never heard her say more than five words at a time, but he'd heard her chatting with *Maummi* Switzer in the kitchen while he stowed his gear in the spare bedroom he'd been assigned upstairs.

What a shame, a pretty young gal like that being a widow. Emma had told him Katie's husband died a year ago, shortly before they had taken him in. He supposed he'd met her back then, but he could recall little of that time. His memory was a blur of shakes and misery as his body demanded the whiskey that had devoured his life every day for the previous five years. The shakes weren't the worst part, though. A fog had descended on his mind during those years of rowdy living, and at one time he'd feared he might never be able to escape it, that his ravaged thoughts might never again be clear enough to focus on anything except how to get the next drink.

With a shake of his head he dislodged the memory of those long, agonizing days and went outside to find Jonas. "You ready to head over to Littlefield's place?"

Jonas fidgeted with his suspenders, an unusually anxious gesture for one who was normally so outwardly calm. "Perhaps tomorrow would be better. To pay a call before the evening meal is bad manners, as though we expect an invitation to stay."

"I don't plan on paying a social call, Jonas. I'm going to tell the man straight up to tear down his fence and get off your property." He smiled. "There's not much chance of us being invited to supper."

Color swept Jonas's cheeks. "*Mader* has prepared a bounteous meal for us here to welcome you." He gestured toward the house, where *Maummi* Switzer could be seen through the wide kitchen window, her attention fixed on some task or other. "She will be angry if we are late."

"Well, I've been on the receiving end of her ire before, and it isn't a place I want to be again." Jesse recalled the cattle drive when a domineering *Maummi* Switzer had nursed him over a busted leg—and was none too motherly. He rubbed the scar on his thigh that still ached when rains gathered on the Kansas plain. Then he leveled a stern gaze on Jonas. "But she said it would be an hour or so, and my job won't take long. If you'd rather stay here—"

Jonas's fingers gripped the fabric of the suspenders that lay across his shoulders. "I thought perhaps..." With a shake of his head, he met Jesse's eye. "I need time to master my anger."

"Anger is good. Littlefield will see it and know we mean business."

"You do not understand." He spoke in the same soft nuance he might use when explaining something to little Lucas. "Amish do not speak in anger. We follow the example of our Lord and treat all men with patience."

"This crook isn't Amish," Jesse pointed out. "We have to talk to him in a language he understands, but you don't have to speak. I will. That's why I'm here."

The worried lines still gathered on Jonas's forehead. "My anger is such that my tongue will not stay tamed."

"Yeah?" Jesse studied the little man who, except for fidgeting with his suspenders, stood completely still and spoke in as even a tone as Jesse had ever heard. If he was as mad as he said, why wasn't he hopping around with a red face and fisted hands ready to pound someone?

"You're doing a good job of handling yourself. You look pretty calm. Me? I'd be fighting mad if a man walked in and tried to steal my land right under my nose. They shoot men for less."

"Oh, no." Jonas shook his head, his placid expression serious. "Inside I am fighting to remember that the Lord loved all, Jew as well as Gentile. Nor did He speak in anger to those who abused Him."

Jesse stared at the man. It was almost laughable to think that inside he simmered with anger while outside he maintained such a peaceful countenance. Could a man really live without ever speaking an angry word to anyone? Even the likes of Littlefield?

Yes, perhaps the Lord did, but He was God. Jesse's instinct was to fight.

Jonas was no coward. Jesse knew that from the time they had spent together on the Chisholm Trail several years ago. And he was a man of his word. So if he said he was struggling to control his anger, Jesse believed him.

I don't need Jonas to go with me anyway. Matter of fact, it might be better if he didn't.

Though he didn't intend for things to turn violent, he needed to be prepared for that outcome. Littlefield wouldn't take the news sitting down, but Jesse was used to defending himself. Having to worry about keeping Jonas safe would be a distraction.

"All right, Jonas. I'll talk to Littlefield alone."

"No." Jonas's jaw firmed. "This is not right. It is my problem, and I want to go with you. But what I ask is simple. Please allow me time to pray and calm my rebellious feelings."

Rebellious feelings. Jesse silently chuckled. *Littlefield doesn't give a whit about rebellious feelings. Only a strong arm and hot lead get through to his kind.*

"Okay. We'll visit Littlefield after breakfast tomorrow."

Jonas's chest deflated, and some of the tension in his forehead relaxed.

"But if you don't mind, I'd like to take a closer look at that fence before I settle Rex for the night. I want to see what we're dealing with."

"*Ja.* I will unhitch the buggy and get a start on my evening chores."

"You do that. I'll give you a hand when I get back."

Jesse pursed his lips and gave a low whistle. Rex obediently left the patch of sweet clover he'd been munching on and trotted over to him. Though lately Jesse had come to regret much of the past ten years of his life, acquiring Rex would never be a cause for remorse. He'd won the horse in a poker game. A rodeo show had come to town, and he'd watched with interest as the traveling troop set up camp and erected an arena and chairs for the upcoming show. Later that night, Jesse found himself seated across a card table from a middle-aged cowboy with a talent for horse training and a lousy poker face. After relieving the man of his cash, he was dealt a hand of pure nothing. Not even a pair of deuces. But a good hand is only a small part of winning at poker, and Jesse had been playing since boyhood. He ended the night several hundred dollars richer and the proud owner of the best horse he'd seen in his whole life. Morgans were known for their calm disposition and sturdy build that allowed them to do double duty as a light draft horse at need. Not that he'd ever worked Rex at anything except driving cattle and carting his drunken carcass all over the Western territories. In fact, there had been a few times when he'd woken up in a back alley from a rowdy night he couldn't remember to find Rex standing guard over him.

He slapped the horse's neck affectionately as he swung himself up into the saddle. "I won't be long," he told Jonas, and then pointed Rex northward and prodded his sides with his heels.

The fence was nothing but a series of posts with a line of ugly barbed wire strung between them. He found the eastern end about a hundred yards northeast of Jonas's pole barn. The small herd of Switzer cattle had aligned themselves alongside the wire, and one brown and white milk cow stared mournfully toward the other side. Beyond the fence, a creek gurgled over a rocky bed. The fence outlined a shallow bend in the creek and headed north, effectively cutting off the cattle's water access. No doubt about the reason for the fence. Littlefield was trying to ensure that his cattle would have access to plenty of water, while Jonas's would have none.

Jesse turned at the corner and followed the fence north. It cut directly across the center of a freshly plowed field. A wide swath of destruction showed on either side of the barbed wire boundary, the neat rows of soft soil showing signs of several sets of hooves, boots, and wagon wheels. Jesse set his teeth together and rode Rex around the unplowed edge on the sturdier ground of green grass.

The Switzer barn and house dropped out of view when he topped the swell in the land that marked the northern border of Jonas's field. The fence continued across uncultivated land. He soon crossed over the trench that Jonas mentioned, the one he'd carved in the land years before to mark his boundaries. Jesse urged Rex into a gallop, following it to the place where Littlefield's fence turned sharply westward. From there he hadn't ridden more than a few minutes when he caught sight of the Littlefield homestead.

He slowed Rex and studied the ranch house before him. Impressive by any standards, the main house was at least three times the size of Luke's place, attractively built of smooth stone and whitewashed wooden planks. A deep covered porch ran the length of the front, and several chairs rested invitingly in the shade. A second building sat a little off to the left between the ranch house and a gigantic barn, a long, low building that Jesse figured was probably cowhand barracks. A second barn had been constructed on the opposite side of the main house, that one obviously to house horses. Apparently Littlefield had an affinity for fences, for a neat split rail fence marked the boundaries of the ranch house, setting it apart from the other buildings. The fence and, indeed, all the buildings had an unmistakable clean, brand-new look, and the smell of fresh-cut timber filled the air. He kneed Rex toward the fence.

As he drew close, a pair of men exited the ranch house. Dressed in trousers and fairly clean shirts, they both wore their holsters slung low around their waists. Across the shrinking distance Jesse caught sight of their unwelcoming stares. They didn't stop on the porch but came forward. Pausing at the small gate, they took up a stance in front of the hitching post, a not-too-subtle sign that he was not welcome to hitch his horse and come in for a visit.

This suited him just fine. He halted Rex several yards away and spoke from the vantage point of the saddle.

"One of you named Littlefield?"

He knew the answer before the question left his lips. A big cattle baron from Texas would dress better than either of these two. They must be hired hands. Mean-looking critters.

The fellow on the left turned his head to spit on the ground before answering. "Who's askin'?"

Jesse remained calm. "I'm asking." His tone said without words, *I'm not talking to a hired hand. Bring me the boss.*

The spitter's hand moved slightly toward his holster. Jesse kept a loose grip on the reins but tensed his muscles in readiness. He could outdraw most any man when he wasn't drinking—and he hadn't had a drink in a year.

The door to the house opened, and two more men exited. There was no doubt as to the identity of the one in the lead. Littlefield wore the clothing of a wealthy man, from his neatly combed hair and waxed mustache all the way down to his polished shoes.

Sunlight glinted off of a gold chain dangling from a pocket in his waistcoat, and a ribbon of smoke curled up from the cigar in his hand. He stepped off the porch and crossed the neat yard toward Jesse with a confident step.

"Hello, sir." Polite words, spoken with the ease of one who enjoys the confidence of an elevated position in life. "Welcome to Circle Star Ranch. Name's Andrew Littlefield. And yours is…" Brows arched over sharp eyes that belied the welcoming smile.

Jesse kept his gaze fixed on the man's face without taking his attention from the three who flanked him.

"Name's Montgomery. I'm here to talk about that fence your boys put up last night."

The smile did not change, but the spark in Littlefield's eyes flared at the mention of the fence. "Are you referring to the fence marking the boundaries of my property?"

"No." Jesse matched the man's conversational tone. "I'm referring to the fence on the land of your neighbor to the south, Mr. Jonas Switzer. Have you met him?"

"I haven't had the pleasure." He lifted the cigar and inhaled. Smoke rose in a cloud from his mouth. "I will dispute the land, though. My employees"—his gesture swept the three ruffians at his side—"and I have scoured this area, and we found no boundary markings of any kind. According to the Homestead Act, I'm entitled to claim one hundred sixty acres so long as I improve the land." He held out his hands to indicate the buildings. "There can be no doubt I've made the requisite improvements."

Though he'd heard of the Homestead Act and the opportunity to claim free land, Jesse wasn't familiar enough with the details to argue them.

"Look, Littlefield," he said in a reasonable tone. "Jonas Switzer is a good man. He's Amish, which means he's peace loving, a man of faith. Why do you want to cause trouble for him? Kansas is a big place. There's plenty of land for everyone. Just move your claim a hundred acres or so to the north and west, and leave him to farm his little parcel in peace."

"Oh, but I can't do that. The land to the west is owned by Mr. Woodard here." He nodded his head toward the spitter. "And to his northern border is Mr. Lawson's property." The thug beside Woodard heaved a laugh.

"Let me guess." Jesse glanced at the fourth rascal, whose slack jaw and dull eyes made him look as though he was playing with only half a deck. "You own the land to the west of Woodard's?"

He turned a questioning stare on Littlefield, who answered for him.

"Actually, Mr. Sawyer's property is north of Mr. Lawson's. The parcel to the west is owned by a dear sweet lady in Boston, a widow whose husband was killed in the war. And beyond hers is land belonging to her sister, a spinster." He took another puff from the cigar and blew it out through a triumphant grin. "Of course, since the poor women are unable to manage the property themselves, I volunteered to do that for them."

So that was the way the wind blew. Littlefield had probably laid claim to dozens of one hundred-sixty-acre parcels by means of working through those he could control. Once the claims were secured, he would no doubt offer to buy the land from the "owners" at a fraction of the value. He'd end up with several thousand acres of prime Kansas land, and poor Jonas would be left with a piece of worthless property with no access to water for his crops and livestock.

He intended to slowly squeeze Jonas off his land.

"And of course none of those acres have convenient access to the creek," he said.

Littlefield's eyebrows arched. "Why should that matter? I have a perfect watering hole on my land, right beyond that ridge." He pointed toward Jonas's property.

Hold your temper, Montgomery. Jesse confidently met Littlefield's eyes and spoke in an even tone. "Your plan isn't going to work with the Switzer place."

"You think not?" The man's eyes rounded with fake innocence, and then the smirk returned. "Who's going to stop me? A pack of mild-mannered religious yokels who refuse to pick up a gun to defend their own daughters or aging mothers?"

A lump of ice slid down Jesse's spine. Obviously Littlefield knew something of the Amish practice of nonviolence, but did the mention of daughters and an aging mother refer to Jonas's daughters and *Maummi* Switzer?

Jesse spoke in a voice as stiff as his spine. "You stay away from the Switzers, you hear me? They may not fight, but their sons-in-laws, who aren't Amish, won't stand by and watch them harassed or taken advantage of."

His words stirred up an instant reaction. Sawyer and Lawson stepped forward, and Woodard's hand actually dropped to his pistol. Rex sidestepped uneasily. The tension was almost palpable in the air around them.

Littlefield, however, merely laughed. "Why would I want to harass a harmless farmer? I mean the man no ill will." His eyes hardened, and he lowered his voice to match. "As long as he stays on his side of my fence."

Jesse returned the cool glare. "Seems our business is finished."

"Seems it is, sir. Have a nice day."

"For now," Jesse clarified. He tightened his knees around Rex's barrel and tugged the reins sideways.

"By all means, do return for another friendly chat, Mr. Montgomery." Sarcasm saturated the gentile Texas drawl. "I've discovered folks in this part aren't so friendly." He chuckled. "Except those Amish. Why, they would give you the shirt off of their backs."

Jesse clamped his jaws down on the parting shot. As he turned, the tail of his eye caught a look exchanged between Littlefield and Woodard, and his insides tensed. This matter was far from over. He urged Rex into a gallop as he rode away, aware that the men stood staring after him. A spot in the center of his back burned from the weight of their glares. He hated turning his back on a pack of no-goods. He turned his head a fraction, enough to see them out the side of his eye, and watched them disperse. Littlefield disappeared into the house along with the third man, Lawson. Sawyer and Woodard were nowhere in sight. They had probably slunk back into whatever hole they crawled out of.

With easier breath, Jesse followed the fence toward Jonas's house, glad when he passed over a hill that hid Littlefield's place from view. At the corner of the fence, he pointed Rex southward and let him settle into an easy canter. What would Jonas say when he told him he'd already spoken with Littlefield? He might be relieved that he didn't have to sit through the uncomfortable encounter. Or he might be upset that Jesse had gone behind his back. One thing was for sure, he'd be unhappy with the outcome. No doubt he'd hoped his neighbor would listen to reason and remove the fence with no further trouble.

Jesse's mind fixed on his thoughts, so at first he didn't see the horses galloping toward him across the plain. They were within gunshot range by the time he noted the sound of hooves pounding the soil. He jerked his head around, reaching for his weapon at the same time, and spotted two men bearing down on him diagonally, coming from the direction of Littlefield's place. *Inside* the fence. Alarm rang in his head and vibrated down his spine. The hair on the back of his neck stood at attention. It was Woodard and the simpleton, Sawyer. And they had guns in their hands.

He made a show of drawing his weapon as he slowed Rex to a stop. Better to face a threat head-on than run from it. He turned and sat stiff in the saddle, waiting for them to come near. They stopped on the other side of the fence, no more than twenty feet away.

Woodard spat before speaking. "We wanted to make sure you made it back home safe, Montgomery."

"Yeah." Sawyer gave a high-pitched laugh. "Shame for you to get hurt by thugs afore you get home."

"That's mighty kind of you. You boys can go on home now to your mamas. I know my way around."

Woodard dropped the pretense. His gaze hardened. "Don't be messing in Mr. Littlefield's business. You tell that Amish man to shut his mouth and keep to his farming, and nobody will get hurt."

Jesse tensed. "And if he pushes the matter, are you threatening the Switzers?"

Their gazes locked together with steel. "I'm sayin' it'd be in his best interest not to find out."

Jesse had run into men like Woodard many times over the years. The saloons were full of them, hardened men who made their living doing the bidding of others by way of their pistols and a show of bravado. Problem was most of them were downright mean enough to shoot a man without thinking twice. And they were decent shots to boot. Not that he was afraid of Woodard or any of his ilk, but it didn't make sense to pick a fight when you were one man against two and there was a peaceful way out.

I sound like Jonas, taking the nonviolent way.

Well, and so be it.

He didn't loosen his grip on his pistol, and he didn't look away from Woodard's glare, but he did give a shallow nod. "I'll be sure and deliver the message."

Was that disappointment in the man's eyes? He'd been itching for a fight. Two against one, the coward.

Slowly, and with exaggerated gestures, Jesse turned Rex, pointed him toward the south, and then prodded him into a walk, leaving the two thugs behind.

"That's it?" Sawyer said behind him, a touch of outrage in his reedy voice. "We're gonna let him walk away?"

Rex kept walking.

"Ah, com'on. Let's get home," answered Woodard.

Sawyer argued in a tone like a whiney child. "But Mr. Little-field said we could—"

"Shut up, you idiot," snarled Woodard.

Mr. Littlefield said they could do what?

Rex took another few steps. The hair on the back of Jesse's neck stood at attention. He strained his ears to catch any sound of movement behind him. No rustling indicative of movement.

"Don't call me an idiot," came the hot reply. "I'm *sick* of being called an idiot. I can hold my own. You jest watch."

The sound that followed erupted in Jesse's ears like an explosion. The click of a gun's hammer. Was the kid getting ready to fire on him?

Woodard's shout. "Sawyer, put that—"

The warning was cut short. An explosion filled the air. At the same moment, fiery pain hit Jesse in the back, high up near his shoulder. Lightning flashed through his brain. The force of the bullet caught him off guard, pitching him forward. He scrambled to grab hold of the saddle pommel, but his nerveless fingers couldn't find a grip. The ground rose up to meet him, and he landed with a breath-battering thud.

"You idiot!" The muted shout seemed to come from far away. "You shot him in the back."

"Come on, let's git out of here!"

A roar formed in Jesse's ears, and the volume increased until he was aware of nothing else. A violent thunderstorm raged inside. He had one coherent thought before he lost consciousness.

Maummi Switzer is going to be mad as a wet barn cat that I missed her fine supper.

When he came to the pain was no longer confined to his back but burned in his chest and radiated throughout his whole body. Grass ground into his left cheek and the side of his head felt as though he'd been hit with a two-by-four. He took a cautious breath, but pain blazed through his lungs and he quickly let it out. *Breathe shallow.*

He cracked open an eye. It was hard to tell how long he'd lain there on the ground. The sun was still a ways above the horizon, but the rays had darkened toward orange. Littlefield's bandits were nowhere around. They'd left him for dead, the lily-livered skunks.

He hurt so bad they might be right. He might be dying.

Well, Lord. Right about now's when I'm grateful for all those sermons I've heard Colin preach over the past year. I never did get around to being baptized, but You remember that night out in the corn field, don't You? I prayed the prayer Colin talked about, and he said You never let that prayer go unanswered. So if it's time to leave this world behind, You're saving a place for me up there, right?

Jesse's question was answered with a deepening of the quiet that surrounded him. No voice, no singing angels or heavenly music, but somehow the silence contained a measure of comfort, as if a cool, gentle hand had reached past the burning in his chest. The next breath came a bit easier, and he closed his eyes.

Then a shadow came over him, and he was aware of movement near his head, the rustling sound of something moving in the grass nearby. A whicker sounded in his left ear, and then a silken nose nudged his cheek. Jesse found himself looking into Rex's liquid brown eye.

"Hey, pal." The words sounded weak and pitiful in his ears, but they were the best he could manage, seeing how he couldn't get a decent breath. "You're watching over me, aren't you? Good boy. That's another one I owe you."

His eyelids felt heavy, so heavy. What he needed was sleep. He let them close.

Rex nudged him again, this time more firmly.

"Sorry, boy. I can't climb up on your back. This isn't like the other times. I'm shot, not drunk."

Another nudge, this time accompanied by the stamp of an iron-shod equine hoof dangerously near his head. Jesse pried his eyes open, irritated. Stubborn horse. Why couldn't he let a man die in peace? Rex's huge head hovered over him. He whickered again and bathed Jesse's face in a spray of horse spit.

"Hey!" Jesse tried to move his head away, but it weighed a ton and the burning in his chest threatened to snatch the breath out of his lungs. "I can't get up, I tell you."

More rustling and the sun suddenly shone more brightly on his face. Rex had been blocking the sun's rays, but he had moved. Instead of standing over him, the horse was easing himself down onto the ground.

"What are you doing, you crazy horse? You pick now to take a nap?"

Once down on the ground, Rex rolled onto his side, his back toward Jesse, legs spread out in the opposite direction. He lifted his head as far as he could and looked over his shoulder, as though to say *What are you waiting for?*

"Well, I'll be..." Jesse would have shaken his head in amazement if it hadn't hurt so badly. The horse had actually laid down to make it easy on him to climb into the saddle. Instinct told him his master was hurt, and he wasn't going to stand around and watch him die.

Jesse had slowly become aware of a large sticky puddle beneath him that didn't come from water. The roar in his ears was getting louder by the second, and every time he opened his eye the world careened crazily around him. If he was any judge, he wouldn't make it more than an hour or two. The exertion of getting himself into the saddle, even with Rex lying beside him, might pump more blood out of him than he could live without.

But he owed a lot to that horse. He hated to let him down now. Rex snorted impatiently, and tossed his head upward.

"All right, all right. But this might take a minute. Hold your horses."

He chuckled at the joke and then drew in a ragged breath. With considerable effort, he lifted his head off the grass. Pain exploded inside, from where he couldn't tell. Everything hurt. Setting his teeth together against a wave of nausea, he edged his body forward, shifting his weight onto his left arm. Agony ripped through his torso, and he couldn't muffle a yell. He intended it to be a bellow, but with no more breath than he had, the sound came out more like a kitten's mewl.

Rex whickered encouragement.

"Okay, okay, okay. We can do this."

Inch by agonizing inch, Jesse edged himself toward his horse. It seemed to take hours to drag his body across the two-foot distance separating them, but at last he found himself nearly flush against the saddle. He rested his head on Rex's neck a moment, his shallow breath coming far too fast.

"Give me a minute." His words rasped, but somehow the horse seemed to know what he said. Rex lay quietly on his side, his only movement a twitching muscle in his shoulder.

Finally, Jesse managed to lift his leg and ease it over the horse's barrel. Somewhere over there was a stirrup, and he needed to find it to help keep himself in place. The only problem was that numbness seemed to be creeping down his right arm toward his hand. He had no idea what that meant, but he was pretty sure it wasn't a good sign. Hurry...had to hurry...Feeling around the horse's side with his leg, he found the flank cinch. Snug, but not too tight. By wiggling his foot he managed to wedge his boot toe inside the strap. Good. With his left hand he grasped the saddle horn, and buried his fingers in Rex's mane with the right. He hugged his body close to the saddle and steeled his jaw.

"Okay, boy. Let's give it a go."

Equine muscles tensed beneath him, and then the world shifted. Agony erupted in his body and a thick fog descended on his brain. In some distant part of his mind he was aware that Rex lurched to his feet quickly and somehow, miraculously, he managed to keep his grip. The horse danced sideways a few steps, giving a couple of torturous twists that resulted in Jesse's weight being more evenly distributed. Then he started to walk.

"Good boy," Jesse managed to whisper. "If I make it, I owe you a great big bag of oats and honey."

Rex answered with a soft whinny.

"Best poker game I ever played." The words left his lips in the moment before the world faded around him.

FOUR

Jonas stood at the back corner of his barn, scanning the wire that sliced his land in two. He searched the length of the hateful boundary, looking for a sign of movement. Where was Jesse? He'd been gone more than an hour, and there was no sign of his return. Beside him, *Mader*'s breath snorted through her nose like an irritated bull.

"My good meal, growing cold on the table. And where is he? Found himself a saloon, no doubt, and joined in the wild *ufrooish* of the *Englisch*." Her mouth formed a tight, crooked line. Like all good Amish women, *Mader* did not approve of the rowdy, riotous behavior of *Englisch* cowboys.

Though his insides had begun to tighten into worried knots, Jonas answered in a calm, even mildly reproving tone. "A saloon in Apple Grove?"

"Long gone from Apple Grove is he." *Mader* jerked her head in a nod, as if the statement was an accepted fact. "Mark my words. We won't see him again for days." If he didn't know his mother so well, Jonas might have missed the hint of worry in the gaze that scoured the fence line. "Come, Jonas, before the meal is unfit to eat."

She turned away, wiping her hands on her apron in a gesture of dismissal. He allowed a quiet sigh. Perhaps she was right. Jesse had ever been an unpredictable man, impulsive and given to capricious behavior. The past year he'd seemed to settle down under the steady guidance of Emma's Luke, but Luke wasn't here, was he?

He started to turn away when he spied movement at the crest of a gentle hill. A horse, not running but walking slowly toward him. Was that Rex?

"*Mader*, look."

She turned, and followed his gaze.

Yes, that horse looked like Rex, but where was Jesse? No rider sat in the saddle. Unless…Jonas shielded his eyes against the setting sun. Was that a man slumped on the horse's back?

Mader threw her hand up to cover her mouth. Without a word, they took off across the field. Jonas held his hat on his head and broke into a run, leaving his mother to hurry after him. The horse seemed to sense that help was near, and picked up its pace a small measure. They met halfway around the fence, and the horse came to a halt.

Yes, it was Jesse, and Jonas spied the evidence that he'd been hurt. Dark, sticky blood matted the left side of his head and covered his back, saturating his shirt and dripping down his side to stain Rex's mane. The source was immediately apparent, a bullet hole in his back. Alarm blossomed in Jonas. Was he alive? Could a man live after losing that much blood?

Mader arrived at his side, her breath coming in heaves. She took in the scene in an instant, her expression grave. With one gnarled hand she reached for the side of Jesse's neck.

"Warm," she told Jonas without taking her gaze off of the wounded man. "He lives."

As if to prove her words, Jesse gave a low, incoherent moan.

Mader rose on her toes in an attempt to inspect his back, but she was not tall enough. "We must get him home. Quickly, before he..."

Her lips clamped shut, but the unspoken words rang in Jonas's mind. *Before he dies.*

Gott help him! It is on my account he is shot.

Guilt nearly dissolved his knees beneath him. Why had Jesse gone alone to speak to Mr. Littlefield tonight? He was impulsive, as Jonas had just been thinking. If only he'd known, Jonas would never have allowed another man to walk into danger because of him. On him lay as much guilt as the one who had held the gun.

But he had not pulled a trigger.

The anger that Jonas nearly buried while feeding his livestock resurfaced with full force. He turned a glare toward the horizon, to whatever lay at the end of the awful fence. What sort of man would shoot another, and in the back? Fury churned in his stomach. The curse of Abel's brother Cain lay on mankind, and even today resurfaced in the actions of evil men. If he could but find this Littlefield man—

No! I must not forget the words of the Confession. I may not return evil for evil.

His hands tightened into fists. Gott, *help me. I am not able to keep this command alone.*

Mader could not guess the struggle that raged within him as she moved to take the horse's reins and tugged toward the house. Rex obeyed, following behind the elderly woman like an obedient puppy.

"Home we will take him," she said without turning her head. "Together we will get him inside, and then you must go for help."

"I will fetch the *Englisch* doctor in Hays City, *ja?*"

"*Ja.*" She nodded, a curt downward jerk of her head. "But first you will fetch Katie Miller. The girl has the healing touch, and our Jesse needs her."

Our Jesse. If he hadn't been so conflicted and worried, Jonas would have smiled. Jesse had long been a favorite with *Mader*, even though he was everything she disapproved of in the *Englisch*. A ray of hope lit the tumultuous darkness that raged in Jonas's mind. Perhaps with the attention of *Mader* and Katie Miller, his friend Jesse would live.

"The bleeding has stopped," Katie said as she gingerly dabbed at the open wound on Jesse's back. Was it good or bad that the bullet hole no longer seeped the sticky red fluid of life? She didn't know. Perhaps he had lost so much he had no more blood to shed. He'd certainly lost a lot, judging by the shirt that lay in shreds on the floor where *Maummi* Switzer had put it after she cut it off of him. And the amount she'd rinsed from his hair. She shook her head. They'd had to empty the wash basin three times while cleaning his head and back.

Jesse lay on the narrow bed in *Maummi* Switzer's bedroom just off the family common room, where Jonas had put him before riding across the fields to fetch Katie. A startling sight he'd made galloping up to the house astride Jesse's horse like an *Englischer*. Papa had looked askance until Jonas blurted out his errand, that his friend lay dying from a gunshot wound acquired while helping him. No more had the words left his lips than he whirled the horse and headed away, Jonas calling over his shoulder that he rode to fetch the doctor in Hays City. Katie had wasted no time in gathering her nursing bag while Papa and her brother Levi hitched their horse to the buggy she used.

Maummi Switzer pressed two fingers against Jesse's neck, and her unsmiling face became even grimmer. "His heart beats too slowly, but at least it still beats."

"Perhaps a tea of red clover tops and goldenseal root?" When Maggie Cramer lost so much blood after the birth of her baby last winter, the midwife had told Katie to give her plenty of tea made from red clover and goldenseal to help rebuild her strength.

But *Maummi* Switzer shook her head. "If the stomach has taken any of the bullet, filling it will do more harm than good."

Katie nodded. She should have remembered that. It was just that she felt so helpless merely sitting here doing nothing while a man clung to life before her eyes. She rinsed her cloth in the basin of fresh water and wrung it out before gently wiping away a spot of blood she'd missed before. The muscles across one shoulder blade contracted when her cloth touched his ribs, and she almost laid a comforting hand across his bare skin. Aware of *Maummi* Switzer's presence on the other side of the bed, she stopped herself. She'd learned that the comfort of a gentle touch did much to calm the sick or injured, but she was an unmarried woman and this man lying before her was only half clothed. And *Englisch* besides.

He was shapely built. Solid and sleek, without a hint of fat in the broad expanse of his back or at his trim waist. Tanned, too, as though he spent much time shirtless in the sun. She'd heard that was sometimes the way of *Englisch* men, to work in the open without proper clothing. Shameless, of course, but only for an Amish man. The *Englisch* had no such prohibition against exposing their flesh to the view of others. Her gaze lingered on his muscled shoulders and then strayed to the row of soft curls that rested against the nape of his neck. Her Samuel had been lean and wiry, his spine in much more evidence than Jesse's. Absently, she pulled a piece of dried grass from one golden brown lock, her fingers lingering perhaps a moment too long on the soft hair.

The sound of a door opening interrupted her thoughts. Guiltily, she dropped the cloth into the water basin and glanced sideways to see if *Maummi* Switzer had observed her study of her patient's form. Fortunately, the older woman seemed not to have noticed. She leaped from the chair she had pulled close to the bedside.

"Finally!"

Katie rose while *Maummi* Switzer hurried toward the doorway, but before she got there a stranger appeared with Jonas close on his heels. Dressed in clean but wrinkled trousers and shirt, the doctor carried a leather satchel at his side. Disheveled gray hair spoke to the haste of his departure from Hays City. A pair of spectacles rested on his nose. With a quick nod of greeting to *Maummi* Switzer and Katie, he hurried to the bedside, where he bent over to examine his patient.

"Lost a lot of blood, has he?" He addressed the question to no one in particular, but *Maummi* Switzer answered.

"*Ja.* The bleeding stopped not long ago."

"Hmm." He glanced at Jonas as he unstrapped the closure on his satchel. "You say this is the same man I worked on some years ago, the one with the broken leg?"

Jonas nodded, his gaze fixed on the bullet wound in Jesse's back.

"Well, it would be a shame to let him die now after I've already patched him up once. Let's see what we have here." From his satchel he extracted a polished wooden tube. The fluted end he pressed against Jesse's skin, and then he turned his head to place the other end, which was rimmed in black rubber, in his ear. His worried expression grew grave.

"He will be all right, *ja?*" Jonas hovered in the doorway and fiddled with the strap of one of his braces just below his shoulder.

The doctor remained silent. He lowered the listening device and with gentle fingers pressed at the skin around the bullet hole. Though it didn't look to Katie as though he'd applied pressure, Jesse moaned, and the arm closest to her moved. His control of the limb was feeble, and it fell off the bed to dangle toward the floor. Katie picked it up and returned it to the mattress. His skin felt warm and dry to the touch. Too warm? The development of a fever this soon after his injury was a bad sign.

The doctor finished his examination of the bullet wound and turned to Jesse's scalp. A gash topped a knot the size of Katie's fist. That wound had stopped bleeding before the one on his back, though it had oozed more deep red liquid while she'd gently sponged the blood from his matted hair.

The doctor replaced the device in his satchel and then turned toward Jonas, his expression grave. "I can suture the head wound, and as long as he hasn't cracked his skull he'll recover from that. He'll probably have a pounding headache for a few weeks. As for the other wound..." He turned back to his patient. "That bullet needs to come out. If he's lucky it didn't puncture the right lung, but what I hear gives me cause for concern. He's fortunate that shot wasn't an inch or so to the left, or it would have hit his spine. How did you say this happened?"

"He rode out to investigate the fence my neighbor has built. When he came back..." Jonas gestured toward Jesse to indicate that this was the shape in which he'd returned.

"My guess is bandits." The doctor's lips pursed. "It's getting so as a man can't take a stroll without worrying about being shot." His gaze slid to *Maummi* Switzer and then came to a rest on Katie. "Are you his wife?"

Startled, Katie's eyes rounded. She took a backward step away from the bed. "No. I-I came to help care for him."

"That's fine. You can give me a hand. I'll need strong soap and clean water, two or three big basins, and some cloths. Make sure they are clean cloths."

Katie started to shake her head and looked toward *Maummi* Switzer for help. The older woman had far more experience at this sort of thing than she. But *Maummi* Switzer flicked a hand in her direction.

"Young eyes are sharper than old ones. On the shelf in the room at the top of the stairs you will find bedsheets and such."

The doctor glanced up. "Old cloths will be just fine, ma'am. When we finish with them they won't be much use anymore."

Maummi Switzer dismissed that with a snort. "Whatever is needful to help our Jesse, that is what we will use. Come, Jonas. We will fetch soap and water."

Katie hurried up the stairs and found the sheets in a starkly furnished bedroom that looked much like hers at home, only no spare aprons or black dresses hung from the pegs. She retrieved a stack of soft white fabric and hurried back to the sickroom to find that the doctor had removed his vest and was rolling his sleeves above his elbows.

"Those will be fine. Put them on that chair. What's your name, young lady?"

Katie deposited the linens where directed and gave a small curtsey. "Katie Miller, sir."

"I'm Dr. Sorensen. Have you ever worked on a gunshot wound, Katie?"

Her gaze strayed toward the half-naked man on the bed, and she swallowed against a dry throat. "No, sir."

"I'd wager to say I've removed enough lead from men's bodies to fill that buggy I saw out in the yard. I doctored in the war." He spoke in normal tones, a shock to her ears after the hushed voices she and *Maummi* Switzer had used. "Why, the bullets from General Bragg's battle in Perryville alone nearly filled up a gallon bucket. If I'd been smart I would have kept them and sold the lead back to the army."

As he spoke he pulled things from his leather satchel and lined them up on the small table next to the bed. A fabric-wrapped bundle clinked metallically as he set it beside a covered jar of liquid. Next, he proceeded to slip a clean sheet beneath Jesse's prone body, gesturing for her to pull it through on the other side until it was fully beneath him. Jesse moaned again during this process, and flailed his limbs.

Dr. Sorensen nodded toward his legs. "That's a good sign. I feared there might be damage to the nerves."

Maummi Switzer and Jonas arrived carrying two buckets of water and several large bowls. With the manner of presenting a gold piece to the bishop, *Maummi* Switzer handed a bar of soap to the doctor.

"Thank you, ma'am." The doctor looked briefly at her and then he turned to Jonas. "I have a very important task for you."

"Me?" Jonas's eyes widened and his hand flew to his collarbone. "I have no skills."

"You won't need any. Open that window over there."

Without a word, Jonas moved toward the room's single window and threw it open.

"Good. Now look here. See this?" With one hand the doctor held up a cone-shaped object that looked as though it was made of fabric, and in the other he had a small glass vial. "This is chloroform. Katie, you and I and Mrs. Switzer will leave the room while Jonas administers the chloroform. Don't worry, Jonas." He forestalled the inevitable protest with a raised hand. "I've already measured the proper amount. All you have to do is empty this vial onto the cone and hold it over his mouth and nose for a minute or so."

For a moment Katie thought Jonas might object. His throat moved as he cast a frantic look toward Jesse on the bed, and then he seemed to come to a decision. He took the items from the doctor and moved to the place where Jesse lay on his stomach, his head facing the far wall. Dr. Sorensen gestured for her and *Maummi* Switzer to precede him out of the bedroom, and they all hurried through the doorway to huddle together in the living room.

"Try not to breathe, Jonas," Dr. Sorensen cautioned from his vantage point.

Although the situation was grave, Katie couldn't help feeling excited. The doctor's practices were beyond anything she'd ever seen. She'd come to recognize which herbs could treat certain disorders, such as Martha Hostetler's occasional stomach upset and Sarah Yoder's headaches. She had heard of chloroform but had never seen it used. Judging by the keen look on *Maummi* Switzer's face, the older woman was as interested as she.

"All right, Jonas, that's long enough. Now, take that cone outside and put it somewhere in the open."

He moved away from the doorway to allow Jonas, holding the cone at arm's length, to pass through the room. Katie noted that the Amish man's anxious frown had relaxed, and he wore a placid, almost happy smile. Perhaps he was pleased to have helped his friend. Or perhaps he'd breathed a little too deeply while administering the chloroform. The sound of the door opening followed his disappearance into the kitchen.

Dr. Sorensen called after him, "When you dispose of that, you might want to lie down and have a nap."

After waiting for a long moment, he motioned for Katie and *Maummi* Switzer to return to the room with him. He marched to the pile of linens, picked up a sheet from the stack, and, with a quick movement, ripped it in two. Katie couldn't stop a gasp. The waste of a good sheet was unheard of. But *Maummi* Switzer did not flinch as the doctor ripped again and then handed her a large square. Then he retrieved the jar from the table and motioned for one of the buckets of water, into which he poured a small amount of the liquid.

"Now, Miz Switzer, if you'll be so kind as to drape this over the edge of that bucket." While she did as instructed, he picked up the biggest basin and placed it on the seat of the chair. "Come, Katie. You and I will both wash our hands."

She followed his instructions and held her hands beneath the flow that *Maummi* Switzer poured through the filter of the ripped bed sheet. A sharp, pungent odor rose from the water. Katie's nose twitched with the unpleasant aroma. Whatever the liquid was in the jar, it was strong. Surely not as strong as chloroform, else the doctor wouldn't risk breathing it himself. They lathered with lye soap, and followed the same procedure to rinse in the odd smelling water.

Dr. Sorensen must have noticed her curiosity, for he offered an explanation. "I expect you're aware of the high rate of infection that results from a wound like this one?"

Katie glanced toward the bed, where Jesse's back rose and fell at an alarmingly slow rate.

"*Ja*," answered *Maummi* Switzer, her tone grim. "Many do not live."

"That's a fact. When I was in school there was a fellow over in England, name of Lister, who did quite a bit of study on infections resulting from surgeries like this one. He put forth the idea that infection, or sepsis, is caused by something invisible to the naked eye in the air and the surrounding area during surgery.

Microorganisms, he said. He came up with a technique to kill those infectious organisms using a solution of carbolic acid."

While he spoke, he ripped the wasted bed sheet into three more squares and dipped them into the smelly water. Carbolic acid. Katie had never heard the unusual term.

"Now, I'll be honest with you, some of my colleagues think Lister is foolish at best, a charlatan at worst." He looked over the top of his spectacles toward the older woman. "They call me the same for practicing his techniques."

Maummi Switzer's mouth pursed. "Cleanliness is next to godliness."

The doctor's gaze became approving. "Exactly, ma'am. On the battlefield we operated in some mighty dirty conditions, and there were a lot of fine young men who never made it home to their families." His lips tightened. "If Lister had been a few years ahead of his time with his antisepsis theory, we might have saved some of them." .

He fished one of the saturated cloths out of the bucket and handed it to Katie, and then he took another for himself. Smelly liquid dripped onto the floor as he turned to the bed. .

"You wipe down his back," he told her, "and I'll do his head. I want every inch of flesh saturated."

She did as instructed, aware that *Maummi* Switzer oversaw her movements with sharp attention from across the room. Jesse did not move, nor did he moan even when she dabbed the cloth around the wound. His back rose and fell in a slow, steady rhythm.

When he was satisfied the area had been thoroughly cleansed, Dr. Sorensen reached for the third cloth in the bucket. From it he dribbled the pungent water directly into the gash on Jesse's head, and then into the bullet hole on his back. A slight sound came from the patient's open mouth, no more than a whispered breath.

"Without the chloroform that would have brought him up off this bed," the doctor told her. He gave a satisfied nod. "Now we can get to work."

Katie had no idea how much time had passed before Dr. Sorensen extracted a lump of metal from Jesse's body. He held it up for her inspection.

"He's a lucky man. The bullet ripped through his muscle but lodged in the pleura instead of puncturing the lung itself. Probably hurts like a billy-o to breathe, and it will for a while. But as long as infection doesn't set in, this cowboy might just pull through."

Katie wilted into the chair, her breath escaping in a sigh. The procedure had been tense and bloody, and her part had mainly been wiping away the fresh blood that ran alarmingly from the wound as Dr. Sorensen prodded and probed along the bullet's path. The man liked to talk while he worked, and she had listened to every word about the rich blood supply to the shoulder, both arterial and venous. Though she had no idea what the terms meant, she'd nodded to indicate she was paying attention and kept her gaze fixed on his hands.

"I'll leave some dried red clover for the blood loss. Steep it in water and give it to him four or five times a day."

She perked up. "I have red clover in my bag. Perhaps goldenseal as well?"

The doctor shrugged. "Can't hurt. My dear granny used to swear by goldenseal. Said it cleanses the blood."

"What of the wound in his head?" She looked at the ugly gash. At least it bled no more.

The doctor bent over and examined the wound through his spectacles. "Doesn't look too serious to me. If I were a betting man, I'd wager he hit something when he fell rather than somebody walloping him." He ducked his chin and looked at her over the top of his glasses. "How are you at stitching?"

Katie's backbone straightened. The doctor, a real *Englisch* doctor, would trust her to stitch a wound? True, she'd only had to sew three or four cuts closed in her entire life, but she had a steady hand, and her quilts were much admired by the ladies of Apple Grove for her small, even stitches. "I can do it," she answered with more confidence than she felt.

"Good. Here's some catgut and a needle. You do that while I go check on Jonas." He gathered his surgical instruments and dropped them into the bucket with the acidy water, and then he reached into his satchel. "I don't have a lot of carbolic acid to spare, and besides, I use that mostly in the surgery. Going forward you'll use the good, old-fashioned way of keeping those wounds clean. Soap, water, and a generous splash of this."

He set a bottle on the table with a *thunk*. Amber-colored liquid gleamed in the flickering light of the lamp.

"What is that?"

"Whiskey." The doctor looked at Jesse. "He'll scream like a wildcat when you pour it on, but do it anyway. If infection sets in..." He shook his head.

Katie swallowed. If infection set in, Jesse would die.

The doctor left the room, and Katie moved to take his place on the bedside where the light was better. She picked up the catgut and inspected it. Always before she'd use ordinary cotton thread, but this seemed stronger, thicker. With a practiced eye, she threaded the needle.

Before she began, she laid a hand on her patient's bare skin. Jesse felt warm beneath her touch, though thankfully not feverish. Was it her imagination, or did his breathing settle at her touch? She formed a silent prayer, as she did every time she nursed someone, but never had she nursed a patient in such grave shape as this man.

Dear God, please do not let him die. Heal him with a word, as You healed the soldier's servant.

Setting the needle against his scalp, she began her work.

FIVE

Awakening to consciousness was like climbing out of a pit. Jesse's body refused to cooperate, and his limbs felt as though they were tied to his sides. His attempts to lift them resulted only in a dangerous swirling inside his pounding skull, and an upsurge of the nausea that roiled in his stomach. Where was he? Not heaven, that much was certain. Nobody could be this miserable inside the pearly gates. Maybe he'd gone in the other direction after all. Trying to pry his eyes open proved to be impossible. They remained firmly closed no matter his effort. His mouth felt as though a herd of Texas Longhorns had trampled through it. And dry. So dry.

He sucked in a breath and pain exploded in his body. Oh, yeah. He realized he'd been dimly aware of the agony of breathing for a while now. How long, he had no idea. A groan rasped through the desert in his throat, and he was surprised to hear the result, a pitifully soft wail barely louder than that of a weak kitten.

Instantly he was aware of a cool hand on his forehead.

"You are awake, then?"

A female voice, soft and low, close by. He tried again to open his eyes, but his eyelids refused to obey. Another agonizing breath, and he managed to repeat his pathetic attempt at a moan.

"Hush, now. She needs her sleep. A full night and day she has kept watch over you."

Who? Who needed sleep? Watched him do what? If only he could open his eyes and see.

"Would you like something to drink?"

Yes! Oh, please, God, I'd give a year's pay for a sip of water.

A hand slid to the back of his neck and tilted his head forward. Jesse ignored the shooting pain that resulted from the minute movement, for something cool and wet pressed against his lips. With an enormous effort he pried his mouth open. The trickle of lukewarm moisture tasted better than any whiskey he'd ever chugged down. He let the liquid slide down his throat, moistening parched tissue wherever it touched. Not water, but something sweeter and infinitely more delicious. He tried to suck more down thirstily, but the mug was removed and his head lowered.

"Not too much at first," the soothing voice whispered. "You must guard your stomach, lest it revolt."

The thought of the physical effort involved in vomiting sent a shudder through his weary body. Exhausted, he sank back into the soft something-or-other behind his head, for the first time aware that he was lying on a padded surface. He tried to decide what it was. Softer than grass, and smooth. A bedroll, maybe? That didn't seem right either, but Jesse had no more time to consider the question. His body rose on a blessed swell of unconsciousness, and he hadn't the strength to fight against it.

He awoke sometime later to a noise somewhere in the vicinity of his feet. Pain still pounded brutally inside his skull, and his back felt as though he'd been kicked by a steer. He took an experimental breath, and at the resulting pain vowed not to try that again for quite a while. His throat was as dry as a Texas plain in August, but this time he was able to open his eyes, and though sharp knives stabbed at his head, he brought them to focus enough to take in his surroundings.

Fading sunlight from a window to his left cast an orange tint on the whitewashed room. His gaze fell on a simple shelf hanging on the opposite wall. Dangling from one of the pegs beneath it was his belt and holster, and resting on top was his Stetson.

Thank the Lord. I paid good money for that hat.

He was propped up on a narrow bed, the tick beneath him stuffed with something soft and moldable to his body. Behind his back was a mound of even more cushiony material, like feather ticking covered with soft cloths. He still felt as if he'd been trampled by a stampede, but at least he was conscious.

A movement near his feet drew his attention. *Maummi* Switzer stood in the doorway, her arms folded in front of her apron and an equally starchy glare on her face.

"Yet again have you nearly died from fighting and needed my care. Will you *Englisch* never learn to practice peace?"

If it hadn't hurt so badly, he would have attempted a feeble laugh. As it was, he settled for a grimace. "Neither time was my fault, you know. First time was a run-in with cattle rustlers, and this time..."

His voice trailed off as the details of his encounter with Woodard and Sawyer swam into focus in his mind's eye. The simpleton, Sawyer, had shot him in the back, and then he and Woodard had left him for dead.

"I guess I owe you another one," he told the scowling elderly woman. "This is twice you've saved my sorry hide."

She shook her head, the straps of her cap thingy waving beneath her chin. "You owe me thanks for changing your soiled clothing. The saving of your hide is thanks to the *Englisch* doctor and Katie Miller."

Two reactions rose in him simultaneously. First was embarrassment. *Maummi* Switzer changed his drawers? He slipped a hand beneath the blanket and felt a thin pair of woolen skivvies that were not his own. A fire erupted in his face. When she'd mended his busted leg several years before, she'd only cut off his britches above the thigh.

Then a second realization stirred a memory from the long, pain-saturated sleep from which he'd just awoken. The soft voice and cool hand had belonged to Katie Miller, Emma's pretty Amish friend who had been at the Switzers' when he arrived yesterday.

Yesterday? Thoughts swirled in his mind. Somehow he felt it had been longer.

He decided to ignore the embarrassing question and ask the easy one. "How long have I been out?"

Before answering she stepped into the room and crossed to his bedside. A gnarled hand, not nearly as gentle or as soft as Katie's, pressed firmly against his forehead. As if satisfied with what she felt, she gave a nod.

"Four days and more."

"Four *days?*" He tried to jerk upright, and immediately regretted the movement. An agonizing blaze began in his head, and his back felt as though it had been ripped open. His breath caught in his throat and he coughed, which sent tortuous flames licking throughout his chest.

"Quiet," *Maummi* Switzer commanded, "lest you undo all the good your rest has done."

He would have argued that unconsciousness couldn't be labeled *rest*, but just then he was occupied with trying to breathe without setting off another agonizing coughing spell.

She stood watching his face, her expression unreadable, until he had regained an even, shallow breathing. Then she picked up a mug from the bedside table and held it to his lips.

"Drink," she commanded.

He drank. The sweet liquid refreshed the starved tissues in his mouth and slid down his throat. The faint taste of honey mingled with something he could not place, and the result was delicious. He drained the mug dry, afraid she might take it away before he'd had his fill.

With a satisfied set to her lips she returned the empty mug to the table. "Keep that down and there will be soup."

He would have protested that *of course* he could keep down a few swallows of sweetened tea, that in his day he'd swigged enough whiskey to float a riverboat and kept it down, but at the moment his stomach felt a bit queasy. Bragging might not be a good idea.

Instead, he closed his mouth and concentrated on not throwing up.

Maummi Switzer slid a straight-back chair across the floor to the bed and lowered herself into the seat. "It has been four days since you were shot," she repeated, "and we feared you dead more than once. Dr. Sorensen came from Hays City and pulled a bullet from your back." She plucked something off the table and showed him a piece of mangled lead. "Katie stitched your head, and together we have kept you clean to guard against a killing fever."

What being clean had to do with fever he didn't know, but his thoughts snagged on one comment. "Did she help...you know." He lifted a hand and pointed toward the blanket that covered his body from waist to feet. "Change my skivvies?"

"*Ach*, no!" The elderly woman seemed scandalized at the thought. "A young widow has no place in such a task. I did that myself, with Jonas to help."

Jesse didn't know whether to be relieved or more deeply embarrassed. He decided on the former. *Maummi* had birthed two babies, and Jonas was a man. Better them than a pretty young woman.

He settled gingerly against the fluffy stuff at his back, which he decided was a small tick stuffed with feathers. Mighty glad he was for it too, because his back was sorer than he could imagine. He'd been shot before while riding the cattle trail, once in the shoulder and once in the leg, but he'd never imagined pain like this.

"Has anybody gone after the no-good scoundrel who did this to me?"

She did not meet his gaze as she shook her head slowly. "It is not the Plain way to retaliate."

If his lungs didn't hurt so badly he would have heaved a sigh. No, of course it wasn't. And now that he looked back on his encounter with Littlefield and his hired thugs, he was glad Jonas hadn't tried to confront them alone. They would make mincemeat out of a mild Amish guy like him. In a few days Jesse would be up and about, and he'd settle his own grudges then.

"That fence still up?"

"*Ja.* Our Katie and the boy help Jonas carry water for the animals morning, noon, and night."

Jesse stared at her. Katie had a son? He'd somehow gotten the impression she'd had no children before her husband went to his rest. "The boy?"

"*Ja.* One of Rebecca's orphans, sent by her Colin to help us." She leveled a stern gaze on him. "Because you are no help and only double the work for us all."

Rather than feel the barb personally, Jesse managed a feeble chuckle. If *Maummi* Switzer felt confident enough to jab at him, she must not be overly concerned about his recovery.

She rose and scooted the chair back across the floor. "Rest now."

"Hey! You said something about soup." He attempted only a weak protest because his head had begun to swirl and his eyelids felt as though they were being pulled closed by an unseen force.

"A good laugh and long sleep are a doctor's best cures." She smiled, not unkindly. "Sleep now. Soup later."

He would have shot back a response, but he couldn't manage to stay awake long enough to think of one.

Katie pumped the handle, watching as water spilled into the bucket. The boy, Butch, stood at her side waiting for the bucket to fill, his expression solemn. Actually, his countenance rarely varied from the grave expression he now wore. The only time she'd seen something approximating a smile was when he'd been given the task of feeding Rex, who had rewarded him by nuzzling his neck.

She stopped pumping when the water level approached the rim, and Butch bent to grab the handle with both hands.

"Knees," she cautioned, just as *Fader* had always warned her when she bent over to pick up a load. "Else your back will ache later."

"Yes'm."

He ducked his head, bent his knees, and lifted the full bucket. Water sloshed over the rim onto his already soaked trousers as he hefted his load toward the side of the barn, where Jonas had set up a watering trough for his livestock. She watched him for a second, a sad little pain in the vicinity of her heart. Rebecca said his parents had been killed by savages while on their way to claim land in the West. His mother had hidden him in the false bottom of their wagon, in a special place prepared for just such a contingency. The poor child had huddled inside, listening to the sounds of the battle that claimed the lives of his parents and all those with whom they traveled. When the wagon in which he'd hidden was set afire, he'd escaped to find the savages gone and his parents' bodies amid the carnage of the devastated wagon train.

Tears stung her eyes, imagining the boy's solitary shock and grief. No one should have to endure such horrors, especially not a child. But that was the way of the world. If only everyone would see that violence was an offense to Christ and would follow His teachings as the Amish did. The only barriers to the peace He bestowed were the ones erected by angry men who refused to practice self-restraint. Her gaze strayed across the field of gently swaying wheat to the fence serving as a physical reminder that even living within the boundaries of a Plain community, violence and greed sought to shatter godly peace.

She'd begun to pump the handle to fill yet another bucket when the door to the house opened and *Maummi* Switzer appeared. "He has awakened."

Finally! Katie released the handle and dried her hands on her apron as she headed toward the house. Though Jesse's brief rise to consciousness yesterday had been reassuring, she would not truly be at ease until he opened his eyes and showed signs of comprehension. A blow to the head such as he'd suffered had been known to make a man feeble.

Maummi Switzer stopped her by holding up a hand. "Sleep has overtaken him again, but he spoke with me for several minutes."

Disappointment halted Katie's step. She'd hoped to be there for his first conversation. "Did he drink?"

"*Ja.* The full mug of tea, and more if I had allowed."

"Is he..." She let the question hang. They had discussed the possible outcome of a cracked skull, and *Maummi* Switzer shared her concern.

A smile deepened the creases in the elderly woman's face. "His words are not garbled, and his mind is clear."

Katie breathed a relieved sigh. "*Gott* be praised."

Butch returned at that moment, the empty bucket dangling from his hand. Katie watched his rounded shoulders and steady gait, her heart twisting at his solemn expression. How unfair for a child to have his laughter stolen by sorrow. If only he would run and laugh and play, instead of this somber attention to the chores assigned him. Perhaps if there were other boys his age nearby? But no, three others lived with Rebecca and Colin in the big house beside their *Englisch* church building, and Emma said Butch was ever on the sidelines, watching the others at play but rarely joining in.

"Butch, a task I have for you." She spoke in a kindly voice as he approached the pump. "Please to take a message to Mr. Switzer. Tell him Jesse has awakened."

Interest sparked in the eyes that flicked toward the house. "He's okay, then?"

The child had expressed concern for Jesse since Luke delivered him yesterday, even going so far as to offer to help with nursing tasks. That Butch thought highly of Jesse was obvious. In a hushed voice, Luke had told her and the Switzers that the boy had practically insisted on being allowed to come and help as soon as he heard of Jesse's injuries. Because this was the first time he'd displayed emotion for a task since being delivered into the Maddoxs' care by a preacher in Hays City, they had not the heart to deny him.

"Apparently he looks to Jesse as some sort of hero or something," Luke had told them, shaking his head. "No accounting for why. It's not like Jesse has spent much time with him, or any of those boys for that matter."

Katie had considered the matter last night, and she thought she understood why. Though Jesse could be engaging and jovial, he was primarily a solitary man, often wrapped up in his own thoughts. The few times she'd seen him while visiting with Emma, she'd noticed a pensive, almost tortured expression on his face when he thought no one was looking. She'd seen a similar expression on Butch's face last evening while he emptied the slops into the hog trough after supper. No doubt the child sensed a common bond in their troubled pasts.

Butch was waiting for her reply.

"Weak, but well." She smiled at the child's obvious relief. "He is sleeping again, as he will do often until he regains his strength, but he spoke with *Maummi* Switzer."

Butch silently set the bucket down beside Katie's half-filled one and headed toward the empty field east of the barn, where Jonas's black-and-white-clad figure could be seen walking in the distance. Katie was happy to note that the child's step had a slight bounce that had been absent before now.

"A good boy is that one," commented *Maummi* Switzer. "Our Rebecca says his grief for his *mader* and *fader* keeps him apart from the others, but she is determined to love him as her own."

With a final glance toward the child, she disappeared into the house. Katie returned to the pump, a familiar ache pulsing deep inside her chest. How well she understood the loneliness of grief. In the months after Samuel's death, she thought she would drown in it, and she would have welcomed death as a way to join her beloved. But even before then she had become acquainted with grief. In all the years of their marriage, the joy of motherhood had been denied her. At first, when her womb did not quicken, there had been little concern. Many waited months before becoming pregnant, her mother assured her. Her body needed more time to prepare for motherhood. Katie consoled herself with the knowledge that the Lord would bless her and Samuel with a child in

His perfect timing. But when month after month passed, and the women at church services began watching her waist for signs of thickening, she grew concerned.

A full year after her wedding day, she quietly inquired of Martha Hostetler, who had birthed every baby in Apple Grove since the first families settled here. Martha had instructed her to drink a tea of oat straw and nettle leaves nightly. Though she'd faithfully obeyed, the first year stretched into a second. Samuel finally suggested that she see an *Englisch* doctor, where she had undergone the most humiliating examination of her life, and for nothing. The doctor had pronounced her healthy with no apparent cause for her barrenness.

Barren. Even now the word brought a bitter taste to her mouth. She pumped with a vigor born of misery, and water sloshed over the rim of the bucket. Five years of marriage, and not a single sign of pregnancy. There had been a few instances when her hopes had risen, only to be dashed when the inevitable proof of her barrenness arrived. At last the curious glances of the women had stopped, and their absence was even more devastating. The pitying looks awarded to Samuel were the hardest of all to endure, but eventually even those ceased. Everyone had accepted the fact that Katie Miller would never bear a child.

Water sloshed into the second bucket, and Katie pushed the pump handle one last time. She picked up both buckets, one in each hand, and made her way to the watering trough, around which a double handful of cattle had gathered for their afternoon drink.

SIX

The next time Jesse woke the pounding in his head had lessened perceptibly. Every muscle of his body ached, but he was able to draw in a cautious breath without feeling as though he'd been stabbed through the chest with a bayonet. He cracked open an eye experimentally, and a flicker of panic threatened when he could see nothing. Had he gone blind? A moment later he spied the faint outline of curtains drawn over the window and breathed a relieved sigh. Night had fallen while he slept.

His mouth again felt like a dust storm had blown through it, and his lips were dry and chapped. Moving cautiously, he turned his head toward the small table and squinted at the contents on its surface. Had *Maummi* Switzer left him a mug of that whatever-it-was she'd given him earlier? Darkness obscured his view, and he couldn't make out details. He lifted his arm in an attempt to feel for the mug.

Owwwwwweeee! The movement sent agony ripping through his back, and he sucked in an involuntary breath that resulted in a torturous paroxysm in his lungs. A groan escaped his lips as he dropped his arm. In a distant part of his mind he took satisfaction from the fact that he'd produced more volume than previous efforts to moan.

The rustling of fabric preceded someone's appearance in the doorway beyond his feet.

"You are awake?" asked a soft voice. Not *Maummi*. Must be Katie.

"Y-yeah." He snapped his mouth shut, embarrassed at his wavering tone.

"Wait. I will fetch a light."

Everyone else must be asleep, for a deep quiet permeated the house. He traced her progress by the faint sound of her footsteps in the room beyond the one in which he lay. A brief scratching noise, and then a yellow gleam illuminated the darkness through the doorway. It grew brighter as she returned and then Katie stepped into his room, her face aglow with candlelight.

She drew near, holding the candle aloft while she inspected him. Whatever she saw must have satisfied her, because she gave a brief nod. "Are you thirsty?"

"Am I ever. I feel like I could drain the Rio Grande." He matched her whispered tone, mindful that *Maummi* Switzer probably slept lightly, and he wanted a chance to talk to Katie without *Maummi*'s watchful gaze. His stomach threatened a rumble. "And my stomach is so empty it feels like the front is touching the back."

A smile curved her soft lips. "I will be back."

She took the candle with her, and he strained to hear signs

of her movements. It seemed hours before a warm halo of light heralded her return. In her hands she carried a tray, and he was relieved to see not only a mug but an earthenware bowl as well.

She seated herself in the chair by his bed and set the tray on the floor. "First, drink."

When she lifted the mug to his lips he started to protest that he could certainly feed himself, but he remembered the agony moving his arm a few minutes before had caused. He drank, cautiously at first and then greedily, downing the contents as quickly as she would allow. She rewarded his efforts with a smile and returned the mug to the tray.

When she lifted the bowl and spoon, he caught a delicious whiff of something. His poor empty stomach gave an eager rumble.

"I've never been so hungry in all my born days." He tilted his head to see over the rim of the bowl.

"'Tis only broth." She held it close for his inspection. "You must go easy at first."

"Broth." His enthusiasm gave way to a scowl. "I could eat a whole side of beef on my own. But at least I can feed myself."

Moving cautiously, he lifted his left arm and made as if to take the spoon from the bowl. But no sooner had he grasped it than his fingers began a mighty trembling. Disgusted, he released the utensil and it splashed back into the broth.

Her chuckle wasn't without sympathy as she picked up the spoon. "Your strength will return in a few days."

"Not if all I'm fed is broth," he grumbled, but he allowed her to place a spoonful inside his mouth. Oh, how delicious. Surely this was the best broth in all of Kansas, rich and savory with just the right amount of spice to satisfy a starving belly. Eagerly, he opened his mouth for a second taste.

"Your head still hurts?" Her glance flickered upward toward his scalp.

"I'll say." He lifted his left hand and pressed gingerly at the sorest place. His fingers found a lump, and a prickly line along a scab. "Whew. I don't think my hat will fit over that hen's egg for a while."

"It is much reduced. Jonas found the rock you fell on, and one side was jagged and sharp. If your head had hit that side..." Her brows rose meaningfully.

What was it *Maummi* Switzer had said about Katie? "Thank you for sewing my scalp back together. And for everything else too."

She rewarded him with a smile as she lifted another spoonful of broth to his lips.

"Any word of those low down, no-goods who shot me?"

"*Neh.*" Despite her denial, she looked troubled and did not meet his eye.

"What?" he prodded. "Something else has happened. I see it in your face."

She shook her head. "Truly, nothing has happened. Only, every day two men ride their horses along the fence and *look* at us."

"They do, do they?" He had no trouble imagining Woodard and Sawyer directing a menacing glare across the wheat field. Pathetic, trying to intimidate an Amish man and a couple of women. Just wait until he was up and around. He glanced toward the place where his holster hung from the wall peg. He'd teach them a thing or two about intimidation. But next time he might need a partner alongside him.

"Any word from Luke and Colin?"

"*Ja.* Jonas sent word of your injuries, and Luke came two days ago. You were not yet awake."

"Yeah? So he got a good look at that fence?"

She nodded.

"Did he happen to say anything about it?"

"He and Jonas talked."

He waited, but she didn't elaborate. That's the way it was going to be, huh? She was going to make him pull every piece of information out of her like pulling rusty nails from an old board.

"And what did they decide to do?" he asked, more or less patiently.

"Nothing." She concentrated on stirring the broth in the bowl. "Jonas has decided to let the *Englisch* cow man have the land."

"What?" Involuntarily, Jesse sat upright in the bed and immediately regretted it. Sharp pains exploded in his shoulder and vibrated through his lungs. He collapsed against the feather tick, weak and gasping shallow breaths.

She chided him with a stern stare that would have made *Maummi* Switzer proud. "Be still, lest you tear your stitches and undo all the good five days of healing have done."

"He can't give up," Jesse protested when he was able to get a breath. "Why would he let that swaggering rooster rob him out of his land without even putting up a fight?"

Katie tilted her head sideways and spoke patiently, as though to a child. "Did not our Lord say, *Und so jemand mit dir rechten will und deinen Rock nehmen, dem laß ach den Mantel?*"

Jesse had grown accustomed to Emma and Rebecca's habit of lapsing into *Deutsch*, as they called it. Many a time he'd come into the house to hear them chattering away in the language they had spoken growing up. So far he hadn't managed to pick up a single word. "You want to tell me what that means?"

Her eyes went distant for a second. "It means if a man takes your coat, give him your cloak as well."

True, he wasn't as familiar with the Good Book as Colin, but personally he'd have trouble with that particular commandment. And speaking of commandments, didn't it say somewhere that stealing from your neighbor was against the law? He started to mention the contradiction but changed his mind. The last thing he wanted to do was get into a Bible-spouting spat. Only a fool showed up at a fight armed with a single bullet.

Instead, he consoled himself by replying, "Well, soon as Jonas gets up I want to speak to him."

Katie's response was to offer another spoonful of broth.

"Hey, *Maummi* Switzer said something about a boy here to help out."

Her face brightened, and he was struck again by how pretty she was, with those soft cheeks and thick dark lashes surrounding round eyes. Twin candles, reflections from the one on the table, flickered in the dark depths.

"Butch is a hard worker. He has taken over many of *Maummi* Switzer's chores without a whisper of protest." She lowered her hands, still holding the bowl, into her lap. "That is a good thing, for she refuses help from most, though she needs it."

Jesse started to protest that he was still hungry for more soup

but then realized his stomach was feeling full, almost uncomfortably so. Then her words registered.

"What do you mean, she needs help?" Concern for the old
woman rose in him. "Is she doing poorly?"

Katie glanced over her shoulder before leaning forward to
speak in an even quieter voice than she had been using. "I grow
concerned about her heart."

"Oh, that." He forced a laugh. "She's been complaining about
her heart for years. It's a ploy she uses to get her way."

The troubled lines did not leave her forehead. "It may once
have been a ploy, but no longer. She is not a young woman."

The idea of *Maummi* Switzer reduced to an elderly invalid was
so disturbing Jesse refused to consider it. Still, once he was up and
around, he'd be sure to lighten her load somehow.

Katie leaned toward the floor to set the bowl down, and then
lifted the tray and rose. "You will sleep now. In the morning perhaps you may have bread with your broth. *Schlofa.*" A quick smile.
"That means *sleep good.*"

"Hey, wait. Stay and talk some more. I'm not sleepy."

But he was surprised at how feeble his protest sounded. And
when had his eyelids grown so heavy? He could barely keep them
open long enough to see her knowing smile before she picked up
the candle and left the room.

Katie slipped through the door into the chilly night air. She
paused for a moment to breathe in the cool fresh scent of Kansas

at midnight, her lungs filled with the scent of soil, growing plants, and the sweet apple blossoms that had recently begun to decorate the trees. The ever-present breeze blew across the plains with little force tonight, though the faint memory of the long winter just past raised chills along her arms beneath the sleeves of her dress. She hurried across the grass to the water pump to *redd* up the dishes before she went to bed.

She set the tray beneath the spigot and pumped the handle until water gushed forth across the bowl and mug. *Maummi* Switzer had encouraged her to retire earlier, and she had promised not to wait up too late, but something had told her Jesse would awaken tonight and need to eat. A healer's instinct, old Martha Hostetler had said before she passed. Katie preferred to think of it as God's nudges, proof she was doing the work He had given her. Fulfilling a purpose, an important place in the Amish community. Because she was denied the responsibility of raising children, at least He could use her to minister to others.

As she wiped the dishes dry, her thoughts turned to her patient. He was a fine man, but again she'd glimpsed a troubled and violent past. Why else would a man long to fight with another?

Her gaze strayed in the direction of the fence, now hidden by darkness. Certainly she understood the unfairness of the *Englisch* cowman's theft of Jonas's land. The injustice rankled deep inside her as well. Truth be told, she understood Jesse's outrage far more than he realized. She too struggled to comply with the Lord's directives with meekness and humility, especially when the violent ways of the *Englisch* world clashed with the peaceful Amish. What safety was there in the world when the *Englisch* threatened not only the Amish way of life, but the Amish people themselves? If they would shoot at each other, would they stop at shooting an Amish man? Or an Amish woman?

The breeze seemed to grow colder, as though it gathered a sinister chill from evil men and carried it toward her and those she loved. She gathered up the clean dishes and headed for the house, her fearful gaze circling the area around her. When she had closed the door behind her, she breathed easier. Here, hidden from prying eyes in *Maummi* Switzer's peaceful kitchen, she felt safe. The Amish way was, indeed, best. Only by separating themselves from the violence of the wider world could they realize even a small measure of peace and safety. Let the *Englisch* stay on their side of the fence, and she would stay on hers.

Once she had returned the cleaned dishes to their rightful places, she picked up the candle and headed toward the sickroom for one final check on her patient. She tiptoed across the room to stand by his bedside and watched the steady rise and fall of his chest. Good. Jesse had slipped into a deep, restorative sleep that would do as much to speed his recovery as the rich broth she'd fed him.

She lifted the candle higher and studied him. In repose his face shed its care and he looked almost childlike. Well, except for the thick growth of stubble that covered his chin and crept up toward high, prominent cheekbones. Another week and his beard would be nearly as full as Samuel's when they had first married. Samuel had always bemoaned the fact that his beard grew soft and thin, like a youth's. Not so for Jesse. She tilted her head and examined the well-formed mouth, slack and tender in sleep. Hair covered the space between his upper lip and nose in typical *Englisch* style. With a tentative finger, she hid the mustache from her view without touching him, her finger so close that warm breath from his nose tickled her skin. If he shaved that small patch of hair, he would make a handsome Amish man.

With a start, she realized the path her thoughts had taken. Jerking her hand away, she hurried out of the room. Lack of sleep had affected her and made her thoughts fanciful tonight. Best to take her own advice and get some restorative sleep herself.

SEVEN

"Ow, woman!" Jesse writhed in the bed away from Katie's ministrations. He ignored the pain in his shoulder, which seemed like a dull ache compared to the fire she'd just let loose on his head. "What in blazes are you trying to do, finish the job those thugs started?"

"I am keeping your wound clean." She returned his glare with a calm stare.

"It's clean enough. Leave me alone."

She was a passel of contradictions standing there beside the bed in her black dress and white bonnet thing—*kapp*, she'd told him it was called—with a folded white cloth in one hand and a bottle of whiskey in the other. Like an Amish barmaid, if such a thing existed, which he doubted.

A chuckle came from the doorway where *Maummi* Switzer stood watching the procedure.

Jesse glared at her. "You find this funny, do you? You always did like torturing me."

Unfazed by the accusation, she returned his glare with a grin while speaking to Katie. "Ever was he a cranky patient. That, at least, has not changed."

Katie spoke in a firm voice. "Now you must turn over and let me clean the wound on your back."

He switched his glare to her. "You're not pouring that stuff on my back." He narrowed his eyes suspiciously. "Where did you get whiskey, anyway?"

She looked at the bottle in her hand. The amber liquid shone richly in the sunlight, about two-thirds full. "Dr. Sorensen left it to clean your wounds."

"Well, you can forget it. I gave up whiskey a year ago, and that includes pouring it on my body as well as down my throat."

No answer, nor was there the slightest hesitation on her calm but resolute face. It appeared she intended to stand there until he gave in, even if it took all day.

"Like a small boy, you are." *Maummi* Switzer clucked her tongue. "Nothing but whining and complaining. Where is the strong cowboy now, I ask?"

He would have shot back a snappy reply if he could have thought of one. Instead, he ignored the jibe and continued to scowl at the liquor-saturated cloth in Katie's hand. Even if he stuck to his guns, she would simply wait until he fell asleep and then set about doctoring him. Could there be a more unpleasant way to wake up than having your back feel as though somebody had held a live coal to it? With a sullen glance at her calm face, he eased himself over on his left side. Even that minor movement robbed him of breath and set his head to whirling. He was careful not to move his right arm as she unwrapped the bandage wound around his shoulder and neck, but he grabbed a handful of bed sheet in his right fist and squeezed until he thought the fabric would shred in his grip.

He heard a soft release of breath. "The wound looks much better."

Was that relief he heard in her voice?

Maummi Switzer left her post by the door to join Katie. "*Ja*. No red streaks, and the swelling is reduced."

"There, see?" Jesse groused. "No need to bother with it. Just wrap it back up and let it heal."

He might as well be speaking to a tree stump. A cool hand touched his shoulder, soft and oddly comforting. "Lean farther, please," Katie directed. "I would not like to wet the bed with whiskey while I pour."

"I've woken many a morning lying in whiskey." Not that he was proud of the fact. He sighed and set his teeth together as he obeyed her, awaiting the inevitable pain. When it came, he prided himself on the fact that only a single groan escaped through his clenched jaw. Actually, the stinging on his back wasn't nearly as severe as on his scalp a moment before.

"There. Not so bad, *ja*?" A cloth pressed gently, and then she began the process of rewrapping the strips of cloth around his body. "The doctor cauterized this wound. Perhaps that deadened some of the feeling?" Her voice rose as if posing a question.

Cauterized. He held back a shudder and thanked the Lord he had been unconscious during the doctor's visit.

Katie finished the bandaging. "There. Rest now. I will bring lunch shortly."

Gathering the soiled strips of cloth, she left the room. *Maummi*

Switzer waited until he had settled against the feather tick and then fussily rearranged the light blanket that lay across his lower half, smoothing out the folds with an expert twist. That done, she retreated to the doorway, where she turned to look at him. Her gaze caught on something, and he saw her eyes widen.

What had she seen? He turned his head in the direction in which she stared, to the small table by his bedside. There rested an unlit candle, a cup of fresh water, and...

A bottle of whiskey. Katie had forgotten to take it with her.

How long had it been since he'd had a bottle of hooch within his reach? Almost a year now. Emma and Luke didn't keep liquor in their home, and he'd taken care not to venture into town without Luke or Colin. Not that he didn't trust himself, but...

He didn't trust himself.

He suddenly became aware of the smell. It was on his skin and in his hair. It had been a long time since he'd smelled like this, but not long enough for the memories to fade. If he let himself think about it, he could feel the familiar, fuzzy-headed fog of drunkenness calling to him, threatening to encircle him. It was not something he would willingly submit to again.

Did that mean he'd licked the liquor habit? When was the last time he'd looked at a bottle of whiskey and not wanted to sink into the enticing numbness it offered?

"*Uh.*"

A guttural grunt drew his attention to *Maummi* Switzer, who studied him between narrowed eyes. He started to say something about the revelation that he'd passed some sort of milestone, but she didn't wait for him to speak. Her face set in a stern mask, she marched across the room and snatched the bottle from the table.

Without a word she turned and left the room, taking temptation with her.

Jesse stared after her, not quite sure how to react. That she didn't trust him was obvious. Should he be offended? How could he be, when she only wanted what was best for him? If he knew her, she'd take personal charge of that liquor bottle to make sure he didn't have the chance at a swig or so. He found himself chuckling at the idea of *Maummi* Switzer trying to sleep with that bottle tucked safely under her pillow.

"*Bass uff, as du net fallscht!*" *Maummi* Switzer barked the command from the doorway, where she stood watching what was proving to be the harrowing task of getting Jesse out of bed.

"Speak English if you want an answer."

"Take care you do not fall."

"*Ja,*" Katie agreed. "I do not want to sew another cut on your head. Please move slowly."

Jesse didn't waste strength answering her. What choice did he have but to go slow, with Jonas bearing most of his weight and setting the pace for their progress? Jesse's good arm was draped over his friend's shoulder while Katie flanked him on the other side, her arm wrapped securely around his waist. His legs seemed to have lost their ability to support him, and he bit back a frustrated curse when he stumbled and would have fallen if not for their holding him up.

"Can't fathom how I could get so weak so quick." He mumbled the comment to cover his embarrassment.

"Six days have you been in bed," Jonas said in an unstrained voice that Jesse envied. "And you are lucky to be up now."

"He should not be." Katie took the opportunity to voice her protest again. "He is as stubborn as my *fader*'s goat, who insists on wandering among *Mader*'s vegetables, though she has threatened to make stew out of him."

"A man can't stay abed all his life." He would have said more, but breath was at a premium just then.

Maummi Switzer obviously agreed with Katie, but at least she didn't voice her opinion. Instead, she stepped back to let them pass and then disappeared up the stairs mumbling something about, "Stubborn is the fool."

They passed through the neat, sparsely furnished living room and the larger kitchen beyond. Katie opened the door, and sunshine shone through. Jesse drank in the sight of it. All of his life he'd been more comfortable outdoors than in. Given the choice, he'd choose a bedroll in the open air over the most comfortable bed in the fanciest hotel. His skin itched to feel a fresh breeze wash over his whole body, not the puny puffs of air that managed to find their way through the window of his bedroom.

By the time they lowered him into the rocking chair they had placed near the porch railing, his legs were wobbling like a newborn calf. He collapsed more than sat, and he had to close his eyes until the world stopped spinning and the pounding in his head receded to a tolerable throb. When he opened them again, Jonas and Katie both watched him with anxious expressions.

"Guess I'm not as strong as I thought." He managed a weak laugh. "Just let me sit here a bit." A familiar sound from across the yard drew his attention. "Rex?"

His faithful horse stood near the corner of the barn, his head high and ears pricked forward. Butch was at his side, running a brush over his back. Rex gave a second whinny and hurried across the grass at a quick trot. He came up to the porch and shoved his head over the railing toward his rider.

"Good to see you, boy." Jesse rocked the chair forward and threw his left arm around the horse's head. Never had he been so happy to breathe in the familiar horse scent he'd complained about during long months on the cattle trail. The sting of tears threatened, and he pressed his face against the white star between the liquid brown eyes to hide them. Rex tossed his head gently and whickered, his horsey breath warm against Jesse's neck.

"Good boy," Jesse whispered, and then he managed to regain composure. He thumped the horse on the shoulder with deep affection. "I haven't forgotten that bag of oats and honey I promised you."

"I'll fix it up for him," volunteered a high-pitched voice.

With a final rub on Rex's muzzle, Jesse gave the horse a gentle shove and turned his attention to the boy standing nearby. Butch was around nine or ten and tall for his age, all skinny arms and legs. It looked as though he'd grown since getting those britches, for they fell short of his boots by a couple of inches, even though the fabric bunched where he'd cinched a rope around his waist to keep them from falling down. Bony wrists peeked from below his shirt sleeves. The eyes fixed on Jesse were filled with shadows but also with an eagerness that bordered on hunger.

"Butch has taken good care of your horse since he arrived." Katie bestowed a kind smile on the boy. "He feeds and brushes him every day."

"And helps with chores as well." Jonas ducked his head at the boy, his expression approving, and he then took a backward step. "I must finish with the hogs now."

With a quick glance that did not quite meet Jesse's eyes, he left the porch and headed toward the barn with the manner of what might be called an escape. Jesse watched his retreating back, sorrow and irritation warring inside him. Jonas had made a point to stick his head into the sick room to check on Jesse several times a day, but only when Katie or *Maummi* Switzer was present. Not a coincidence, Jesse figured. Jonas knew he'd be pressed to explain his decision to let Littlefield get away with his thieving, and he didn't relish the discussion.

Jesse tore his gaze from Jonas and returned his attention to the boy. "I owe you one for taking care of Rex. This isn't the first time he's saved my hide. He's a special horse."

"Yes, sir, he is. Real smart too."

"You know, he used to do tricks in a traveling show. I've seen him toss an apple into a basket from four feet away, and he can dance better than me. The man who owned him before could stand barefoot on his back and shoot at a target while Rex galloped smoother than a stone skimming over a pond." He caught a glimpse of Katie's alarmed expression behind the boy's head. "Don't try that, though," he cautioned.

Butch shook his head. "I won't."

Jesse didn't think he would. If this boy ever had a streak of mischief in him, it had been buried by the avalanche of sorrow he'd suffered in his short life. "If you could mix up a mash of oats and honey for him, though, I'd consider it a personal favor."

The boy looked at Katie, as if for permission.

"I saw a full jar of honey in the kitchen." A smile touched her lips. "I think *Maummi* Switzer will not mind sparing some for a horse that does tricks."

Butch nodded again, though his forehead did not lose the ever-present crease between his eyebrows.

"Tell you what," Jesse told the boy. "You can do me a big favor, if you've a mind. Have you ever ridden before?"

"Yes, sir. My pa taught me when I was little, before..." His throat moved with a swallow. "I ride Preacher Maddox's horse whenever he lets me."

"Good. It'll be a few days before I can climb back in the saddle." Katie opened her mouth to protest his estimate of a "few days," judging by her aggrieved expression. Jesse continued before she could say anything. "I don't want Rex to get fat and lazy. What he needs is somebody to ride him every day to give him a bit of exercise."

Hope dawned on Butch's face as he realized what was being asked of him. "You want *me* to ride him?"

"If you're of a mind to, and if you can spare the time from your chores around here."

"I'll get up before the sun comes up." The child's back straightened, and he turned wide eyes on Katie. "I'll take him out before watering the cows in the morning?" He said it as a question, as though asking her permission to accept the offer.

She appeared to consider and then gave a nod. "I will inform Jonas and *Maummi* Switzer of your new responsibility."

The first smile Jesse had ever seen on Butch's face ignited a light in his eyes. Something stirred in Jesse's heart to witness the excitement that made the boy rise up on the toes of his boots.

"I'll exercise him real good, sir. He won't get fat, I promise."

"That'll be fine." A thought occurred to him. Katie had said that Littlefield's men had been seen riding along the fence every day. That might only be a show of bluster intended to intimidate Jonas and the women, but if those blackhearted villans would shoot him in the back, what would they do to a child alone? "Do me a favor, though. Ride him that way." He pointed toward the road that marked the southern boundary of Jonas's property, in the opposite direction of the fence. "And don't go too far, all right?"

"Yes, sir. C'mon, Rex. Let's go see about those oats."

He whirled on his boot heel and with a cluck toward Rex, he took off toward the barn at a run. Rex regarded Jesse with one liquid dark eye. Though Jesse knew horses didn't laugh, he could have sworn Rex was chuckling.

"Go on, boy. And watch out for him, okay?"

His head bounced up and down twice as though replying in the affirmative before he turned and trotted off after Butch.

Katie's jaw dropped as she watched the horse disappear into the barn. "I almost believe he understands."

"Of course he does." Jesse settled back in the rocker, fidgeting gingerly until he found a comfortable position for his injured back. Overhead the sun blazed in a cloudless sky of deep Kansas blue, but the covered porch provided pleasant shade. "I think I'll spend the afternoon out here. It's a far sight more pleasant than lying around in bed, don't you think?"

She studied him a moment, eyes narrowed. Then she disappeared into the house without a word. A moment later she returned carrying a wooden straight-back chair with a basket resting on the seat. When the chair was in place by his side, she seated herself and leaned over to pick up a piece of fabric from the basket. He watched her thread a needle with a quick, expert motion and then go to work on the fabric.

Was that where she learned how to sew? He gingerly pressed a finger along the scab on his head and indulged in a cautious breath, enjoying the earthy smell carried to him on the breeze. A few days ago he couldn't have done that. He could barely get enough air in his lungs to keep himself alive. Katie had told him what Doc Sorensen said, that the bullet had lodged in the lining of his lung. Another quarter of an inch and it would have ripped a hole in his lung, an injury from which he would not have recovered, more than likely. The constant headache and occasional dizzy spell let him know he hadn't fully healed from cracking his skull, but mostly the pain in his head was easy to ignore. Many a time in years gone by he'd risen early and put in a full day's work with a pounding head left over from a night of drinking.

No, what bothered him most was the weakness in his right arm. Nearly a week and still he could barely lift it without searing pain in his back and shoulder. Worry niggled at his mind. What if Littlefield's boys returned and he needed to hold a gun? He'd never been good at shooting left handed.

He became aware that she was watching him.

"*Wie geht's?*"

"What?"

A quick apologetic smile flashed onto her face. "I am sorry. I forget sometimes to speak English. I asked how you were."

"I'm good. I can actually get a decent breath now." He inhaled again to prove it. "Uh, did the doc say how long it would be before my arm stops feeling like it's being ripped off every time I use it?"

She shook her head, her attention on her stitching. "He did not say, but the muscle in your shoulder was injured. Muscle takes time to heal."

Her offhand manner comforted him a bit. At least she seemed to think he would recover in time. He lifted his right arm experimentally, setting his jaw against the resulting pain. Was it not quite as sharp as before? Maybe he'd better practice shooting with this other hand.

"What are you making there?" He nodded toward the fabric in her lap.

In answer, she picked it up with both hands and held it up for his inspection. A tiny garment, with little sleeves and a long skirt.

"Baby clothes?"

"*Ja*. A gown for Rebecca's little one. See here?" She held the garment toward him. "An M to stand for his last name."

"His?"

A shrug. "I think the child will be a boy."

Tiny white flowers surrounded the letter and circled the loose collar of the gown. Jesse had no idea about women things like stitching, but even he could admire the beauty of the intricate work. "That's real pretty." He raised a boyish grin toward her. "Maybe the next time I crack my skull you could sew JM into my scalp."

That elicited a laugh, a sound Jesse enjoyed immensely. Though Katie frequently wore a shy smile, he'd rarely heard her laugh. He found himself trying to think of ways to make her laugh again.

"I hope Rebecca does not mind the design."

"Doesn't mind?" Jesse shook his head. "Why would she mind?"

Her expression grew serious. "It is far too fancy for an Amish baby, but Rebecca is no longer Amish. I have seen fancy stitching on her *Englisch* dresses, so perhaps she will be pleased."

Though Jesse knew more about the Amish now than he had when he first met the Switzers, he realized he knew little of their beliefs. He was aware of the obvious, that they dressed only in black and white, and the men shaved their mustaches but not their beards, while the women hid their hair beneath those starchy *kapps.* But why?

"Is there some sort of law in the Bible against fancy stitching?" He pressed his toe on the boards beneath his boots, and the chair rocked gently.

Katie returned to her work, her gaze focused on her hands as the needle wove in and out of the fabric. "Not *die Bibel,* but the *Ordnung* cautions against anything that may lead to pride. Instead we choose to model Christ in simplicity of dress and lifestyle."

"Huh?" Jesse didn't follow. "I admit I don't know much about the Bible, but I don't think Christ wore black trousers and suspenders."

He snapped his mouth shut. She might think he was poking fun and take offense. Instead, her smile deepened and he breathed easier.

"*Neh,* Christ did not wear trousers and *braces,*" she glanced up at him as she spoke the word, "but He was a simple man, without conceit or vanity in any form. To live like Him, Amish avoid opportunities for vanity. We dress alike so no one has cause to take pride in their garments."

"Really?" Actually, the explanation made sense. He'd seen some pretty prideful women strutting around the streets of town in their fancy getups. "Is that why you all drive the same kind of buggies too?"

"Ja. They differ only in size." She tugged at her needle to tighten a stitch and then raised her work to bite off the thread.

"So why black? Why not brown or something else?"

"Black is a modest color." She leaned toward him and spoke in a low, conspiratorial tone. "I have heard that some districts in the East allow gray and even blue dresses. And shirts for the men as well." She turned the garment around and began plying her needle to one tiny sleeve.

Ah, sleeves. "And why long sleeves, even in summer?"

"To bare our skin to the view of others would be improper." A faint peachy stain colored her cheeks. "There are some sights a woman reserves only for her husband." She bent forward over her work, presenting him with a view of the top of her *kapp*.

Jesse turned his head, sorry to have embarrassed her. He'd never given much thought to the reason behind the funny clothing Jonas and the other Amish wore, but now that she'd explained, it made sense. A cowboy on the trail learned quick to hide any possession he took pride in or it would get stolen by some jealous cowpoke or other. He once saw a man get shot over a pair of high-priced boots that a trigger-happy bandit admired. There was something to be said for not having anything different than the fellow who bedded down next to you.

He would have asked more questions, but a movement on the road caught his eye. A man on horseback topped the hill. By instinct, his right hand inched toward his side, but not only was he not wearing his holster, the slight movement produced a sharp reminder in his shoulder that he wanted to use care before he did that again.

"We have company."

Katie's head rose, concern apparent on her face. In the next moment, her rigid posture relaxed. "And also an Amish visitor."

Sure enough, a buggy came into view. They followed the horse and rider, who Jesse noted was maintaining an unhurried pace, obviously traveling with the buggy. When they neared, he recognized the man.

"It's Luke." He sank back in the rocker. "I wondered when he'd manage to get back over this way."

She folded the little gown and laid it in her basket before rising to her feet. Gazing at the buggy, a smile broke free on her face. "It is also Amos and Sarah Beiler. The children too. I will tell *Maummi* Switzer."

The door slammed shut behind her as she hurried into the house. Jesse watched the little troop's arrival at the front yard. On the buggy's front bench sat Amos, his round-brimmed straw hat perched on the top of his head, his black-and-white-clad wife seated beside him. With a flick of the reins he guided the horse toward the shade of the huge tree that dominated the Switzers' yard. Before the wheels had stopped moving, a boy leaped from the rear bench to the ground, where he landed in a crouch.

The woman half rose, her expression alarmed. When the child bounced to his feet, her shoulders deflated. "Karl Beiler, how many times have I told you not to do that? You're gonna break a leg one day."

"I am sorry, *Mamm*." Though the words were contrite, Karl

looked anything but. Mischief glinted in the close-set eyes that, like his father, looked slightly crossed.

Luke guided his horse beside the buggy and jumped down from the saddle with an ease that Jesse envied. While Amos climbed down and then turned to help his wife, Luke lifted the two Beiler daughters to the ground. Pretty little girls, they looked like miniature adults in their matching Amish dresses and white *kapps*.

Luke crossed the grass toward the house with a huge smile plastered on his face. "That's more like it. You look almost normal again." He hopped up the steps onto the porch and covered the distance to the rocking chair in two long strides. "Don't bother getting up."

"Wasn't planning to." Jesse turned a grin upward and rocked. "Decide to see if I'd kicked the bucket yet?"

"Something like that." Luke leaned against the railing, his long legs stretched out before him. He took his cowboy hat off and smoothed his hair down. "Emma sends her best."

"How's she doing?"

"Pretty as ever."

Jonas had apparently heard their arrival, for he rounded the corner of the barn at the same time Butch emerged from inside. Then the door to the house opened, and Katie and *Maummi* Switzer came out to greet their guests.

The Beilers arrived on the porch, each carrying a bundle. Amos offered an arm to his wife, who leaned heavily on it while she climbed the two stairs. Her round belly bulged beneath the black dress, and Jesse glimpsed a swollen ankle when she stepped onto the porch. Unless he missed his mark, she was closer to dropping her baby than Rebecca. She looked plumb tuckered out, her face red and slightly damp. A mass of blond curls had escaped the confines of her *kapp* and were performing wild gyrations around her face in the wind. Jesse's instinct was to jump up and offer her the rocking chair, and he rocked forward, ready to haul himself to unsteady legs.

"Don't you dare." Sarah pointed at him and speared him with a look every bit as forceful as *Maummi* Switzer's. "You just set yourself down there and stay still."

Luke raised an eyebrow in mock alarm. "You'd better listen to her. I heard she once wrestled a two-hundred-pound outlaw to the floor of the saloon and held him there until Colin arrived to haul him off to jail."

Dimples creased her cheeks. "Aw, go on with you. That was Sassy who done that, not me."

Her gaze flickered toward Amos, who did not seem at all upset at the reminder that Sarah, his Amish wife, had once been an *Englisch* barroom singer named Sassy. Instead, the tender look he bestowed on her kindled a flicker of envy in Jesse.

"This is for you." Sarah thrust the basket she held into *Maummi* Switzer's hands. "They're crunchy sugar cakes. Don't mind the burned edges. Amos says he likes them that way."

Amos's gaze dropped to the floorboards, giving Jesse the impression that he didn't like the treat quite as much as she claimed, while *Maummi* Switzer took the gift with a gracious nod. "*Danki.*"

"*Gern gschehne.*" Sarah's wide grin spoke of her pride in knowing the proper response. "And there's more too. Girls." She motioned for the girls to deliver the parcels they carried. "A loaf of cornbread I fixed just this morning, and *snitz* pie, and a jar of apple butter we put up in the fall. The girls did most of the work," she admitted. "Better'n me, truth be told."

"Come inside." *Maummi* Switzer turned toward the door. "A fine snack we will fix for the men."

"Oh, goodie." Sarah clapped her hands together. "And we can visit while we're fixin'."

Jesse watched the women file into the house, Katie holding the door open until the others had passed inside. A bemused smile hovered around her mouth as she looked after Sarah. Jesse couldn't imagine two more opposite women than Katie Miller and Sarah Beiler. As different in temperament as looks too. Sarah boasted a boisterous, rowdy personality that matched her untamable blond curls and buxom figure that no amount of black Amish garb could hide. By comparison, Katie was quiet to the point of almost being shy. No, that wasn't right. Not shy. Serene. Her unassuming manner seemed to exude peace. And as for her looks, she was quite simply the loveliest girl Jesse had ever known.

Before she started for the inside, her glance slid toward him. Caught staring at her, Jesse's face warmed. He started to look away but found himself unable to turn from her beautiful eyes. Thick lashes fluttered modestly downward before she disappeared into the house.

EIGHT

Katie pulled the door shut and paused with her hand on the latch while willing her pulse to slow. Jesse's gaze had sent blood racing through her veins in an all-too-familiar rise of emotions. Not since before Samuel's death had she felt the giddy lightness that came from the admiring attention of a handsome man.

An Englisch man, she reminded herself. *Not Amish. And not for me.*

Years ago she had given her life to the church. She'd knelt before the bishop in front of the whole Apple Grove district, repeated the Confession, and been anointed with the waters of baptism. She had not made that commitment lightly. She and Samuel had discussed their decision many times during their courtship. Never had there been the slightest doubt that they would both be baptized. It was the life she had been raised to, the only way she had ever known, and not once had she considered another. For all her life she would follow Christ in the way He had called her to follow Him, as an Amish woman.

Of course, she'd always imagined she would have Samuel by her side. They had knelt in baptism together as they intended to live—side by side, sharing every joy and every burden.

Tears threatened, and she squeezed her eyes shut against the sting. At moments like this she missed him with an intensity that threatened to pull her back into the dark cave of grief in which she'd lived during the months following his death. And yet...

She opened her eyes and noted the sunlight gleaming through the small window high in the door. What she missed most about Samuel was his friendship. They had been close friends from childhood, at play and at school and at Sunday night singings. But if she were honest with herself, never had his glance sent the blood racing through her veins like Jesse's.

"Are you coming, Katie?"

Sarah's call provided a welcome distraction from her thoughts. Katie left the door and entered the kitchen, where *Maummi* Switzer stood at the work surface arranging a mound of burned sweet cakes on a tray. The tight set of her lips spoke loudly of her opinion of the overcooked treats. Or perhaps her disapproving scowl was for Sarah. Draped over a chair at the table, Sarah sat with her legs spread wide beneath her dress and her arms dangling at her sides. Katie scanned her flushed face, concerned with the swelling she saw there.

"Honey, I don't know how much longer I can keep this kid in." Her lower lip protruded and she blew upward to sweep the loose strands of hair from her blues eyes. "I swear I feel that if I squatted down in the corner he'd slide right out."

Maummi Switzer looked toward the corner where she pointed and then fixed a scandalized glare on her guest. "Ugly words soil a pretty mouth."

Sarah shrank back. "You mean I shouldn't a said that?" She looked at Katie for an answer.

Katie shook her head. "'Tis considered unbecoming to speak of the miracle of birth in such a manner."

Confusion colored her face. "Even among women? I'd never talk like that in front of the men, a'course, but I figured I was safe here." She cast a hurt glance toward the older woman, who had returned to her task.

Katie spared an understanding smile for her friend. Nearly a year ago Amos Beiler had fetched the woman he had fallen in love with from a saloon in Lawrence, Kansas, to be his wife and mother to his children, and to live a Plain life in Apple Grove. She'd embraced Amish customs with an enthusiasm that many girls born to the faith never exhibited, but her improper behavior was, at times, shocking. Katie had befriended her and undertaken the task of instructing her in acceptable Amish ways, but at times even Katie was surprised by the crass and unacceptable comments that came from Sarah's mouth.

"Purity is not a garment we don to impress men or even other women," she explained in a patient tone. "Purity is a way of life. An Amish woman's mind must focus on Christlike thoughts and reject coarseness in any form."

Sarah's shoulders slumped. "I might as well give up, then. You'd be shocked at the thoughts that never make it outta my mouth. Some would probably curl your toes up right inside your shoes."

Katie caught a flash of amusement on *Maummi* Switzer's averted face.

"A good thing, then, that you have learned to control your tongue." She tilted her head and studied Sarah through narrowed eyes. Her baby was still at least two months from birth, so the swelling of her fingers and ankles, and the puffy skin beneath her eyes, was faintly disturbing. "How do you feel? Are you drinking the raspberry leaf tea?"

"Every day, though I can't abide the taste without adding a couple a dollops of honey. Amos says I drink more honey than tea."

That might explain the puffiness. Perhaps it was not so much swelling as added weight, resulting from overindulgence in sweets. Still...

"Do not eat so much salt pork," she advised. "Stick with fresh, and cook without seasonings for a week or two."

Maummi Switzer nodded in agreement, and a satisfied feeling settled over Katie. Though the older woman was not a midwife, she'd done a lot of doctoring in her lifetime.

"*Das gut.*" The elderly woman set a platter piled with treats on the table between them.

"Why I swan, would you look at that?" Sarah eyed the platter with delight. "You made my burned-up sweet cakes look like a feast. That bread looks so fluffy and light, not like mine a'tall. But is that my apple butter in your pretty little dish?"

"*Ja.* The bread is fresh this morning and tasty with apple butter." She glanced at the two wrapped bundles still on the work counter. "We will have those for our supper tonight. *Danki* for the bounteous gift."

Sarah preened, obviously pleased with herself. Katie considered telling her that one or two offerings was considered sufficient when paying a social call, and in fact more made the visitor appear overeager for the host's approval, but she didn't have the heart to deflate the woman's pleasure in her successful visit.

Maummi looked at Katie. "Reach down cups for the water, please."

She left the table and crossed the room to the shelf where the cups lay in neat rows. Rising on her toes, she reached up and grasped the first two.

"Oh, look at you, so slender and pretty." Sarah's sigh held a note of longing. She spread her fingers and encompassed her huge round stomach like a cage. "I used to have a waist like yours. Someday I will again, the good Lord willin'."

Though she knew Sarah's words were kindly meant, the prickle of impending tears stung her eyes. For years she had longed for her flat belly to swell with a precious child, but it was not to be. For a reason unfathomable to her, the Lord had willed that his daughter, Katie Beachy Miller, was not to know the joy of motherhood. And because she could not inflict her barrenness on another, neither would she know again the joy of marriage. An image bloomed, of Jesse's brown eyes admiring her across the porch. She thrust it away and quickly turned her back to the room, lest anyone see the tears that blurred her vision.

After the women disappeared into the house, Jesse saw the three Beiler children eyeing Butch. The younger girl looked to be around his age, though he was nearly as tall as the older one. But it was Amos's boy, seven-year-old Karl, who took control of the situation.

"You got a creek around here?" he asked Butch.

With a quick glance toward the fence, Butch shook his head.

"How about chickens?"

Butch cocked his head. "Yeah, we got chickens."

Mischief sparkled in the younger boy's eyes. "Will you show me?"

"Karl." Amos leveled a stern gaze on his son. "Do not chase Jonas Switzer's chickens. If they stop laying eggs, as ours did, I will send you to peel a switch."

"*Ja, Fader.*"

The boy's shoulders slumped forward in submission, but from the angle of his rocking chair, Jesse saw the spark of mischief flare even brighter. He bit back a chuckle. A rascal like little Karl was exactly what Butch needed to stir up his boyish tendencies.

"I will watch him, *Fader,*" the older girl promised. No doubt the mantle of responsibility fell on her shoulders quite often, with a brother like Karl and a mother like Sarah, who was just as likely to fall in with his lively ways as correct them.

"There are some kittens in the shed out behind the barn," Butch offered. "The mother hid 'em, but I found 'em yesterday."

The younger girl's eyes lighted. "Will you show us?"

He nodded, and the children left the porch. The men watched until they disappeared into the barn. Jesse noted the faraway looks on his friends' faces. No doubt they were remembering similar times from their own childhoods. He'd never had much of a boyhood himself. Pa died when he wasn't too much older than Butch, and he joined his first cattle drive in order to send some money back home to Ma. Not much place for mischief-making on the trail.

"So, Jonas," said Luke when the four men were alone, "I see the fence is still in place. You had any more trouble from Littlefield?"

Jonas shook his head, but Jesse noticed he avoided meeting anyone's eye.

"No trouble?" Jesse twisted his lips. "Not unless you count those thugs of his riding along the other side of that fence every day, glaring this way and upsetting the women. Soon as I can get back up on my horse, I'll show them an upsetting thing or two."

Jonas turned an alarmed face his way. "And be shot again?" He shook his head so hard the round hat slipped down on his forehead. He resettled it. "*Neh.* Land is not worth the cost of a man's life." A teasing smile tweaked at his lips. "Even an *Englisch* man like you."

Jesse ignored the jibe for what it was, an attempt to distract him. "But it's your land. You can't let Littlefield get away with stealing."

Signs of an internal struggle played across Jonas's face, but beside him Amos's expression remained placid.

"You do not understand Amish ways." Amos spoke not as one who sought to convince, but matter-of-factly, by way of explanation. "Peace is valued above all. Without peace, no amount of land matters."

"I understand, truly I do." Luke leaned against the porch railing, his long legs stretched out and his boots crossed at the ankle. "Living with Emma these six years past, I've started to understand a bit about the life here. But you're not talking about fighting with a peaceful man, Jonas. Littlefield isn't one of your Amish brothers."

"All men are our brothers in Christ," he replied instantly.

Jesse bit back a scowl. That sounded to him like a rote reply, something memorized from that *Ordnung* of theirs. And yet Jonas's voice rang with conviction.

"Even a man who'd shoot a friend in the back?"

Troubled eyes fixed on him. Jonas nodded with obvious reluctance. "Even that man."

"Well, I don't understand that at all," Jesse snapped.

Luke gave him a quick warning look, and he then spoke in a level, reasonable tone. "Look, do you think Littlefield will stop at stealing *your* land? If he gets away with this, he'll move on to someone else."

The conversation standing in front of the house stirred in Jesse's memory. "Luke's right. He's already taken advantage of a pair of widows back East, using their names to secure more land than he's allowed and no doubt cheating them out of what they're due."

"He won't stop with them, either," Luke said. "I've been doing some checking, and the word I got is he's conniving and greedy. Once he beats you down he'll move on to someone else, and he won't stop until he can lay claim to every bit of land in this whole territory."

"He'll run you out of here, Jonas." Jesse looked at Amos. "And you may be next."

They wore twin troubled expressions at the idea, but neither of them looked convinced yet.

"I don't know about you," Jesse said, "but I for one am not

letting Sawyer get away with shooting me in the back. If he'll do it to me, he'll do it to someone else."

"That's right," agreed Luke. "And Littlefield's the one who sent him after Jesse, you can count on that. If we don't do something to stop him, we might as well be aiming the gun at another man and pulling the trigger ourselves."

"How'd you like to have that on your conscience?" Jesse held first Jonas's gaze and then Amos's.

"I..." Jonas closed his mouth and then his eyes. Jesse had the impression he was praying, and when he opened them again, he saw resignation in the troubled depths. "What would you have me do?"

It was not agreement but an earnest question. He wanted to know what steps they were suggesting he take. Problem was, Jesse didn't have a clear idea, and from the look his friend was giving him, neither did Luke.

"Not a thing," Luke answered after a minute. "We respect your ways, and neither of us wants you to do anything contrary to your beliefs. Let us handle Littlefield. You carry on here like you have been."

That seemed to relieve them both. Jonas nodded. "It is a matter for one *Englisch* man to discuss with another."

The door opened just then, and *Maummi* Switzer's head stuck out. "Jonas, fetch for us a table from the barn. It is a nice day to sit outside and enjoy the air with our treat."

She disappeared back inside, and Jesse watched the three men start for the barn. He, of course, could only sit by helplessly and watch them do the work.

Jonas waved Luke back. "Stay and talk with your friend. We will get the table."

Luke relaxed against the porch railing, watching their retreating backs.

"So what *are* we going to do next," Jesse asked in a low voice when they had moved out of earshot.

Luke shrugged. "I'll stop in Hays City on my way home and pay a visit to the sheriff there. Shooting a man in the back is a crime. If he arrests the one who did this to you, that'll send the message to Littlefield that we don't intend to back off."

Though Jesse would prefer the message be clearer, preferably in the form of a show of force, he knew for now he'd have to settle for Luke's plan. "It's a start."

⁂

Jonas entered the barn with Amos at his side. The children were not in sight, though he heard the distant sound of childish voices drifting through the open doorway at the back side of the barn. He nodded toward the side wall, where they kept the barrels and boards they used as tables when they had church meals at their house, and Amos moved toward the opposite end of the nearest board.

Before he grabbed hold, Jonas looked at him. "They are *Englisch*, but their words make sense, *ja*?"

Worried creases appeared above Amos's close-set eyes. "It is not our way to resist evil done to us, and yet what they propose is not resistance." The crease deepened. "At least, not by us."

"Is it wrong to grant them permission to follow their own

plans?" Though he was Amos's elder by at least fifteen years, Jonas respected the wisdom the younger man had accumulated over the years and valued his opinion in matters of propriety and faith.

Amos shook his head. "As long as you do not lift a hand against another man, you are not guilty of wrong. Of that I am sure."

Relief settled over Jonas, but doubt still nagged at a corner of his mind. "Bishop Miller advised gifting the property to the *Englisch* cow owner."

"Advised?" Amos's eyebrows arched high. "Or directed?"

Jonas thought back to the conversation a few days ago, when he'd taken his buggy to the Miller farm with the news that Jesse had been shot while acting on his behalf. The bishop's exact words had been, *"Much prayer is required in this matter. Perhaps it would be best to make the land a gift."* Jonas had been hard put to restrain signs of the anger and injustice that rose up in him at the words.

"Advised," he replied firmly. If the bishop had directed him, he would have had no choice but to obey.

"Ah, then."

Each man grasped the wide board and, with a silent signal, lifted in unison. They headed toward the opening with their burden between them, Amos walking backward in the lead.

When they arrived at the opening, Amos stopped. The look he gave Jonas was troubled, and he had difficulty maintaining a direct gaze. Instead, he fixed on the place where Jonas's hands grasped the wood.

"Have you wondered lately if our bishop is..." He paused to swallow. "Distracted?"

Guilt flew at Jonas on powerful wings. The thought had

occurred to him many times over the past months. Before the lot had fallen to him, John Miller had been a jovial man, full of humor and laughter. The role of bishop was one he had accepted with a sense of commitment that few displayed, and the Lord blessed his leadership of Apple Grove. His administration of the district was done with care and the same good-natured humor he had possessed since boyhood. But now the man never laughed. Jonas couldn't remember a time when he'd so much as smiled recently. Instead, he went about with a perpetual scowl carving lines in his sagging cheeks.

But discussing a bishop in a negative light was serious business. Jonas chose his words carefully. "Samuel's death haunts him still. Hard, it must be, to lose your only son."

"Hard for Ella too," Amos persisted, "yet her soul has once again embraced the peace of Christ."

Though guilt buzzed inside his mind, the truth of Amos's words resonated in a deeper place. "*Ja.*" He nodded. "The bishop seems to cling to grief with clenched hands."

Amos raised his head then, and Jonas found himself caught in a wretched gaze. "A bitter heart leaves no room for compassion. And is not compassion necessary for leadership?"

Jonas considered Amos's meaning, and to his sorrow found himself in agreement. They had all witnessed Bishop Miller's harsh judgment in stopping the traditional youth singings because he claimed they led to "inappropriate fellowship" between young, unmarried men and women. The entire district knew, though no one said, that the true reason had lain in the fact that his daughter-in-law, Katie, had emerged from mourning and attended her first singing since Samuel's death. And had Bishop Miller's harsh judgment not threatened to infuriate Jonas not more than a week past?

But to accuse the bishop of letting his grief stand in the way of his administration of the duties *Gott* had bestowed on him?

Jonas did not filter the conflict from the gaze with which he returned Amos's. Nor did he wish to continue this disturbing conversation.

"We must pray for our bishop," he replied in an even tone.

A moment's pause, and then Amos nodded before continuing to walk backward through the doorway with the table for their afternoon snack.

NINE

Jesse opened his eyes Thursday morning and, for the first time since the shooting, he didn't feel like throwing up. A good sign. He turned his head, testing the pain, and was pleased when the movement resulted in no more than a dull ache.

He spied something on the bedside table that drew his attention. Once again, Katie had forgotten to take the whiskey bottle away after cleaning his wounds the night before. *Maummi* Switzer's vigilance was slipping. He indulged in a grin as an idea occurred to him. He could have a little fun plaguing her.

Soft female voices drifted through the doorway that had been left cracked open a couple of inches. He heard the clink of a dish and then the sizzle of something frying on the stove. Bacon, judging by the delicious aroma that stirred up a rumble in his empty stomach. If he was real quiet, and they were intent on their tasks, he might have time.

Moving slowly, as much for stealth as caution for his weakened state, he rolled onto his side and then pushed himself upright. His vision swirled dangerously, and he squeezed his eyes shut until the world stopped spinning. There were only a few steps between here and the window, where the curtains waved gently in a cool morning breeze. The window looked out over the garden west of the house, so the sun was not yet visible, but a few clouds overhead glowed with a pink light that let him know the day was underway.

He grabbed the bottle by the neck. Standing required an effort that sent the world careening crazily again, but he managed not to fall or make any undue noise. Thank goodness for the empty chair someone had left beside his bed. The sturdy wooden back provided the support he needed to leave the mattress behind and cover the three or so feet to the window.

Once there, he kept a firm hold on the sill. Grasping the cork between his teeth, he twisted the bottle open. A soft *pop* set his heart to thudding, and not merely because he feared being overheard. The sound called to mind a passel of memories, not all of them unpleasant. For one moment, the sharp smell of whiskey overpowered the aroma of frying bacon, and he was tempted. One taste would do no harm, surely.

But when had he ever stopped with just one drink? Jesse knew that first taste would lead to another, and another, and another. This half-full bottle would be empty in less time than it took to sing a verse of "The Ol' Cow Hawse." And he'd be lost in a drunken fog once again.

With a hand that trembled from more than physical weakness, he thrust the bottle outside and tipped it. Amber liquid trickled out to wet the grass below him. Not all of it. No, that would be sure to cause a ruckus. Only a little, enough to rouse *Maummi's* suspicions.

That done, he recorked the bottle and, moving as cautiously as before, returned to bed. Only when he had seated himself and arranged the blanket over him did he set the bottle on the table—with an audible thud. Then he leaned back on the feather tick to wait.

Sure enough, they had been listening for him. The door opened and Katie entered. But where was *Maummi* Switzer?

"*Guder mariye.*" Katie's smile brightened the room more than any candle could. "You are well this morning?"

He returned her smile absently, his gaze fixed over her shoulder. "Truth be told, my stomach's a bit uneasy. Might have been something I ate yesterday." He straightened his neck and projected his voice to carry past her. "Or maybe something I drank."

As he had hoped, *Maummi* Switzer came scurrying into the room. She paused in the doorway, her gray brows gathered low over her eyes as her gaze swept over him.

Concern settled on Katie's features as she crossed to his bedside. "Have you a fever?" Her hand felt cool against his forehead.

"Nah, I'm sure it's nothing. I'll be fine."

Sure enough, the old woman's gaze settled on the whiskey. With a sharp look in his direction, she strode to the table and snatched up the bottle. Her eyes flickered from him to Katie, and he clearly saw the struggle on her face. Should she say something or keep silent? Jesse had a hard time trying to hold back a snicker.

Finally, she turned and marched through the door, mumbling something about "*redding* up the room." Chuckling, Jesse relaxed into the soft feathers. She'd fret about that whiskey all morning.

"I'm fine," he told Katie. "It's probably nothing more than an empty stomach tempted by that bacon I've smelled for a while now."

She continued to study him for a long moment, and then she gave a small satisfied smile. "I will bring a plate soon."

"No need for that. I can eat at the table like everybody else." He couldn't lie abed forever, could he? As long as they continued to mollycoddle him, he'd never get his strength back.

Her eyebrows arched, and he expected her to deny him. He released a sigh when she replied mildly, "I will prepare a place for you."

After checking the wound on his back and placing a clean shirt and his boots within reach, she returned to the kitchen. As he slowly donned the shirt, he contemplated her response with a certain amount of satisfaction. If she'd still been worried about fever and infection and the like, she would have protested. He must be getting better. Certainly the whiskey she'd poured on his scalp last night hadn't stung nearly as much as before, and he could hardly feel it at all on the bullet scar.

Time to get up outta bed, cowboy, and get back to work.

Work. He paused in the act of easing the fabric over his weak right arm. And what work would that be? Protecting Jonas and *Maummi* Switzer from the conniving machinations of Littlefield was his immediate task, but what about afterward? Would he return to Luke's place? The thought left him cold. Though Luke and Emma had gone out of their way to make him welcome, a man couldn't live off of his friends forever, could he? Maybe he ought to claim his own hundred-and-sixty-acre parcel and start up a farm. True, in all the years he'd run cattle up and down the Chisholm Trail he'd never had much respect for sodbusters, but in the past year he'd learned to enjoy working the dirt. There was a certain amount of satisfaction in harvesting a crop a man had planted with his own hands. And who said he couldn't start up a small herd of cattle, as Luke had done? He could even build himself a house, like he'd helped Colin and Rebecca build theirs after the church was finished.

He slipped the shirt over his head and tucked the tail into the waistband of his britches. What good was a house without a family to live in it? On his own he didn't need more than a privy and a one-room shack for when snow froze the ground and made it too uncomfortable to sleep outdoors. No need to build a whole house without a wife, and no decent woman would have him.

A noise from the kitchen drew his attention, a low female laugh. Katie. His head jerked up and he stared hard at the doorway, as though he could see through it and catch a glimpse of her smiling face and trim figure as she went about the task of preparing breakfast in *Maummi* Switzer's kitchen. Speaking of decent women, there was a fine one right here under the same roof as him. But of course she wouldn't spare a second thought for him. He had nothing to offer her.

But if I did lay claim to land, and start up a farm and a herd of cattle...

He shook his head to dislodge the spark of hope the thought produced. He'd spent his good years in rowdy living, rolling in muck so disgusting he'd never get the stink of it out of his nostrils. Taking up with her would sully the fresh wholesomeness that was Katie's nature. Besides, she was Amish, and he, most definitely, was not.

Emma used to be Amish before she married Luke. The thought crept unbidden into his mind. *And Rebecca too, until she met Colin.*

But somehow he sensed Katie was different. When she spoke

of her Amish beliefs, he sensed not a shred of hesitance, not a single whisper of desire for any lifestyle other than the one she lived. He knew better than to expect a woman of her character to give up her whole life for a rowdy cowpoke like him.

With the gloom of certainty gathering to form a lump in the vicinity of his chest, he shoved his foot into a boot and thrust the disturbing thoughts from his mind.

❦

Katie bit off the final thread and smoothed the wrinkles from the tiny white gown on her lap. There. Her gift for Rebecca's babe was finished. Though after Sarah's visit yesterday, perhaps she should have made something for the new Beiler daughter—Katie was positive Sarah carried a girl, though she could not pinpoint the exact source for her certainty—before Rebecca's. No doubt Sarah would deliver first. Katie closed her eyes and formed a silent prayer that the Lord would seal Sarah's womb long enough for the little one to be born healthy.

She opened her eyes to find Jesse observing her. He had resumed his place in the rocking chair after breakfast, and had watched her and Butch make a dozen trips from the water pump to the trough with a scowl. The unaccustomed exertion of joining the rest of them at the table had exhausted him, and he dropped off to sleep while she performed the rest of her chores. When she finished, she'd moved a chair quietly to his side to work on her sewing.

"You are rested after your nap?"

A grimace squeezed his features. "Whoever heard of a grown

man taking a morning nap after a full night's sleep?" He scrubbed at his eyes with his left hand. "I've got no more strength than a newborn lamb."

"You sleep less now than three days past," she pointed out. "Your body is working to make up for the blood it lost. A man with less strength would not have recovered."

He considered the statement, and then his expression softened. "It's thanks to you I'm alive at all."

She found herself unable to return his frank stare and fumbled to fold the baby garment. Fortunately, before she finished, the sound of a horse's hooves clopping in the distance announced the arrival of a visitor. Welcoming the distraction, she stretched her sight to catch a glimpse of the approaching Amish buggy. A lone man on the bench this time.

When the figure drew near enough to recognize, her spirits sagged. Bishop Miller had come to pay a call. Or had he come to check on her? As he drew near, she became aware of his sharp gaze fixed on her. With a quick glance at Jesse, she rose and hastily shoved the gown into the sewing basket. She could go inside and prepare a light meal. Surely *Maummi* Switzer would want to offer the bishop a bite to eat and a cool drink. But though she intended to head for the door, she found herself held in place by the unsmiling countenance of her father-in-marriage. Her arms pressed the sewing basket into her stomach, and she had to lock her knees to keep them from trembling.

"Hey, you okay?" Jesse's inquiry held a note of concern.

She gave a shaky nod. "It is the bishop come to call."

"Yeah?" He turned narrowed eyes on the buggy. "I met him once, a long time ago."

Later she might be curious about that, but at the moment she was too busy battling a fit of nerves as she watched the bishop stop his buggy in the same shady spot the Beilers had taken the day before.

Why am I anxious? I have done nothing to bring his disapproval.

She spared a quick glance for Jesse. He was the reason behind her jittery stomach. Though she did not fully understand why, she did not want the bishop to see her talking with the *Englisch* cowboy.

Too late for that.

Maummi Switzer, who had been in the vegetable patch teaching Butch to recognize the difference between weeds and bean plants, rounded the corner of the house wiping her hands on her apron. Katie relaxed her clutch on the basket. No one intimidated *Maummi* Switzer, not even the bishop.

Fader Miller climbed down from the buggy and called a greeting toward the older woman. "A pleasant morning to you, Marta."

"And to you. Always a treat to see our bishop."

The two reached the porch at the same time. *Fader* Miller studied Jesse as he might inspect a lame horse someone was trying to sell him. Finally, when his brooding silence began to feel awkward, he dipped his head.

"I heard of your injury. I trust you are recovered." Not a trace of sympathy appeared in the stern countenance.

Jesse replied with an easy smile. "I'm getting there, thanks to the care of these fine ladies. Without them I'd have been a goner."

"Thanks are due to our Katie." *Maummi* Switzer beamed at her. "She has an uncommon healing touch, and she has not left his side since she arrived."

Katie kept her eyes lowered. Though she appreciated the good word, she wished the older woman had not chosen this moment, and this audience, to deliver her tribute. *Fader* Miller's gaze, full of speculation, slid to her for a moment before returning to Jesse.

"Jonas will arrive in a few moments." *Maummi* Switzer waved toward the field east of the barn, where Jonas could be seen making his way toward them. "Please sit here in the shade. Katie and I will bring a cool drink." She indicated the chair beside Jesse's rocker that Katie had vacated a moment before.

"A drink would be most welcome." Bishop Miller cleared his throat. "Though I would like to speak privately with Katie first."

Sparse gray eyebrows rose high on *Maummi* Switzer's wrinkled forehead. She glanced at Katie before replying, "*Ja*, of course."

Fader Miller looked at Katie. "Perhaps a walk in the shade of the apple trees?"

Though he posed the question as an invitation, she knew she had no choice but to accept. Her stomach tensed into knots. What could he want to say privately? Rarely had he spoken to her since Samuel's death, and then always in the presence of others. Swallowing against a throat tight with nerves, she set her basket on the porch near the door and followed him down the steps. She spared a passing glance at Jesse, whose questions lay heavy on his brow.

The bishop remained silent as he led her to the small stand of apple trees. Blossoms still clung to the branches, though many had fallen in the past week or so. A thin layer of wilted petals covered the ground, and tiny apples no bigger than a pea had begun to appear amid the leafy foliage. The petals swirled around Katie's feet as she dragged herself after the bishop, and their sweet scent lingered in the air around her.

Once they were inside the grove, he ended his silence. "He is recovered from his wounds, this *Englisch* man?"

Katie had suspected that Jesse would be the topic of this conversation. "He is recovering," she answered carefully.

He glanced toward the house. "I see no lingering signs of his injuries."

"He lost much blood. The doctor said it will take weeks for him to fully regain his strength."

"Weeks?" He halted and looked down at her from his towering height. "You would stay here for weeks, caring for this *Englisch* man?"

"Not weeks," she replied. "One week more, perhaps."

"Already you have spent a week. Marta Switzer is a capable woman. Why not leave him in her hands?"

"*Maummi* Switzer's heart grows weak with age." She sent a concerned glance backward to the house. "I fear placing an undue burden on her would be harmful."

"She appeared well a moment ago." His eyes narrowed. "Tell me, is there more behind your care than concern for an injured man?"

She found herself the object of intense study, and her thoughts turned to yesterday, when her pulse sped up in response to Jesse's gaze. Her heart began a heavy thudding in her ears. Could the bishop see guilty thoughts on her face? A warm blush threatened to creep upward beneath the high collar of her dress.

"His injuries are extensive, and he is *Englisch*." She nearly wilted with relief at the calm, measured tone she had managed to maintain. "What else would I feel but concern for his health?"

His eyes narrowed, and then he gave a tiny nod. He resumed his slow pace, hands clasped behind his back. "It would be unseemly for my son's wife to spend more time caring for an *Englisch* man than for one of our own."

Thoughts raced in her mind. Was he accusing her of neglecting her Amish friends in order to care for Jesse? If so, it was an unjust complaint. "I am not aware of illness or injuries that need tending among those in our district." Her reply contained the faintest hint of the insult that rankled inside.

The thin lips tightened. "Sarah Beiler complains of pain in her back."

"Sarah was here yesterday." A touch more heat slipped into her voice. "I advised a change in her diet to guard her health and her babe's."

"The cut on my Hannah's hand—"

"Was closed and healing well when I saw her eight days past. Has something changed since then?"

She saw from his expression that it had not. She also saw that he was growing impatient with her, and guilt niggled at the realization. One should not argue with the bishop. To do so was disrespectful to him and to his appointed position of leadership.

But he is wrong!

Shame flared at the sinful thought. Wrong or not, he was the bishop.

He continued his slow pace, though she was aware he watched her closely from the corner of his eye. "Do you know what will occur seventeen days from this one?"

Seventeen days from now? Today was Thursday, so that would be the second Sunday of the month. It would be the week for church, and if she remembered aright, it was her parents' turn to host the church meeting. Was he giving her until then to return home?

"I will be home to help my family prepare for the meeting," she promised.

He came to a stop and pierced her with an icy stare. "You do not remember. It is the twentieth of May."

She closed her eyes. Yes, she had forgotten the date for a moment. May twentieth, the day her Samuel pressed a tender kiss upon her forehead before he went out to plow the far field and never returned.

"You dishonor the memory of my son."

Katie's eyes flew open, startled at the harsh accusation in his voice. "I-I merely forgot the date, that is all."

"You have forgotten far more than the date. You have forgotten your place as Samuel's widow."

Her irritation of a moment before swelled. "And what place is that? To go about my days with a long face and bitter disposition? How would that honor Samuel's memory?"

"Never have you shed a tear for him." The bishop's nostrils flared, and spots of color appeared high on his cheeks where his graying beard grew thin.

Breath entered her lungs with an outraged *whoosh*. "What do you know of my tears? Of the mornings I have woken with my bed stiff from salty tears shed in the night?" She snapped her mouth shut. Her private moments of grief were hers alone, not to be trotted out and displayed for approval by this man or any other. "Samuel loved laughter and pulling pranks and the joy of being the first to smile at the rising sun of a morning. Tears do not honor his memory." She straightened and looked him full in the face, letting him see the anger there. "Nor does a life lived in a dark cave of pro-longed bitterness and grief."

"You would chastise me for grieving his loss?" His eyes nar-rowed to slits. "You, who ensured that his line would die with him? It is thanks to your barren womb that he has no son to follow him. When I am gone, his memory will disappear with me, and that is your doing alone."

Katie stepped backward as though slapped. The harsh words, sharpened by his fury, flew straight at her heart and hit their mark. Pain erupted inside her ribcage, so vivid it robbed her of breath, and she raised both hands to press against her chest.

The bishop's shoulders heaved, whether from anger or unshed tears, she did not know. He tore his gaze from her face. "You have spent enough time tending this *Englisch* cowboy. Today you will return home."

The pronouncement barely penetrated the heavy cloud that had invaded Katie's thoughts. Because his piercing eyes continued to watch her for a sign that she understood, she managed a nod. He turned and retreated in the direction they had come, leaving her alone beneath the apple trees. His heavy footfalls receded into silence behind her.

Katie collapsed against a tree. Rough bark prickled the cheek she pressed to its trunk, and salty tears ran in tiny rivers down its length. The bishop's harsh words battered her mind over and over. Barren womb. No son to follow. Her fault.

Dear God, if I could change, I would. You know I would.

But nothing could change the fact of her barrenness. The only thing she could do was make sure no other man suffered the child-less fate of her beloved Samuel on her behalf.

An image arose in her mind, of Samuel's laughing face, his eyes shining with admiration for her. In the next instant she realized it was not Samuel's eyes she saw, but Jesse's.

⁘

Jonas intercepted Bishop Miller as he stepped from the shade of the apple trees into the open sunlight. He had been walking off the plot of land at the eastern border of his property—on *this* side of the *Englisch* man's fence—in preparation for plowing. That field had remained uncultivated in all the years since he had moved his small family here, providing good grazing for his cows and goats. Though saddened at the necessity, he planned to plant his corn there next week because his cornfield was denied to him. The bishop's arrival provided a welcome interruption to his work.

"*Guder mariye.*" He called the greeting as he neared. "A pleasant day to you."

The man halted his walk toward the house and turned. Jonas nearly stumbled at the fury he spied on his flushed face. Did the bishop come bearing bad news? Or was he ill, perhaps? Before he could form a question, Bishop Miller spoke.

"I have instructed Katie to return home. Long enough have you kept her here to tend your *Englisch* friend."

Jonas stared at the man while trying to make sense of the words. Was the bishop accusing him of holding Katie here against her wishes? Nothing could be further from the truth. "I did not—" He snapped his mouth shut on the explanation, stunned at the raw display of emotion on the face before him. Surely inappropriate for an Amish man, and doubly so for a bishop. The man was not thinking clearly. Best not to explain, lest the explanation be mistaken for argument.

"Of course her family misses her at home," he replied instead. "We have been grateful for her help."

The bishop made a visible effort to get himself under control. His shoulders heaved with several deep breaths, and when he next spoke, the sharpness of his tone was much reduced.

"How long will the cowboy remain in your care?"

Jonas glanced toward the porch, where Jesse sat rocking slightly, watching them from a distance. "He is weak still but gaining strength every day. I believe Katie mentioned that it would be several weeks—"

"One week." Bishop Miller snapped the words. "By then he should be strong enough to return to his own home."

Jonas took special care to keep his expression calm. That the bishop wanted Jesse gone, far from Apple Grove, was obvious. What had occurred to set him against Jesse? A movement behind his shoulder drew Jonas's attention. Katie walked beneath the apple trees, her shoulders drooping and her head bowed. The reason for Bishop Miller's behavior became clear.

"It is because of me that Jesse Montgomery was hurt." He spoke mildly, hoping as he did so that the bishop would not take offense. "Is it not my Christian duty to offer aid to my fellow man?"

His tactic did not work as planned. The man's chest swelled with a swift indrawn breath. "Do you venture to instruct me on Christian duty?"

"No," Jonas rushed to say. "I only thought—"

"Your thoughts give me much concern." Bishop Miller's mouth formed a tight disapproving line beneath his clean-shaven lip. "Word has reached me that you are not, perhaps, as dedicated to obeying the *Ordnung* as you once were."

Jonas's jaw dropped. How could anyone doubt his dedication? He had devoted his whole life to Amish practices, to living as Christ instructed. He was still casting about in his mind for a response to the stunning accusation when the bishop continued.

"Did you ride astride the *Englischer's* horse?"

For a moment his mind was blank. Then he remembered. He'd ridden Jesse's horse to the Beachys' farm, and then to Hays City to fetch the doctor. "Only in the interest of saving a life. Had I tarried to hitch the buggy and travel at the slow pace of my horse, my friend would have died."

"Is there a weapon in your house at this moment?"

"Yes." He answered truthfully, if reluctantly. "But it is not mine. It belongs to my injured friend."

"Your friend." The bishop's gaze strayed toward the porch, his nostrils flared wide. "You have many friends among the *Englisch*. And family too. I grow concerned that their ways may entice you from your Amish faith. Is this not the very reason we insist on separation from the world, so that our lives will not become corrupt from their evil practices?"

An anger that rivaled Bishop Miller's rose from deep in Jonas's gut. A dozen answers came to mind: that men's actions must be ruled by charity; that Christ urged love for others, sinners as well as righteous, Amish as well as *Englisch*; that his daughters might not follow the Amish practices in which they were raised, but they were *not* evil. Because he could not muster the strength to speak in a peaceful voice, he held his silence.

"One week," the bishop repeated. "By then the *Englisch* cowboy should be well enough to return home where he belongs."

Without a word of farewell, Bishop Miller left Jonas standing alone in his yard, his arms dangling helplessly at his side. Stunned by the conversation, he watched the bishop climb up onto the seat of his buggy and pick up the reins. A moment later, the horse started forward. As the buggy turned in the yard and headed toward the road, *Mader* came through the door, a laden tray in her hands.

"Jonas," she called across the yard. "Did you not ask him to stay?"

Jonas couldn't answer. All he could do was watch the bishop's retreating back, the words still tumbling like stones in his mind.

TEN

I don't understand." Jesse's tight grip on the straight-back chair was born out of necessity. "That man can march in here, tell you to pack your stuff, and make you go home?"

A smile curved Katie's soft lips. "You do not need me anymore. Look at you, standing under your own strength and taking meals at the table beside everyone else. It is time for me to leave."

He considered releasing his grip on the chair so she could judge for herself how weak he still was, but pride kept him upright. She'd already seen evidence of his weakness more than he liked to think about. Besides, Butch stood nearby holding her horse's lead. He hated to embarrass himself in front of the boy.

"That isn't the point. If you want to go home, go, but decide the timing for yourself instead of jumping when someone tells you to jump."

"I want to go home. I miss my family."

He didn't believe her, not when she refused to look him straight in the eye when she said it. And why was the tender skin around her eyes red and slightly puffy?

The door behind him opened and *Maummi* Switzer exited with a cloth-wrapped bundle in her hands.

"For your *mader*, to thank her for loaning her daughter to us." The elderly woman handed the bundle to Katie. "It is apple bread with walnuts and a jar of blackberry preserves."

"*Danki.*" She took the gift with her free hand, her other holding the rim of her sewing basket. "You will send for me if need arises?"

From the gaze that searched the older woman's face, Jesse knew that Katie wasn't only referring to him.

Maummi Switzer waved a dismissive hand in his direction, more than likely purposefully misunderstanding. "Him! If he gives me trouble, I will take my broom to his backside."

The corners of Katie's lips turned up. "I left red clover in the kitchen. See that he drinks the tea each day." Her smile faded into a meaningful look. "And hawthorn berry as well."

The older woman busied herself with brushing an imaginary speck of dirt from her apron, but when Katie continued to stare, she finally jerked a nod. "*Ja*, I know."

The door opened again, and Jonas exited. He picked up the bulging bag Katie had set on the wooden boards near the step and carried it to her buggy. The trio on the porch watched him store it on one side of the bench.

Katie crossed the two steps that separated them. "Please sit down so I can leave without fearing that you will fall."

He started to argue, but he gave in to the imploring look on her face. Gritting his teeth, he managed to round the chair and sit without falling, though a faint buzzing in his ears threatened a return of the dizziness.

"*Danki*." She stood looking down at him. "Take care, Jesse. Do not lose patience with your healing. Remember that a babe first creeps and then crawls before he walks."

He scowled. "If you think I'm going to crawl on the floor like a baby, you don't know me."

A faint smile curled the soft lines of her mouth. "I know enough to know that you will try to run before you walk."

She started to turn away. He was gripped by a sense of urgency that bordered on panic. When would he see her again? He grabbed her arm to stop her. Surprised, she turned a questioning glance on him.

"I wanted to thank you for...you know." He shrugged. "For all you've done."

The smile broke free, and a curious lightness invaded his mind.

"*Gern gschehne*," she replied. "You are welcome."

She turned away, but not before he glimpsed the glitter of moisture in her eyes. Or maybe he had imagined it.

Maummi Switzer moved to his side, and together they watched as she approached Butch. Her tone, but not her words, carried faintly on the breeze. The boy glanced at them on the porch, and then he returned his gaze to her face and nodded. Then she approached the buggy, and Jonas lifted her up onto the bench. With a final wave, she flicked the reins and the horse lurched forward. Jesse watched her leave, afraid to blink lest he miss the moment if she turned and waved again. Was it his imagination, or did the sun's rays darken as she turned the buggy onto the road, heading away from them? Away from him.

When Katie passed out of view, *Maummi* Switzer turned a stern gaze on him. "Your wounds are clean enough," she announced. "I will pour the liquor out this minute."

At another time Jesse might have teased her and told her how he'd tricked her into thinking he'd taken a couple of swigs from the bottle, but at the moment the idea of a shot of whiskey didn't sound all that bad. It might ease the tightness that had gathered in his chest. "Maybe you should." For the first time in months he didn't trust his judgment. Butch and Jonas strode side by side to the porch.

"You want anything?" the boy asked, his expression intent.

Jesse shook his head. "I'm good, thanks."

"If you need something, holler for me. I'll listen for you."

Jesse nodded, and Butch ran off toward the barn. A moment later he appeared with two buckets, crossed to the pump, and began filling them.

Jesse became aware that Jonas was studying him.

"A fine woman, our Katie."

Because the statement didn't require a response, Jesse kept his gaze fixed on the road down which she had traveled. How far was it from here to the Beachy place? He would have asked Jonas, but he didn't want to say anything to cause that probing stare to turn to concern.

A moment later Jonas went inside the house. He returned with Jesse's belt, the holster and six-shooter dangling a few feet above the porch. "I must move this to the barn."

Jesse arched a brow. "Why?"

Jonas looked embarrassed and did not meet his gaze. "It is against our *Ordnung* to house weapons that may be used for violence."

"You have guns. I've seen them."

"Not pistols," he returned quietly. "Rifles for hunting only, and not kept in the house."

"A rifle can kill a man same as a pistol whether it's stored in the barn or the bedroom." Jesse shook his head. "It's that bishop, isn't it? He's been on you because I'm staying here."

Though his friend didn't answer, Jesse saw from the misery in his kind eyes that it was so. Frustration gripped his stomach with a fist. Their ways were different, but disarming a man who was fighting a war could lead to real trouble.

Jonas spoke in a calm voice, his expression tranquil. "I submit to God's authority."

"You mean to Bishop Miller's authority," Jesse corrected.

"The one is the same as the other. He was chosen to lead Apple Grove, to ensure our adherence to the *Ordnung*."

"I respect your belief, Jonas, but letting one man control your life...I'd have to question that practice."

Though Jonas maintained his trademark placid mask, one hand rose to tug at his beard in an unconscious gesture of discomfort. "Since his Samuel's death, the bishop grieves. And who would not, to lose his only son as a young man?"

Jesse tried to understand the point. Not having children he couldn't put himself in the bishop's boots directly, but he could imagine the grief of losing someone you love. Hadn't he wanted to dig a hole and crawl in when his pa died, and then again a few years later when Ma followed? That's when he'd had his first taste of whiskey, as a twelve-year-old boy who had just learned of his mother's passing. But not everybody who lost a child turned into a sour-faced tyrant who took his grief out by bossing others around. "Jonas, Katie was telling me that some Amish are allowed to wear blue shirts instead of white. Do some keep their rifles in the house as well?"

Jonas cocked his head sideways to consider. "*Ja*, I suppose this is so."

"So what you're saying is that the rules here are more demanding than they are other places." When Jonas didn't answer, Jesse continued. "Who sets these rules, anyway?"

"Many are dictated by the Confession, and *die Bibel*, of course."

"And the others?" Jesse prompted.

The fingers tugged at the beard with renewed energy. "The others are defined by the *Ordnung*, the practices by which an Amish community lives."

"And that *Ordnung* is written by the bishop?"

"The *Ordnung* is not written," he said quickly. When Jesse continued to stare, waiting for an answer, he nodded. "It is given to shape the lives of the Amish, to build community and help prevent temptation so we can live like Christ. *Ja*, the bishop provides leadership by helping us apply the *Ordnung* to everyday situations." He leaned forward, and Jesse sensed his desire to convey the depth of his belief in the words he spoke. "The bishop is appointed by God's own hand. We who live by the *Ordnung* must follow his leadership. It is the only way to ensure a Plain life, a life of peace and simplicity."

Jesse stared at the man, moved by the sincerity, the passion in the eyes fixed on him. Peace. He'd had enough violence, enough rowdy living, to fill five lifetimes, and he would like nothing more than peace.

If I were Amish, I might have a chance with Katie. The thought rose unbidden in his mind, bringing with it a longing that had nothing to do with passive living. He shoved it away, but it sprang back like a coil.

A chance with Katie? He frowned. The head wound must have addled his brain. What would that pure, wholesome girl want with a no-good like Jesse Montgomery?

"I don't know, Jonas." He spoke slowly, shaking his head. "I think if I were Amish, I'd start looking for a district where the rules made sense."

Jonas started at the words, his fingers frozen in the act of tugging on his beard. After a long moment he turned and left the porch, mumbling something about getting to work on his field.

"That's it, boy. Just one more round." Jesse wasn't sure if he was talking to himself or Rex, but his grip on the saddle horn was tighter than a fat foot in new boots. A bead of sweat rolled down his temple, followed by another. His teeth ground together in the effort of putting one foot in front of the other. Rex was more carrying him than supporting him, but he did his best not to let on to the boy walking beside him, watching him with an anxious expression.

The horse slowed his pace to that of a sheep grazing in a clover field, but he obediently continued his fifth circuit around the Switzer house. Good old Rex. Jesse would have given him an affectionate slap on the neck if he could have done it without falling.

"You sure you don't want to set a spell?" Deep creases lined Butch's youthful forehead. "You're looking kinda greenish."

That's because I'm fighting not to heave my breakfast.

But Jesse gave a curt nod and saved himself the effort of answering. A man couldn't get well sitting around in a rocking chair all day. He had to keep blood pumping through his veins. Already he could tell a difference in his strength, and this was only the second day. His shoulder was healing. When he did sit, he'd taken to moving the joint around as much as he could tolerate. This morning he could lift it higher than yesterday. What would Katie say about his efforts?

Katie.

Only two days had passed since she left, but it felt like weeks. Amazing how the absence of her quiet, serene presence and her sweet smile affected everyone. Life went on around the farm as usual. Jonas was plowing a new field, so he'd turned over the responsibility of feeding and watering the animals to Butch. *Maummi* Switzer performed her chores in the house and kitchen with the same quiet efficiency he'd always known her to have. Jesse pitched in wherever he could, when he wasn't napping, and he had even taken a chair and Jonas's hunting rifle out to the garden yesterday afternoon to stand guard against a pack of jackrabbits that had shown too keen an interest in the tender plants. He hadn't managed to hit anything left handed yet, but at least the noise kept them on the run. But without Katie, everything seemed...quieter. More solemn.

"Look there, sir." Butch's quiet voice interrupted his thoughts.

Jesse followed the boy's gaze across the wheatfield, where a pair of horses trotted along the fence line. Their riders' heads were turned toward them, though at this distance Jesse couldn't identify either one. Could it be Woodard and Sawyer? His anger flared and he paused. Rex came to a halt. Let them see that he wasn't afraid of any cowardly scum who would shoot a man in the back and leave him for dead. And let them report back to their boss that Jesse Montgomery was upright and not afraid to stand his ground.

After a moment, they turned and headed away, across the creek, in the direction of Littlefield's homestead.

Jesse leaned heavily against Rex's side. Butch stepped closer, concern etched on his young face, but Jesse waved him off. "I'm all right. I think I'll head back to the porch to rest a minute, though."

Instead of continuing on their circuit of the house, the two turned and retraced their steps.

"Mr. Switzer is a nice man." Butch turned troubled eyes on Jesse as they walked. "And Miz Switzer wouldn't hurt a living soul. How come these men are pestering them?"

"Because some men would rather take what they want instead of working for it. They'll look for someone they can tyrannize, who won't put up a fuss. That's the worst kind of yellow streak there is, son." Jesse pressed his lips together. He could list a few choice descriptions of people like Littlefield, but they wouldn't be proper for young ears.

"They didn't teer...teeruh...They didn't bully you."

"They tried." His expression turned grim. "Right before they shot me." Ordinarily he'd never turn his back on a man. Why had he dropped his guard that day?

They continued on a few steps.

"They ought not be allowed to get away with it." Righteous indignation sounded in Butch's tone. "We ought to do something."

Jesse turned to look at him. Out of the mouth of babes..."We'll let the sheriff sort this out. It's both cowardly and against the law to shoot a man in the back. My first instinct is to shoot back, but that isn't the way to live. One shooting leads to another and then another."

He glanced toward the house. Jonas and his family had the right idea, though he didn't think he could ever follow their paths. Be nice if he could. Be real nice to settle back and let God handle the big stuff.

"We'll let the sheriff sort this out," he told the boy. "It's just been a few days since Luke rode over to Hays City and told him about the shooting. I expect we'll hear something any day now."

They arrived at the porch. Rex paused alongside the steps, and Jesse was grateful. It was all he could do to climb them, pulling his weight along the railing. He collapsed into the rocking chair.

Good job, Montgomery. You're only years away from full recovery.

❧

After dinner, *Maummi* Switzer told Butch to put a chair beside the hand pump, and then she assigned Jesse the task of washing up the dishes. Though he made a point of grumbling about being given women's work, he'd done cleanup duty on cattle drives more often than he could count and privately appreciated the chore. When he first came to stay with the Switzers, he'd intended to work alongside Jonas to earn his keep. He couldn't yet handle a plow, but he could certainly manage a few dishes.

When an unknown horse hugging close to the fence topped the northeastern ridge at a canter, Jesse sat upright in the chair, his senses on full alert. He automatically felt for his holster and found it missing. He should have demanded that Jonas let him keep his pistol nearby. The man in the saddle caught sight of Jonas, who walked slowly behind a plow pulled by Big Ed, leaving even rows of freshly turned soil behind him. Jonas paused, exchanged a word with the stranger, and then waved in the direction of the house. When he returned to his work, the horse headed his way and Jesse relaxed. Jonas wouldn't react so calmly to one of Littlefield's men.

Jesse watched as the animal drew close enough to see a tin star pinned to the rider's vest. The sheriff. And he was coming from the direction of Littlefield's place.

"Sheriff," he acknowledged as soon as the horse drew near enough for speech. "Wondered when we'd be seeing you."

"I got out here as soon as I could." He swung his leg over his horse's back and stepped to the ground, and then he came toward Jesse with an outstretched hand. "You'd be Jesse Montgomery?"

"That would be me." Jesse got to his feet and, with a grimace, gingerly extended his right hand.

Instead of shaking it, the sheriff waved the gesture off. "Heard you're recovering from a gunshot. Sit down, son, before you fall down. I'm Ben Wiley, the sheriff over to Hays City."

Jesse didn't know whether to be relieved or embarrassed at the invitation to sit, but he gratefully obeyed. "Ripped up my shoulder pretty good," he said. "They got me in the back."

Wiley took his hat off and smoothed his balding scalp. "Yeah. A man's got to be pretty low to do that."

Jesse arched an eyebrow. "You talked to Sawyer?"

The sheriff shook his head. "I just came from Littlefield's spread. The man who shot you lit out of here right after. They ain't seen or heard from him since. Scared of the law, they say."

"Left?" Jesse figured as much. A man who would shoot another man in the back wouldn't hang around long.

"Littlefield said he was feeble. You know." The sheriff tapped the side of his head with a finger. "Bucket's half empty. He'd hired him on out of pity, but if he'd known the boy was dangerous, he would have sent him packing long before."

"What about Woodard? Did you happen to see him while you were there?"

"I did. He told me what happened. Said he witnessed the whole thing. Said you two exchanged a few heated words, and then Sawyer drew on you after you turned away."

"Did he explain why he rode off and left me for dead on the ground?"

The older man's expression grew solemn. "No. The way he told it, you were shot but still on your horse and riding for home. He said he was sure you'd make it, seeing as how it wasn't that far."

"He's lying. I hit the ground." He pointed to the head wound. "Fell on a rock and knocked myself senseless."

Wiley's hand rose to his lips while he thought. "I don't hold with leaving a wounded man without help, but there ain't no law against it. Woodard didn't strike me as a charitable sort."

Jesse almost laughed at the idea. "No, I wouldn't call him charitable." He sobered. "Littlefield is trying to run my Amish friend off his land. He's strung wire and cut off his water rights. You saw the fence."

Wiley nodded. "But that's not the way Mr. Littlefield tells it."

"I'm sure it isn't."

The sheriff's eyes narrowed, and his jaw hardened.

So *that* was the lay of the land. Littlefield had gotten to him.

Probably not a bribe, because Wiley didn't look like the kind of man who would take part in an underhanded scheme, but he'd been won over to Littlefield's camp. Maybe nice manners and polished words impressed him. Jesse knew the cattle baron was capable of both.

"Every day a couple of his boys ride by trying to scare the family. The have the womenfolk upset, not to mention the extra work they've added."

"There's no law against riding on your own land."

"No, there isn't," Jesse agreed. "But we can't stand by and let them terrorize the family. Right now they have to haul water to the stock; that's mighty hard to swallow when they were accustomed to having their private water supply."

Apparently Sheriff Wiley wasn't willing to discuss the point further. He straightened. "Well, I wouldn't worry none. The fella that shot you is long gone, and the water rights—well, that's something the Switzers will have to talk to Littlefield about. He seems like a reasonable sort. Surely they can come to some suitable agreement."

Jesse's gaze swept the house, the garden, barn, and beyond, where Jonas toiled behind the plow. "This place has been here for years. Littlefield's house is so new the roof hasn't even seen a good rain yet. How can his claim be valid?"

"Look, I don't know about land boundaries and the like. That's up to the folks involved." He placed the hat back on his head. "I'd say they'll get it worked out."

Jesse clamped his mouth shut. Though he was so frustrated he could snarl, he'd better not antagonize the lawman. They might need him before this thing was over.

Sheriff Wiley mounted his horse. "Oh, I nearly forgot. Mr. Littlefield asked me to convey his hope that you're feeling better soon. He said to let him know if there's anything he can do."

He can move that fence. But Jesse held his tongue. The sheriff kneed his horse and took off in the direction of the road.

So much for his help. If anything was done about the matter, Jesse would have to do it.

ELEVEN

Katie's father circled his buggy in front of Leo Stolzfus's barn and stopped near a group of black-clad, bonneted women. Noah, Leo's sixteen-year-old son, came forward to help first Katie's mother down from the front bench and then Katie. She allowed herself to be lifted from the back bench by large hands that nearly encircled her waist, and she awarded the young man a smile of gratitude when he set her on the ground. With a tug to straighten her skirt and a quick check to be sure her church bonnet was in place over her hair, she hurried to join the ladies and leave the way clear for the next arrivals. *Fader* flicked the reins and the horse lurched toward the barnyard, where many identical buggies already formed neat rows. As he pulled away, another horse trotted into his place.

Katie found herself surrounded by young women.

"We heard an *Englisch* man is staying at Jonas Switzer's house."

Interest gleamed in Edna Eicher's wide eyes. "And that he was *shot* with a gun."

"And we heard you were there," said Bertha Schrock.

Charity Wagler, whose thin frame and gangly height showed signs of matching those of her older brothers, bent at her waist to lean close to Katie. "Is it true? Did you see him being shot?"

"I see you have been listening to gossip." Katie pressed her lips into a disapproving line. "What you do not see with your eyes, do not witness with your mouth." It was one of *Maummi* Switzer's favorite proverbs.

"*Ja, ja*," answered Bertha, unimpressed. "But is it true?"

"No, it is not true." Three sets of shoulders sagged with disappointment before Katie continued. "'Tis true he was shot, but I was not witness to the shooting. I merely tended his wounds, along with *Maummi* Switzer."

Their interest flared once again.

"I heard my papa say that a rich *Englisch* man intends to drive Jonas Switzer off his land." Charity's eyes rounded with dismay. "If he succeeds, the rest of us may soon lose our homes as well."

"Is it so, Katie? Is Jonas refused access to his land by a fence?" asked Edna, clearly distraught at the idea.

"*Ja*. That much is true."

Silence fell on them as the women exchanged worried glances.

"I heard the *Englisch* man who was injured is a cowboy, and that he intends to fight rather than let Jonas's land be stolen from him." A grin appeared on Bertha's face. "Is he handsome, this cowboy?"

Something in the line of buggies waiting to unload their passengers caught Katie's eye. A tall figure wearing a light-colored oblong hat, which stood out from the round, black hats Amish men wore to church like a duck egg in a hen's nest. No, surely that was not Jesse. He could not possibly be coming to an Amish church meeting. When she last saw him three days ago he could barely sit upright in a chair for more than a few hours without sleeping. Yet there was a young boy about Butch's size seated next to this man, and that was Jonas on the front bench, and *Maummi* Switzer beside him. A flutter began deep in her stomach. Jesse was not Amish, and she knew he was skeptical of Amish practices. Why, then, come to church? Perhaps this was an attempt to please his host? Or—the flutter increased—perhaps he'd come to see her.

"Well?" Charity interrupted her thoughts. "Is he handsome, this cowboy?"

Katie wiped damp hands on the rough fabric of her dress. "You may judge for yourself. There he is."

They turned in time to see Jonas's buggy approach. Edna drew in a breath, and delight sparkled in Bertha's eyes.

"*Ja*," whispered Charity. "Not at all hard on the eyes, for an *Englisch* man."

The buggy rolled to a stop and Noah came forward to lift *Maummi* Switzer down. On the other side, Butch hopped to the ground and came around the rear. Katie noticed he wore a new pair of broadfall trousers that fit him much better than his old ones. His shirt was of *Englisch* style, and his hat was a miniature of Jesse's. The boy came to a halt on this side of the buggy and looked up, waiting for Jesse to climb down.

He moved slowly and, she noted, used his left arm to grip the buggy's side as he lowered himself to the ground. His right arm he kept protectively close to his body. When his feet were firmly on the ground, he waved at Jonas and watched him pull away. Then he turned, his expression guarded and his eyes darting around the crowd, whose attention was fixed on him. Katie felt a wave of compassion. No doubt he was embarrassed, being let off up front with the women, but she could see by his slight waver that he was not yet fully steady on his feet. Though the barnyard where the buggies were left during the meeting was not far, if he'd had to walk the short distance he may have collapsed from the strain.

His gaze fell on her. A slow smile transformed his expression, and she knew there could be no other reason for Jesse's presence at an Amish church meeting. He had come to see her. An answering warmth spread through her insides, and a smile broke across her face. The buzz of women's hushed whispers sounded in her ears. Their silent exchange had been noted. She could not muster the urge to care.

Butch had also caught sight of her and rushed forward.

"Katie! I've been looking after him like you told me. He's walking more and more, and last night he even took Rex out for a ride!"

She tore her eyes from Jesse to smile down at the boy. She had not seen him this animated since he first arrived at the Switzer farm. "You have done well, Butch. And look at you." She made a show of examining his new clothing. "I see that *Maummi* Switzer's needle has not been idle."

Butch started to reply, but at that moment he became aware that they were the center of attention. His cheeks reddened, and he mumbled something about his old clothes being fine for farm work. Then he returned to Jesse's side.

Jesse apparently noticed the staring eyes of the women. He put on a wide smile and spoke in a voice intended to be overheard. "Good morning, Katie Miller. I've come to show you what your efforts have done. I'm almost good as new, thanks to you." His gaze slid toward *Maummi* Switzer. "Both of you."

The older woman peered up at him through narrowed eyes. When her gaze shifted to Katie, the younger woman kept her expression calm and ignored the speculation she saw there.

But *Maummi* Switzer's attention was nothing compared to the penetrating stare of *Fader* Miller. Katie felt the hot fury of the man's scrutiny all the way across the yard from where he stood near the door of the house. Even from this distance she could see anger in his rigid posture, in the hands fisted at his sides.

Maummi Switzer had noticed as well.

"Butch, do see you those boys yonder?" She pointed to a corner of the yard where a small cluster of children had gathered. "You will enter with them. Jesse, wait there for Jonas." Her finger switched to a place not far away, near the entrance to the barn. "He will show you where to sit."

Jesse turned a confounded look on her. "You mean I can't sit with you?" Though he did not add the words or look in her direction, Katie knew he wanted to say, "And Katie?"

Maummi Switzer looked scandalized at the idea. "With the women? *Neh*! Go with Jonas, and mind you stay awake."

With a quick glance toward the bishop, she hooked an arm through Katie's and marched into the midst of the group of women. As she was dragged away, Katie spared a backward glance. Jesse and Butch stood close to each other, staring after them with lost expressions. She flashed Jesse a quick smile before a half dozen black bonnets blocked him from view.

Jesse's backside was completely numb. If only he could say the same for his injured shoulder muscles. These Amish sure didn't believe in comfort in their church services. A cushion to sit on would have been a blessing. He squirmed on the hard bench and then shot the man next to him a glance of apology when he brushed against his leg. They had been introduced while standing in the yard before the meeting began, but his name had immediately melded with all of the others he'd heard. John, maybe. There were several Johns and a couple of Adens as well. Only one Jonas, though, and one Amos. He switched his attention to the front of the crowded living room, where he could see the back of his friend Amos's head on the front bench.

This was an odd church service. These folks might call themselves Plain and claim to love simplicity above all things, only their rules were anything but. In Colin's church, families milled around before the service talking to each other until the kid whose turn it was rang the bell. Here the men and women clustered in their own separate groups outside, waiting until the bishop gave the signal that it was time to go in. Then they couldn't just go inside and find a seat. A man couldn't enter the meeting out of place. First the bishop and preachers, followed by men in order of age. Jesse had felt out of place following Jonas inside while men his age were somewhere behind him in line, but Jonas assured him that because he was a guest, he was not expected to adhere to the regulation.

No church building here, either. They were meeting in a regular house. The family who lived here had moved out the furniture, and the big room was stuffed full of hard, backless benches, definitely not built for a man getting over a gunshot to the back. When they entered the house, Jonas had offered to set a proper chair over against the wall for him, but just at that moment Jesse had glimpsed a steely-eyed look on Bishop Miller's face. Jesse would rather chew nails than show weakness in front of that man. He squirmed again and found a position that relieved the injured muscles.

Actually, meeting in a home appealed to Jesse. Though he appreciated the church building he had helped Colin and Rebecca build, meeting in a house made the service feel more welcoming somehow. More like a family gathering than a formal affair. Though pressed between two men was not to his liking.

He leaned back so he could see the benches on the other side of the room. That's where the women sat, following the same age order as the men. *Maummi* Switzer's place was near the front, on the second bench. His gaze was drawn across the aisle and back two rows, where Katie sat beside Sarah Beiler, whose pretty voice had dominated the singing earlier.

The hymns had been sung in German. Amos had kindly handed him a book, but because Jesse didn't read German any more than he spoke it, following along was impossible. Slow and laborious, but nice in a mournful way, the songs had filled the room and flew through the open windows toward the neat rows of wheat in the fields surrounding the Stolzfus home.

The bishop and several other men, including Amos, had left the room during the singing, and when it was over, they filed back in. A man who had been introduced as John Somebody-or-Other spoke for close to twenty minutes in a measured, lulling tone, every word in German. Just when Jesse thought he might drift off, the man stopped and Amos rose to take his place. He opened the pages of a leather-bound Bible and read a lengthy passage in a passionate voice that stirred Jesse's spirit, even though he didn't understand a single word.

Then came the painful part. Bishop Miller stood. Though he, too, spoke in German, Jesse had no doubt from the fire in the man's tone that the message was a blistering one directed at him.

Katie glanced sideways, and their gazes connected. He let her see his slow smile and enjoyed watching two spots of red appear high on her cheeks in response. With arched eyebrows, she turned her head pointedly toward the front of the room, but not before he saw the corners of her mouth curve appealingly upward. Satisfied, Jesse leaned forward and returned his attention to the bishop, who had been talking for at least forty minutes and showed no signs of letting up.

When the service finally ended, Jesse felt as if he'd been dunked in a deep river and twisted dry. Sitting on a backless wooden bench was twice more exhausting than *Maummi* Switzer's rocking chair, and a hundred times worse than a full day in the saddle on the Chisholm Trail, but he'd done it! He hadn't understood a single word spoken from the front of the room in the past three hours, but because he'd caught several blushing smiles on Katie's face, and had twice looked back to catch her watching him, he left the Stolzfus home feeling pretty good.

He followed Jonas outside to find the bright Kansas sun high overhead.

"Well, that was interesting."

Jonas's face was a mask of amused indulgence. "You enjoyed the meeting, then?"

Jesse was unwilling to lie about church. "I didn't understand a thing," he admitted, and Jonas chuckled.

The women had begun to file out of the house, and Sarah Beiler caught sight of them. She pushed her way through the milling crowd and hurried toward them, waddling like a duck. "Jesse! I didn't get a chance to speak to you before. We was late." She aimed a scowl at her bulging belly. "I don't move so quick anymore. Anyhow, it's good to see you up and about."

"Thank you. And may I say you're looking fine, Mrs. Beiler?"

Not true, actually. Dark smudges marred the puffy skin beneath her eyes, as though she hadn't slept well, but she gave him a wan smile anyway.

"Thank ye, though I'll be mighty glad when this—" Her mouth snapped shut, and she tossed a guilty glance over her shoulder.

Approaching were *Maummi* Switzer and Katie. Jesse couldn't stop a grin. He'd hoped for an opportunity to speak with Katie after the meeting. Not the same as their long talks on the porch while she stitched a piece of sewing, but he would love to see her smile. As they arrived, Amos also joined their group and greeted Jesse and Jonas with a bob of his round head.

"I didn't know you were one of the preachers," Jesse told him, referring to his role in the service.

"Not a preacher," *Maummi* Switzer corrected. "A deacon. He is charged with reading the Scripture. An important role."

Amos looked properly humble, his gaze fixed on the ground, while beside him Sarah beamed with pride.

"I was just about to tell Jesse how much better he looks today than when we were over that way a few days ago." Sarah grinned at Katie. "You must be a mighty fine nurse."

"She is," Jesse agreed, enjoying the way pink roses bloomed in her cheeks at the compliment. "It's all that tea she makes people drink."

She opened her mouth to reply, but before she could speak she caught sight of something behind him. The pink spots on her face turned red, and her gaze dropped to the ground. Jesse glanced over his shoulder and into the stern countenance of Bishop Miller.

"A pleasant good day to you." The greeting, though friendly enough, was spoken in a cold voice that belied the gracious sentiment. The temperature in the little group dropped noticeably as he joined them. Even Jonas lost his pleasant smile and began tugging at his beard, though his expression remained placid as ever.

Jesse answered in an even tone. "And to you, Bishop."

The man regarded him with a speculative stare. "A surprise to see you here this morning. Did you enjoy our church meeting?"

"Yes. Yes, I did." Jesse said. "In fact, I might come back if it's all right with you."

"*Ja*, visitors are welcome." The man's gaze turned brittle. "The next time you find yourself in Apple Grove, please join us again."

An awkward silence fell, during which Katie kept her eyes lowered and even Sarah seemed without words. Finally, Jonas cleared his throat.

"There are chores waiting at home. Where is the boy?"

"Butch?" Sarah nodded toward the barn. "I saw him running off with Karl and a bunch of others a while ago."

"I will fetch him," Katie said, and wasted no time in hurrying away.

Jesse watched her go, disappointed that their visit had ended so soon. He caught a satisfied gleam in the bishop's eye when he turned back. He tightened his lips. Called by God or not, he disliked the man nearly as much as he disliked Littlefield.

Jesse was seated on the front porch late that afternoon cleaning his saddle and checking the leather straps when a familiar pair rode into the yard. Butch knelt on the floorboards beside him, rubbing an oil-soaked rag over the cinch straps as Jesse directed. When they got home from church Jesse had rested while *Maummi* put together the noon meal, and even now, several hours later, he had to fight back a yawn. Apparently the Amish church service took more out of him than he realized. "Looks like we got company."

The boy straightened. "Hey, that's Preacher Maddox."

Luke and Colin dismounted beneath the shade of the tree and approached the porch, Colin carrying a bulging bag in one hand.

"Well, would you look at that?" Luke grinned toward the mound of tack scattered on the porch. "He's only got one kid doing his chores for him. What happened? Did that pretty nurse of yours get wise to your wild ways and desert you?"

Jesse grinned. "Katie's gone home. And I'm teaching Butch, not using him. He's good help."

The boy nodded, his expression serious. "Jesse's a good teacher."

Colin stepped up, his hand outstretched. "You're looking better than expected."

"I'm feeling better, thanks." Jesse shook the man's hand, though he tensed his muscles to shield his shoulder from undue movement.

Colin thrust his hand toward Butch. "How you doing, son?"

Obviously pleased, the boy jumped to his feet and grasped the hand, man-to-man. "Real good, sir. I've been exercising Rex and helping Mr. and Miz Switzer around the place. I'm earning my keep."

Colin cocked his head, a tender smile hovering in his eyes. "I'm sure you are."

The door opened and *Maummi* Switzer appeared, wiping her hands on a towel. With a quick glance at the horses, she looked up at Colin. "Rebecca is well?"

Colin snatched the hat off his head. "Oh, yes, ma'am. And here." He handed her the bag he carried. "She had the boys pick you some dandelion greens this afternoon. We have more'n we can eat."

"*Danki.*" Looking pleased, she took the bag and then fixed an inquiring gaze on Luke. "And our Emma? She and the little ones are well?"

"She couldn't be better." A smile crept across Luke's face. "Lucas took his first turn ringing the church bell this morning, and you should have seen how proud he was." The smile became a chuckle. "'Course, it took him a few tries, but once he figured out he had to put his whole weight into it, that bell rang far and wide."

She nodded, an indulgent smile playing around her lips. "You will stay for the evening meal?"

The pair exchanged a grin. "We were hoping for an invitation, if it's not too much trouble."

Maummi Switzer's curved backboned straightened, her eyes sparking with pleasure. "I will make apple dumplings."

"Now you're talking." Luke slapped his thigh. "That's my favorite."

The door slammed shut behind her when she disappeared into the house with an eager step.

Jesse eyed his visitors. "You two didn't ride all this way for apple dumplings. And unless I'm mistaken, you didn't come to visit the sick, either."

Their expressions sobered. "Where's Jonas?" asked Colin.

Butch looked up from his polishing. "He's out behind the barn, checking on one of the cows who is about to calf. You want me to fetch him?"

"You'd better," Luke said. "He needs to hear what we have to say."

They watched the boy duck under the porch railing, jump to the grass, and then take off at a run across the yard toward the barn.

"He's looking better than I've seen him since he came to us." Colin glanced around the farm. "This place must be good for healing all kinds of injuries."

"He's a good kid," Jesse said. "Too good, if you ask me."

Luke's eyebrow cocked upward. "How so?"

"When I was his age, I was getting into mischief every day of my life. Snitching my daddy's cigars and stuffing frogs down the girls' dresses. Butch doesn't have a rebellious bone in his body."

Colin shook his head, sadly. "That boy's been through a lot and seen more killing than me, even with years of being a lawman, including his own parents. It has to weigh on him."

Butch returned with Jonas in tow. The two crossed the yard, Jonas's troubled gaze going from one of his sons-in-law to the other. He joined them on the porch and nodded a silent greeting.

Luke reached around to his back and pulled a folded newspaper from beneath his vest, which he handed to Jonas. "You'll want to see this."

The expression on Jonas's face darkened as he scanned the newspaper. When he finished, he handed it without a word to Jesse.

It was a copy of the *Hays City Sentinel*. The paper was opened to a list of notices. A bad feeling settled in Jesse's stomach as he glanced down the page until his eyes stopped on a name he recognized.

> *Andrew W. Littlefield hereby claims one hundred sixty acres of Kansas land, the southern border of which lies approximately forty miles west of Hays City under the terms of the Homestead Act of 1862. The boundaries to said land are established and marked with a fence. Improvements have been made in accordance to the Act in the form of homes and barns erected beginning November 1885. Claim filed with the land management office of Hays City, Kansas.*

Jesse's mouth tightened. Below that notice, several identical ones identified the claims of Matthew Woodard, Harold Lawson, and even the now-absent Saul Sawyer, as well as a handful of women whose addresses were listed as Boston, Massachusetts.

"That snake." His teeth ground together as he handed the paper back to Luke. "He thinks he can get away with it by putting a notice in the paper?"

Colin and Luke exchanged an uncomfortable glance.

"Well, that depends," Luke said. "Jonas, did you ever file a claim to this land?"

Jonas nodded vigorously. "I wrote a letter and sent it to Washington, DC. There was no office in Hays City then. The *Englisch* man who helped us told us about digging the trench to mark our land, and we did. Me, John Miller, Eli Schrock, and the others."

"A trench is a legal boundary in Kansas," Colin said. "As good as a fence. I know that from when we laid claim to our place."

"I dug a trench too," agreed Luke.

Jonas shook his head wearily. "Perhaps it is best to give my neighbor what he wants."

"No, Jonas." Jesse's eyes fixed on the Amish man. "No."

Luke took a deep breath. "Jonas, you can't do that. This is your land, your home."

"*Ja*, it is." Jonas's expression was troubled but serious. "And when I am gone, who will have it? I have no sons. My daughters are gone and have homes of their own." He spared a quick smile for each of his sons-in-law. "I planned for my girls to marry Amish husbands. Perhaps one would be his *fader*'s second son. He would move here to help me work my farm, and one day take over. I would build a *dawdi haus* there," he pointed to a narrow strip of land between the garden plot and the wheat field, "and live out my days as a *grossdaadi*. But now?" He shrugged his suspender-draped shoulders.

"But to give in to Littlefield isn't the answer. Would you have him treat your neighbors the same? Steal their land and endanger their stock?" Jesse shook his head. "You can't do that."

The look Jonas turned on him could be considered mildly

reproving. "He is my neighbor. Did not Christ instruct us to love our neighbors and let naught come between us?"

Jesse was glad when Colin, the preacher, spoke up. "He did, and you're to be commended for following His instructions, but Christ also told us to look out for one another. If you give in now, what's to stop Littlefield from moving the fence again? You might get up in the morning and find his cattle grazing in your wheat field."

Creases appeared beneath the rim of Jonas's straw hat.

"Think about it," Jesse said. "The way he's grabbing up land, he might not stop with you. Who's your neighbor that way?" He pointed to the east.

Jonas cast a quick, worried glance in that direction. "Zacharias Schrock. And beyond him is John Beachy."

Jesse's ears perked up. Katie's father lived two farms away? He filed that bit of information away for future reference.

Colin chided his father-in-law in a reasonable tone. "If Littlefield gets away with driving you off your land, he might decide the Amish make an easy target and he'll go for theirs next."

Though he was still clearly troubled, Jonas shook his head. "Conflict is not the Amish way. We keep ourselves separate from the world in order to escape the corruption that is found there."

"You're not going to stay separate for long if the corruption takes over your land and throws you out of your home," Jesse pointed out.

Colin's expression softened. "Jonas, we don't want you to do anything that goes against your beliefs. We respect everything you stand for." They all nodded, even Butch, who had remained silent but had followed every word. "We want to act on your behalf. You don't have to do a thing."

"Just give us a chance," Luke said. "Let us try one more thing. No fighting, either. Would you agree to that?"

After a long moment, Jonas's head dipped in a slow nod, and Luke and Colin exchanged a triumphant glance.

Jesse studied the pair. Something was cooking between those two. Some plan—most likely as ruthless as Littlefield's. Luke was staring toward the visible marking of Littlefield's fence, his fingers tapping absently against his thigh. Jesse had seen that expression on his friend's face many a time in the years they rode together, and he knew it meant Luke had decided to do something he wasn't entirely comfortable with.

"I know that look," he said. "What have you two come up with?"

"Littlefield is partial to fences." Luke's jaw was set with grim determination. He glanced at Jesse and smiled. "We're going to do a little fence work ourselves."

TWELVE

A breeze ruffled Katie's hair as she placed the tip of her needle against baby-soft fabric for the next stitch. Many of the women in Apple Grove insisted that sewing on the Lord's Day was sinful, but she didn't agree. If her task had been a joyless one, such as mending ripped seams or darning worn socks, that would definitely be work and therefore forbidden. This kind of sewing was different. Making gifts for precious newborns or new brides helped her relax. She'd long since learned the trick of letting her fingers do the work while her mind wandered.

Today she had brought a chair out to the yard to sit in the sunlight and breathe in the fresh Kansas air. Her thoughts strayed to the morning's church meeting while her gaze fixed on the western horizon, past the neat rows of corn *Fader* had planted while she'd been at the Switzers'. Jesse's arrival at church had taken her by surprise. She'd had a hard time focusing on the preaching, even though Bishop Miller's message about the necessity of observing the rules of propriety had been specifically for her benefit. That the *Englisch* cowboy had come to see her was obvious, and the fact had not gone unnoticed—by the bishop or by *Maummi* Switzer. The memory of *Maummi's* shrewd and slightly disapproving stare had lingered into the afternoon.

A noise behind her alerted her to a presence. The slow, almost silent footfall on the grass could only be one person. A smile took her lips, and she placed the next stitch, though her ears were attuned to the sound. Wait. Wait. A little closer.

At exactly the right moment she leaped to her feet, turning with her hands out and her fingers curved into the shape of claws. "*Raaaaahhh!*"

Levi started, his wide-eyed expression every bit as shocked as she could hope. Then he threw his head back and moaned. "I thought this time I could do it. I made no more noise than a rabbit, and my shadow is behind me."

Katie laughed, enjoying his consternation. "Even a rabbit makes noise, *bruder.*"

He scowled. "*Ja*, and has long ears. Like yours."

She refused to take offense at his taunt, though she had been sensitive about her ears from girlhood. Which he knew, the pest.

Levi dropped to the ground while she returned to the chair and took up her sewing.

He plucked a long blade of grass before looking up at her. "I saw your *Englisch* man at the meeting today."

"He is not my *Englisch* man," she chided, "and do not say that around others. The gossips are already whispering about him.

'Twould do no good, and maybe even harm, to have my name spoken in the same sentence."

"It already is." The blade of grass went into his mouth, the end waving in the air as he chewed. "I heard it said that you are sweet on him and even spoke with the bishop about leaving the Amish to marry him."

Katie's hands fell still as her mouth gaped open. "Who voiced such a *narrisch* notion?"

He shrugged. "It does not matter if the notion is crazy or not. It is being said, and some are paying it credence." The grass waved for a second or two. "Is it true?"

"*Ach!* That my own *bruder* would ask such a question!" His expression of inquiry did not change. She answered with more force than strictly necessary. "Of course it is not true. I would no sooner follow *Englisch* ways than..." She cast about for a suitable example. "Than Bishop Miller himself."

He studied her for a moment more, and then gave a satisfied nod. "*Gut.* I told her so."

Katie leaped on the word. "Her?"

Now it was her turn to study him, and she was amused to see the tips of his ears turn pink. Which could only mean one thing. "Mary Schrock you mean. I saw you hovering around her after the meeting."

"I did not hover. We talked."

She hid a smile. That her little brother was enamored with the pretty Schrock girl was apparent to anyone with eyes. For the past year the two had been seen standing off to the side at every community gathering, never far enough from the crowd to draw censure but isolated enough to exchange private words. Judging by the increasing red stain that spread across Levi's face, those words had lately turned to more than the idle passing of time.

"Will we hear an announcement soon?" She focused on her hands where they held the soft fabric.

Though he did not answer, his smile betrayed him. Katie had a hard time not squealing with excitement. Last fall Levi, Mary, and three other young people had completed the required classes and been baptized in the Amish church. At the time she'd wondered if one of those young women had caught her brother's eye. After baptism an Amish man and woman could declare their intentions and marry. Often they waited until a few weeks before their desired wedding day to visit the bishop and receive his blessing on their union. Only then would the families be informed, and the excitement of preparations would overshadow everything from that moment forward until the marriage was accomplished.

At twenty years, Levi was old enough to marry. Mary, if she remembered correctly, was his junior by only one or two years, the same age she had been when she and Samuel were wed. A good age to start a family. A wave of sorrow threatened at the idea of children, but she brushed it aside, as she did more and more often lately.

"Well, please be sure to correct Mary about the rumor." She grinned. "I would hate for my future sister-in-law to believe such a thing about me."

The blush erupted full force on his face. He whipped the grass from his mouth. "How did you pry this out of me when all I intended was to ask you about the *Englisch* man? Not a word before we speak to *Mader* and *Fader, ja?*"

"*Ja,*" she agreed, though not without a teasing glance.

He lumbered to his feet, and she shielded her eyes with one hand to look up at him. When had he grown so tall? Only yesterday he was a small boy.

An awkward expression dawned on his features. "One day soon you will find someone, Katie. You are too young to be a widow forever."

Her answer was a wistful smile. That was a subject she preferred not to discuss with her brother or with anyone else. "Will you do a favor for me?"

His strong body straightened. "Name it."

"Fetch this chair to the house for me. I've stitched until my fingers are numb."

She stood and watched Levi lift the chair, the muscles in his arms bulging like a man's, no longer the puny, thin sticks she used to tease him about.

Jesse's arms are even bigger with muscles.

The thought brought sudden warmth to the tender skin on her neck. Levi headed for the house, but she dallied behind. Her gaze strayed once again to the western horizon. The sun had crept low in the sky while she worked. Not many miles in that direction lay the Switzer farm. And Jesse. The rumor Levi had heard echoed in her mind.

When Levi and Mary were wed, the bride would come here to live. Levi would continue to work the farm with *Fader*, gradually taking on more and more responsibility until, years from now, he would take charge. Then *Fader* would build a *dawdi haus* and he and *Mader* would move into it, leaving the family home to Levi and Mary and, by then, their children.

And what of Katie? A feeling of desolation threatened as an

image of herself, the unmarried aunt who occupied the small bedroom at the top of the stairs, loomed in her mind.

If Jesse asked me to leave the Amish, would I?

The answer rose up in a heart already heavy with sorrow. No. This was the life she loved, the one God had given her. She could not live any other way than the way she had been raised.

Besides, Bishop Miller's accusations hammered at her heart, as painful as when he'd first said the words. Her barrenness was a curse she would not inflict on another man.

Swallowing past a lump that seemed to lodge in her throat more often than not lately, she turned her back to the west and headed for the house.

※

Jesse stood beside Rex, his left hand on the pommel, and took a minute to gather his nerve. Rex turned his long neck to fix him with a brown eye as if to say, *Well, what are you waiting for?*

"Are you sure about this?"

Luke, who was already seated in the saddle, spoke quietly. There was something about the darkness of night and the song of the crickets that called for hushed voices, even though they weren't being watched. At least not yet.

"I'm sure. There's no way on God's green earth I'm letting you boys have all the fun tonight."

Colin's soft laugh sounded from beyond Luke. "You call digging postholes in the dark fun? I've said before you had pickles for brains, and this proves it."

Jesse grimaced in his direction, though no doubt he'd just wasted a good scowl. The dark was thick as mud tonight. Clouds covered the stars, and though the moon occasionally peeked through a misty break, its random appearance was no help.

"I may have spent years trying to pickle the rest of myself, but my brains are fine, thank you."

Butch spoke up from behind. "You want me to get the milking stool?"

Luke chuckled, and Jesse rounded on the boy. "No, I don't need a milking stool to get on my horse!" He instantly regretted his harsh tone, but if Butch told Luke and Colin he'd used a stool yesterday, he'd never survive the ribbing. He went on in a kinder voice. "I'll get up there on my own. I still have one good arm and a couple of strong legs."

He turned back to the saddle, but not before giving Rex a loaded look. *Help me out here, boy. I'd hate to end up on my backside on the ground.*

He tightened his grip on the saddle horn and placed a boot in the stirrup. His right arm wasn't completely useless. He'd been working to strengthen the abused shoulder muscles, and though it hurt to lift his arm overhead, he managed to grab onto the saddle. Setting his teeth, he gave a giant heave, pushing off with his right boot. Pain stabbed at his shoulder, but he bit back a groan and pulled, trying to take the weight on his left boot. He wavered, and for a second he thought he'd end up on the ground after all. But then Rex skittered sideways, and he felt pressure on his backside. Butch gave a shove, and Jesse managed to swing his leg over. Not the most graceful move he'd ever made, but at least he was in the saddle.

Once he had his balance, he nodded at the boy. "Thanks, son. Appreciate the help."

"I can be more help if you'd take me with you. I'm stronger than I look, and I'm a good digger."

Jesse looked down into the boy's upturned face. Being left behind while the men rode out to a sneaky midnight job would be a bitter disappointment to any boy. He wouldn't have stood still for it when he was that age, but he knew Butch would obey the way he always did. Maybe letting him tag along would be good for him.

Jesse glanced toward Colin, who was the boy's guardian. "What do you think?"

Colin cocked his head sideways, his face hidden in the shadow of his hat. "We do have a lot of work ahead of us. Another pair of hands would be mighty welcome."

Jesse indulged in a smile. Colin understood a boy's feelings as well as he did.

Butch nearly hopped with excitement. "You mean I can go?"

"Yeah, you can go. But first run in the house and tell *Maummi* Switzer so she doesn't worry."

The child raced toward the house as though a wildcat were on his tail.

Luke chuckled. "I like that boy. Reminds me of myself at his age."

Jesse poured his scowl into his voice. "Yeah, but don't worry. We'll train that out of him."

The men enjoyed a laugh, and then Jesse kneed Rex toward the house. When Butch ran out, he was waiting beside the porch, which was higher than the milking stool. "Hop on up here."

"Yes, sir!" He ducked beneath the railing and, grasping the

hand Jesse extended, swung up into the saddle. He settled in behind Jesse and got a grip on the sides of his belt.

Colin raised a hand and pointed westward. "How far does the fence go in that direction?"

Jesse shook his head. "I never got to check it out. I'm thinking we should start at this end, though. It's not likely we'll finish the job tonight. Better to clear the way to the creek first."

The three horses headed out at a walk. Soon they had left the house behind them, and skirted around Jonas's barn. The goats stirred as they passed, but the cattle had settled farther away, their bodies a dark cluster of shadows on the ground edging the wheat field.

The men approached the corner of the fence east of the place where the stream narrowed and turned toward the north. The sound of rushing water filled the night.

"I don't understand." Colin said. "That stream runs from the north. Why wouldn't Littlefield stake his claim farther up?"

"The creek bed's a lot narrower up there, no more than a trickle." Jesse had noted the distinction when he last traveled along the fencerow. "I figure there must be an underground feed close by somewhere, because it's not near as deep as it is here. And the bank is steeper up a ways."

"Not good for watering cattle," Luke noted. "Especially when there's a nice, wide place right there." He pointed to the west, where the stream broadened and gained depth, a perfect watering hole.

Jesse agreed. "If you're a power-hungry cattle baron who's used to getting what he wants, why not take advantage of a prime source?"

They approached the narrow trench that marked the boundaries of Jonas's farm, and halted. Colin and Luke dismounted and set about pulling tools from their saddlebags. Behind him, Butch swung his leg over and dropped to the ground, and then he stood looking up at Jesse.

Jesse studied the ground. Once he got down, he might never get back up again. With a sigh, he shifted his weight to his left boot in the stirrup, grabbed a handful of Rex's mane, and stepped down. He counted it a blessing he didn't fall but landed on two feet.

Luke stood peering northward toward a rise in the land that was distinguishable only by a slightly lighter shade of black. "How far would you say Littlefield's place is?"

Jesse knew what he was thinking. "Far enough that he won't hear us."

"What about his thugs?"

"Let's hope they've drunk themselves into a stupor. They won't be expecting trouble from Jonas, and they think I'm worthless at the moment."

"Hey, this is good news." Colin's voice, barely above a whisper, drifted to them from a few yards away, where he'd gone to inspect the fence. "Look here."

Using two hands he hefted one of the posts, which was nothing more than a long spike, up out of the ground.

"They must have barely pounded them in," Luke commented.

"They were in a hurry," Jesse said. "They did most of this in a single night."

Colin turned his head at the same moment a break in the clouds let the moon's rays through and illuminated his wide smile.

"That's a dirty thing to do, but let's copy them. Come on, fellas. We have a fence to move."

Jesse imagined Littlefield's fury when he discovered that his boundary line had been repositioned. Oh, how he wished he could be there to witness that moment.

By dawn Jesse was not only thanking the Lord that he'd had a nap after church but wishing he'd slept a few hours more. In fact, he'd petered out after thirty posts or so, even though his job was only to hold the post in place while Colin pounded it into the ground. They set him on guard duty, and he couldn't swear he hadn't drifted off once or twice.

But the job was done. The fence was moved, more or less following the faint furrow in the land that Jonas had cut two decades before, though they'd had trouble finding it in places, so overgrown was the fertile land. Their gloves were in a sorry state, and every one of them bore wounds from wrestling with the barbed wire, though Luke's hands looked the worst. They had taken care to wash them in the creek before settling on the ground to await the dawn and the inevitable moment when their night's work was discovered. Finally, the sun rose above the eastern horizon, painting the clouds overhead pink.

Jesse shivered against the morning chill, and shifted his weight in a vain attempt to find a more comfortable position on the hard, rock-strewn ground. In the dawn of light, he realized he wasn't all that far from the place he'd lain after being shot. Had it really been eleven days ago? He extended his right arm until he felt the painful pull in his shoulder. Seemed as though it had been months.

"I'm hungry." Sleep weighed down Luke's words, making them slow and drowsy. "Wish we'd thought to get *Maummi* to pack us something for breakfast."

"Mmm." Colin's hat muffed his voice. It covered his face as he lay prone on the ground, his arms cradling the back of his head. "What I'd give for a stack of Becca's hotcakes right about now."

"Hey, Luke, remember McCann's breakfasts back on the trail?" Jesse could almost hear the sizzle from the cook's frying pan and smell the bacon mixed with smoke from the campfire.

Luke groaned. "Don't remind me. My stomach thinks my throat's been slit."

A loud snore issued from the place where Butch had curled up in a ball, bringing a quiet laugh from all three men.

"How can a kid that skinny make a noise that loud?" Luke asked.

Jesse chuckled. "I think he's been taking lessons from *Maummi* Switzer."

"Boys," came Colin's quiet voice, "we have company. Get ready. The party's about to start."

A pair of riders topped the ridge to the north and came to a halt, their silhouettes standing out starkly against the empty Kansas sky. Jesse cast a glance sideways at Colin, who had taken the hat off his face, his gaze fixed in that direction. His voice sounded calm and even, but there was no mistaking the underlying note of tension. "Hold off, gentleman. Let them make the first move."

Jesse nudged Butch's back to rouse him before climbing to his feet, his senses on high alert. His pistol, retrieved from Jonas's barn, hung from his belt. Though he'd spent time yesterday practicing drawing with his left hand, he was nowhere near ready for a confrontation. *Lord, I'd be much obliged if it doesn't come to that.*

As though he heard Jesse's thoughts, Luke spoke in a low voice, his stare fixed on the pair in front of them. "Jess, you and Butch saddle up. At the first sign of trouble, you take the boy and hightail it out of here."

Jesse would have argued, but his gaze fell on Butch, whose round eyes were still foggy with sleep. He caught sight of the men, who had made no move to approach them. If anything happened to the boy, he wouldn't be able to live with himself. With a quiet whistle to Rex, who had strayed a few yards away in search of fresher grass, he spared a hope he could climb into the saddle without shaming himself.

Rex covered the distance between them, and Jesse positioned the horse between himself and Littlefield's men. He exchanged an anxious glance with Butch and then hooked his foot in the stirrup. He heaved himself into the saddle on the first try, and without Butch having to give him a shove. Butch's ascent to Rex's back wasn't nearly as smooth and nearly unseated Jesse, who had misjudged his ability to swing the boy up with his left arm, but after a scramble they were both astride.

Luke whistled for his horse and mounted while Colin stood watch, and then he swung his horse around beside Rex. When Colin grabbed his horse's reins, Littlefield's men spurred their mounts forward.

Jesse's stomach tightened. Butch's thin body trembled against his back. Between his thighs, Rex's muscles twitched, attuned to his rider's mood. Colin was in the saddle before the men reached a distance to be recognized. When they did, acid rose in Jesse's throat.

"Well, what do you know?" He pitched his voice to broach the distance. "I thought I recognized that yellow streak running down your back, Sawyer. Sheriff Wiley is going to be interested to know you've turned up again."

Sawyer held his tongue as he cast a nervous glance at his partner.

Woodard didn't spare a sideways glance but kept his stare fixed on Jesse. They came to a halt several yards away, on the other side of the newly erected fence. The animosity in the man's face started an itch in Jesse's palm, and he fought the instinct to reach toward his pistol.

"I can't hardly believe my eyes," the man said, his voice gravelly. "Looks like you boys are aiming to get somebody kilt."

"No, sir. Just protecting a friend's property."

"This ain't yore land. Tear that fence down. Now."

"That sounded like a threat to me," Luke said. "What about you, Sheriff Maddox?"

Sawyer started and stared at Colin through rounded eyes.

"Hard to tell," Colin replied in a conversational tone. "Could be he's making polite conversation, only he sure sounds rough."

Woodard turned his head and spit, though his eyes didn't leave Jesse's face. Jesse's blood picked up speed, racing through his veins with the dim rumble of a distant rainstorm.

Sawyer had the look of a man who could barely keep his tongue in his mouth. "What's this fence doing here?" he blurted. Woodard silenced him with a quick glare.

Jesse watched Sawyer out of the corner of his eye, but kept his gaze fixed on the older man. "Why, don't you recognize it? You ought to, since you boys put it up not two weeks ago. This here's Mr. Littlefield's fence."

"This ain't our fence." The younger man rose up in the saddle and pointed toward a place behind them. "Our fence is back that a way."

"Shut up, idiot," Woodard growled, and though Sawyer shot an angry glance, his mouth snapped shut.

Colin spoke in a pleasant voice. "Well, see, here's the thing about that fence. It seems there was a mistake in where it was put up. It cut straight through our father-in-law's land. Cut him off from his watering rights. You boys probably missed the trench marking the boundaries of Jonas's farm since it was overgrown. It'd be an easy thing to do."

"My wife got real upset when she heard about her daddy's trouble." Luke matched Colin's reasonable tone. "Fellas, I can't abide my wife being upset."

"Me, neither," Colin agreed. "All those tears break my heart. I hate to see a woman cry. Now, I'm sure Mr. Littlefield wasn't aware of the mistake, but you boys tell your boss not to worry. We've set things right now."

A storm gathered on Woodard's face. His gaze slid from Colin to Luke, and finally came to a rest on Jesse. "You don't know who you're messing with. Mr. Littlefield's a powerful man. He owns five thousand head of cattle and a spread down in Texas that would put this puny little farm to shame. Nobody crosses him and gets away with it."

Jesse scowled. "Only problem is, this is Kansas, not Texas."

A scornful laugh escaped Sawyer. "We know we're in Kansas. We're not stupid."

Woodard growled, "Shut your trap before I nail it shut."

If he hadn't been the same slimy varmint who had shot him in the back, Jesse might have felt sorry for the younger man. He ducked his head between his shoulders and slumped in the saddle, casting a resentful glance at his partner.

Behind Jesse, Butch's breath came shallow and fast. His own pulse raced, and his fingers twitched, senses on high alert while he watched for movement. He didn't think either of the two would try something when the odds were three against two, but he knew better than to count on them using good sense.

"You have a message to deliver." Jesse tossed his head in the direction from which they had ridden. "What are you waiting for?"

When they still didn't move, he added in a dry tone, "I'm not leaving until you boys are out of sight. I learned a thing or two about turning my back on a pair of low-down prairie dogs like you."

Beside him, Luke shot him a warning glance, which Jesse ignored. After another long glare, Woodard turned his horse and moved off in an unhurried retreat, Sawyer following behind.

When they had topped the ridge and dropped out of sight, Colin turned an exasperated frown on Jesse. "If I didn't know better, Montgomery, I'd say you were doing your best to get them to draw down on us."

Jesse answered with more confidence than he felt. "I knew they wouldn't. They're the kind of men who are quick on the draw when the numbers are in their favor, but not when the odds are against them."

Colin didn't look convinced. "Let's get back and tell Jonas what we've done. I need a cup of coffee. It's been a long night."

He turned his horse and pointed it toward the Switzer home, Luke following. Jesse spared one more look at the horizon in case Woodard and Sawyer decided to double back and pull another dirty stunt like last time. The only movement he spied was a wood-chuck making its cautious way through the grass.

Behind him, Butch's stomach growled.

"All right, all right," Jesse said with a laugh. "Let's get home and get some breakfast in you."

He nudged Rex into movement, turning him after Luke and Colin, and headed for Jonas's place. With luck, their act of defiance would show Littlefield that he was dealing with more than a single peaceful Amish man, and he'd back off.

Jesse glanced over his shoulder. Somehow he doubted it would be that easy.

THIRTEEN

"You're sure you can handle things around here?"

Jesse returned Luke's searching gaze with a nod. "It's been three days since we moved that fence. If Littlefield was going to do anything, he would have done it by now."

He spoke with more confidence than he felt and saw from the look in his friend's eyes that Luke wasn't fooled. But he also saw Luke's struggle. He'd left his wife and kids alone for three days. When Colin left Monday morning, he'd promised to keep an eye on them and handle things around the farm, but he had his own place to run. Jesse pushed back envy. Luke and Colin, though not Amish, lived a peaceful life. They both had families. If Jesse would admit it, he was tired of roaming. Tired of single life. Yet there wasn't a wife in sight unless he considered Katie, and that was a foolish dream. She'd been good to him and nursed him back to health, but he'd bet all he owned no other man would ever take Samuel's place. Bishop Miller would see to it.

The past three days had been edgy and anxious for all of them. Jesse couldn't keep himself from searching the horizon, expecting any minute to see a pair of riders heading their way bent on trouble. Luke, too, had been jumpy while he helped Jonas plow his new cornfield. That had irritated Jesse, because Jonas already had a plowed field ready for planting, but he had to admit he understood the man's hesitance. Littlefield's boys could do a lot of damage to new corn plants in the distant field before Jonas could get there. At least this one was near enough to the house that they could keep a closer eye on it.

And at least they no longer had to carry water to the trough for Jonas's animals. He glanced in that direction now, where a dozen or so milk cows sauntered along the bank of their favorite watering hole.

Luke shuffled his weight from one boot to the other, his struggle apparent.

"Go home," Jesse urged. "Emma needs you more than we do."

He finally relented, barely hiding his relief behind a mask of real concern. "If you get wind of trouble, or if you need anything at all, get word to us, okay?"

Jesse nodded and then watched his friend cross the yard toward the cornfield to tell Jonas of his decision, his step lighter and stride longer than it had been in days. A smile twitched at Jesse's lips. If he had a good woman and a couple of great kids waiting for him, he'd be in a hurry to get back to them too.

Butch exited the barn and came to stand alongside Jesse, his gaze fixed on Luke. "Is he going home now?"

"Yeah." Jesse eyed the boy. "You want to go with him?"

His head jerked sideways. "No. I really like Colin and Rebecca, but I-I'd like to stay here if I'm not a bunch of trouble." He looked away again. "I like it here."

"You're not any trouble, son. You're a real help around the place. I don't know what Rex would do without you." Given the violence Butch had witnessed when his family was killed, there was little wonder he liked the peaceful atmosphere around the Switzer home. Actually, Jesse had seen enough violence in his twenty-five years to fill a couple of lifetimes. His gaze roamed the yard, the house, and then the field where Jonas had halted his horse and stood talking to Luke. A peaceful life had a lot to offer a man.

He ruffled Butch's hair, grinning. "I'd hate to leave too."

When *Maummi* Switzer was informed of Luke's impending departure, she called for Butch's help as she scurried around the house putting together a pair of bundles to send to her grand-daughters. She supervised Butch tying them to Luke's saddle, giving each a firm tug to test the security of the knots. Only when she was satisfied did she nod her approval for Luke to climb into the saddle. Smiling indulgently, he did.

"Tell our Rebecca to send for me when the little one arrives." She shielded her eyes to look up at him. "A girl needs help at such a time."

She'd said the same thing to Colin three days earlier. Luke nod-ded. "Yes, ma'am. And thank you for feeding me so well the past few days." He rubbed his stomach. "Emma's going to have to let out my britches when I get home."

"Bah." She waved a wrinkled hand in dismissal. "It's good to have hungry men at the table. And hungry boys," she added, with a smile in Butch's direction.

Luke nodded farewell to Jonas and Butch, and then he looked at Jesse. "You take care, buddy."

"Always."

Luke dug his heels into the horse's sides. They stood watching until he'd cantered out of sight.

When Jonas started toward his new cornfield where the horse and plow stood waiting, Jesse stopped him.

"You think you could teach me how to work that thing?"

Jonas's eyebrows inched upward. "You are well enough to plow?"

Every day Jesse noticed more improvement. The waves of dizziness had stopped, though an almost constant headache still plagued him sunup to sundown. He'd finally given up on trying to shoot left handed, figuring his efforts were better spent getting his right arm back to normal.

"I figure hard work's about the only way to regain my strength." Jesse lifted his arm above his head to demonstrate. "Might as well make myself useful, seeing how you just lost one of your helpers."

Jonas looked toward *Maummi* Switzer in a silent request for approval. Her answer was a shrug.

"All right, then."

Jesse grinned. It was strange how eager he was to put his hand to a plow, the ultimate sodbuster activity. But anything was better than sitting around watching the grass grow.

And how hard could plowing be?

Jesse moaned, but then bit it off when the sound came out louder than he thought and filled the dark bedroom with proof of his aching muscles. He held still, listening for signs of activity on the other side of the door. The straw tick in this bedroom wasn't nearly as comfortable as *Maummi* Switzer's feather tick downstairs. He hadn't noticed it so much in the three days since he had vacated her room and moved upstairs to what he was told used to be Rebecca's bedroom, but before tonight his muscles hadn't been as sore as a green bronco rider after his first rodeo.

He swallowed another groan and eased himself over onto his side. Jonas made plowing look easy, but holding that blade straight as it carved through hard soil that had never seen a plow had proved to be a skill requiring strength and endurance. When he got to the end of his first row, he'd been embarrassed to see the zigzagging furrow alongside Jonas's straight ones. And he'd lost as much sweat today as a hot day in the saddle on a cattle trail. His back ached so that he worried he'd ripped something open in there. Finally, after two rows, Jonas had taken pity on him and set him the task of clearing the rocks unearthed by the plowshare.

His throat was drier than dirt. No way would he get back to sleep with his tongue stuck to the roof of his mouth. His aching muscles protested when he rolled over and put his feet on the cool floorboards. He glanced at the peg on the wall, where his britches and shirt hung. Nobody was up at this time of night. His long johns would be clothing enough to get him down to the kitchen and back again.

Moving as silently as a cat on the prowl, he crept across the floor and cracked the door open. The sound of muffled snores came from two directions. Down the hall, from behind the door to the room where Butch slept, and the quieter snores that drifted up the stairway from the direction of *Maummi* Switzer's room. He tiptoed downstairs, easing his weight onto every stair with care for a telltale creak. That woman had ears like a jackrabbit.

In the kitchen he headed for the water pitcher she kept sitting on the work surface. He filled a cup and downed it in a single draught. Still thirsty, he filled the cup a second time and drank more slowly. His thirst finally slated, he wiped the cup dry with a towel and covered the pitcher the way *Maummi* always did.

As he turned away from the high table toward the stairs, something caught his eye through the window. Moonlight illuminated the yard and glimmered off the leaves of the big tree. Branches swayed, stirred into an eerie nighttime dance by the ever-present Kansas wind. Gyrating shadows skittered across the grass. But to the left, in the direction of the barn, the black of night was relieved by an orange glow.

Jesse planted his hands on the sturdy wooden worktable and leaned forward for a better look. His stomach clenched.

"Fire!" He whirled and bolted across the room, his hands clenched into fists. "Jonas, wake up. The barn's on fire!"

He directed his shout up the short staircase, pounding on the wall for good measure. The snores came to an abrupt halt, both from *Maummi* Switzer's room and from upstairs. Good. He wasted no more time but sprinted for the door.

Part of his brain burned with a fury that rivaled the flames now visible through the open barn door as he ran barefooted across the grass. This was Littlefield's doing. He didn't doubt it for a minute. That scheming skunk had retaliated in the most cowardly way possible, striking under the cover of darkness.

He focused on the task at hand, rescuing the terrified animals who had been corralled into the barn for the night.

"Rex!"

He ran into the barn and made straight for Rex's stall. Smoke filled the dark interior, pungent and heavy. It seeped into Jesse's lungs, a menacing presence that threatened to steal his breath permanently. With a sickening realization, he detected another odor. Kerosene.

The horse stamped with fright, his breath snorting through his nose when he caught sight of his rider. Jesse threw open the stall door.

"Go on, boy. Get out of here!"

Rex galloped off while Jesse dashed to the second stall, where white rims showed around Big Ed's eyes. Jesse released him too, and the horse hurried after Rex. From here he could see where the fire had started. Hay filled the barn's upper level, dry from sitting all winter and spring, the perfect kindling. Jesse searched for the source of the orange glow. If the fire were contained to the straw, maybe they could shovel it through the high opening on the back of the barn.

No good. Though smoke billowed from the straw, he caught sight of flames licking up the wooden back wall toward the pitched roof and heard the crackle of burning wood.

A figure brushed past him toward the two stalls in the rear. Jonas.

"I'll get this one," Jesse shouted.

While Jonas ran to the stall on the left, he dodged right. Inside, the frightened bleating of goats drowned out the snapping fire. Jonas confined his small herd in the barn at night to keep them from *Maummi*'s vegetable garden. Jesse opened the door and the terrified animals rushed away from him to cower together at the back of the stall. He ran inside to shoo them out. They joined their brothers and sisters, released by Jonas, in a stampede for the exit.

"Get the buckets!" Jonas motioned toward the place where they were stored as he shouted, and then grabbed a pitchfork and began climbing the slat ladder.

"Be careful up there!" Jesse shouted after him, and then he lurched for the buckets.

As he exited the barn, a slender figure joined him. Butch, holding his shirt out from his stomach to form a pouch, the inside full of squirming kittens.

"Go for help!" Though the sound of the fire was not loud out here, Jesse shouted in a voice fueled by urgency. "Take Rex and ride south." He pointed down the road toward the next Amish farm.

Butch's gaze darted to the barn. "The saddle's in there."

"There's no time for saddles. Just go." Jesse put a hand on his back and gave a gentle shove in the direction of the road as he continued running toward the pump. "And tell them to bring buckets."

"Yes, sir."

The boy scrambled toward the porch with the kittens, yelling for Rex. He passed *Maummi* Switzer, who ran at a speed Jesse wouldn't have thought possible for a woman her age. She rushed forward and thrust a bundle into his arms.

"Here."

Jesse realized she'd handed him his clothes and boots. He'd forgotten he was only wearing his skivvies. Grinning his thanks, he turned the task of filling the buckets over to her while he pulled on his britches.

It seemed as though half of Apple Grove showed up to help the Switzers put out the fire. The first wagon arrived in what felt like only minutes after Butch galloped away on Rex. Before long a parade of buggies and wagons, the horses trotting at top speed, began arriving. Men and women alike formed a solid line from the pump to the burning barn, buckets passed from hand to hand as quickly as they could be filled. Even the children helped by running empty buckets from the barn back to the pump. The Amish of Apple Grove worked tirelessly, calling directions to each other and to those inside the barn struggling against the flames.

They would have succeeded in putting out the fire if the people who started it hadn't saturated the entire upper level of the barn with kerosene.

Finally, when it became obvious that their efforts would prove ineffectual, Jonas called a halt. Amish men, their clothes covered with ash and reeking of smoke, filed outside, coughing and taking in great draughts of clean air. The task at that point became ensuring that the flames did not spread to the house, a frightening prospect that appeared all too possible due to the winds. Sparks flew on the breeze, a few coming dangerously close to the upper floor of the Switzer home.

Jesse sat in the grass beneath an apple tree, his back leaning against the rough bark, and watched the men on the roof of the house pouring water down the siding. Around him were scattered half a dozen men in various poses of rest. His limbs felt heavy, and exhaustion vibrated through his veins. The sun had not yet risen, but the sky in the east was beginning to lighten. A day of plowing and hefting rocks, little sleep, and then several hours of frantic work were taking its toll. His eyelids closed against his will.

"Would you like a drink?"

He pried his eyes open at the soft, familiar voice. Standing above him, a pitcher in one hand and a cup in the other, stood Katie. She smiled, and for a moment Jesse thought surely he was caught up in a dream.

"Thirsty?" She offered him the cup.

He took it, embarrassed when his hand trembled as she filled it from the pitcher. Water sloshed onto his pants.

"Sorry. Guess I'm kind of tired."

"You are well?" She searched his face, her expression concerned. "Your shoulder is hurting?"

He heaved a laugh. "No more than the rest of me."

The water quenched a powerful thirst he hadn't realized until that moment. He would have downed it quickly, but then she might leave and move on to the next thirsty man. He lowered the cup, still half full, but did not return it to her. Instead, he used it to gesture toward the men at work around the house.

"Pretty amazing, the way everybody showed up to help."

"Amazing?" She shook her head. "It is what we do, we Amish. The need of one is the need of us all."

"I thought it was only Jonas who felt that way, back when I first met him." His gaze followed the tireless workers. "I'm beginning to see that there are others like him."

"*Ja*, it is our way. If two are stronger than one, as *die Bibel* says, then how much stronger are one hundred?"

"I have to say, that sounds better than the way most folks behave." He ducked his head toward the barn. "Folks who'd pull a stunt like this would stoop to anything."

Startled, Katie followed his gaze. "This fire was not an accident?"

Jesse answered with a bitter laugh. "Not unless you can think of a way kerosene would accidently get spread over hay and a match struck."

She regarded him with round, solemn eyes. "It was the *Englisch* man who wants Jonas's farm?"

"I think that's a safe bet." He spotted a man breaking away from the others and heading in their direction. Bishop Miller. And judging by the rigid set of his spine and his jerky pace, he wasn't happy.

He got to his feet so he could look Katie in the face as he spoke quietly, aware that they had only a minute before they were interrupted. "Katie? Have you ever considered leaving Apple Grove?"

"Leaving? This is my home."

"I know, but..." Behind her, the bishop stalked toward them. Jesse spoke in a rush. "Not only leaving Apple Grove, but leaving the Amish. You know, like Emma and Rebecca."

Shock appeared on her face and she took a backward step,

clutching the pitcher close to her chest. "No. I will never leave. Ever."

He almost reached out to grab her, to hold her in place before she could run away. He would have, except for the menacing presence of Bishop Miller advancing on them.

He took a deep breath. He hardly believed the words that came out of his own mouth. "What about if I joined up? You know. Became Amish."

Her jaw dropped.

"I've given it some thought lately. It's a good life, a peaceful life, and I want that. If I had to choose between living like Jonas and going back to my former life, I'd choose this." He spread his arms wide to indicate Jonas's farm around them, and then he held her gaze with his. "Especially...if you were to agree to see me..."

Though the sky had lightened with dawn while they spoke, shadows still lingered beneath the apple trees, shading part of her face. He couldn't be sure, but were those tears sparkling in her eyes?

Her shoulders straightened and her neck stiffened. "No." The word, though small, carried the weight of certainty. "I have been married. I miss my Samuel too deeply to ever consider another. I will not marry again."

She turned and fled, leaving him alone. Nor could he go after her, for Bishop Miller arrived to take the place she vacated.

The man looked after her, and then he turned back to Jesse, his eyes narrowed to slits. When he spoke, it was not in reference to Katie.

"This is your doing." He waved a hand backward, indicating the barn. "You and your *Englisch* friends."

Though reeling from Katie's rebuff, Jesse set his teeth and focused on the man in front of him. "Are you accusing me of setting fire to my *Amish* friend's barn?"

"Yours was not the hand to light the fire, but the fault lies with you." He did not bother to control his voice, and the men scattered around the area stirred uncomfortably.

Jesse met the bishop's eyes, though he was aware that two men were headed their way from the barn. The rage that rose in him was only in part a result of the man's accusation. He made an attempt to shrug off the hurt and confusion Katie's words had caused.

"We have helped a friend in need. You refused to help him." He narrowed his eyes. "I still don't understand your ways, Bishop. Isn't that your job, to help the people who look to you for leadership?"

The man's expression became even grimmer. "Your question shows your ignorance of our ways. And the foolishness of yours."

They were joined then by Jonas and Amos. Both wore somber expressions as their gazes flickered from Bishop Miller to Jesse.

The bishop's rigid posture relaxed, and he made a visible attempt at control. "Jonas, what does the Confession say concerning the spoiling of our goods?"

Jonas hesitated, clearly unwilling to answer, but at a quick look from Bishop Miller, he swallowed. "*For the Lord's sake we must flee from one city or country into another, and suffer the spoiling of our goods; that we must not harm anyone, and, when we are smitten, rather turn the other cheek also, than take revenge or retaliate.*"

He glanced at Amos beside him, who looked troubled but nodded his agreement.

"So have we confessed and pledged." The bishop clasped his hands behind his back and tilted his head toward the sky. His voice carried to all in the vicinity. "Therefore, it is clear to me that Jonas must leave this farm and flee to another."

Gasps sounded from a few of the men nearby. Amos's mouth fell open in disbelief. Jonas stared at Bishop Miller, his expression stunned.

"Have you lost your mind?" Jesse couldn't believe his ears. "You can't mean that—"

The bishop ignored his outburst and addressed Jonas. "Caleb Weaver's farm on the eastern end of Apple Grove lies untended since his passing last fall. Elizabeth has expressed a desire to move to Troyer, where her sister's family has invited her to live with them. Because she and Caleb had no children of their own, the farm must pass to other hands."

"But..." Jonas's mouth snapped shut, and he struggled visibly for control before attempting to speak again. "I have not the means to pay for a new farm."

Bishop Miller waved that concern aside. "The district will help, if need be."

No one spoke. Though Jesse could hardly credit his eyes, Jonas, looking miserable, appeared ready to concede.

"Jonas. Can we talk?" Jesse couldn't keep quiet, not when the scene unfolding in front of him stretched credibility. "You can't be serious. This is wrong! It's exactly what Littlefield is hoping for. You can't give him your farm, your home. You can't let him win."

Jonas refused to meet his eye. Jesse glanced around, trying to find someone who would stand with him against the madness of Bishop Miller's edict. Though they were the focal point of the

Amish men within listening distance, nobody would look directly at him. He stepped sideways, in front of Amos. "Surely you see how wrong this is." Amos was a level-headed man. He would see reason. "Tell them they have to fight this. Littlefield will be coming after them next."

Though Amos' looked troubled, he shook his head almost sadly. "You do not understand our ways."

"Oh, I understand." Bitterness made his voice carry far on the cool morning air. "Littlefield has won. All this..." He motioned to the barn and beyond, to the unseen fence that started the conflict. "He won't stop at Jonas's land. His goal was to frighten you so badly you would let him take what he wanted, and he won."

Jonas looked up then, his eyes so full of conflict that Jesse's throat constricted in sympathy.

"It is not about winning." He spoke in the same calm, gentle tone he might use to correct an errant child. "It is about following Christ's example. In that way only can we find true peace."

He turned then and walked away, leaving Jesse to stare after him. Every fiber in Jesse's being screamed that this was wrong, that a great travesty was about to occur.

He forced himself to turn back and meet Bishop Miller's stern countenance. He was surprised at what he saw there. The man's gaze was fixed on Jonas's back. Orange flames reflected in the dark depths of his eyes, and something else smoldered there besides.

Instead of the triumph Jesse expected to find, he glimpsed a flicker of respect.

❧

The sun was fully up and rising toward its apex before Jonas's barnyard emptied of buggies and wagons. The barn's roof had collapsed just after dawn, and the danger of the fire spreading was contained. The heap of ash and charred wood that used to be the barn was a bleak reminder of Littlefield's intent. The women had put together a bountiful meal for those who had worked tirelessly to battle the fire. Jesse's appetite had gone up with the flames. Sour acid churned in his gut, fed by the travesty that was about to take place. Jonas would lose his farm, and there was not a thing he could do about it. He was sure he was not the only one who felt that way, though he was the only one to voice his disagreement. Gloom settled on the men and women. Even the children went about with subdued expressions.

Three buggies remained after the rest had gone. Chairs had been brought from the house and placed in the shade of the big tree. Jesse sat in one next to Jonas and John Beachy, Katie's father, who seemed as disturbed by recent events as Jonas himself. Amos also sat beside them, head bowed. His shoulders were slumped, his face hidden beneath the brim of his hat. If Jesse had to guess, he would say the man was praying.

Most of the women were inside the house cleaning up after the huge meal, all except for Katie and the two Beiler girls, who were occupied in washing the dishes at the pump. Jesse considered joining them to lend a hand but dismissed the idea. He hadn't seen an Amish man ever do a woman's chores, at least not openly. Common sense told him to approach Katie cautiously. Her words spoken beneath the apple tree still stung. Apparently, he'd figured her kindness for affection and had spoken too soon. He shouldn't have spoken at all. The injury still muddled his mind. A woman like Katie—an Amish woman and him? What had he been thinking?

"John, what do you know of Caleb Weaver's farm?" Jonas's question broke the heavy silence.

Katie's father pursed his lips before answering. "It's not as well situated as this one. Caleb had little interest in farming, other than what was needful to put food on the table."

Amos nodded. "Only one field did he keep plowed, for wheat."

Jonas's shoulders lifted in a small shrug. "Land can be plowed." His gaze strayed toward his new cornfield.

"It is not level land," John observed. "Caleb used to jest that in all of Kansas there was only one steep hill, and it belonged to him."

"There is a stream for the livestock?" Jonas asked.

John shook his head. "Not that I have seen, though I have not walked the boundaries."

"Wells can be dug." Amos attempted a positive tone, which fell flat.

Jesse could no longer hold his peace. "I still can't believe you're talking this way. I mean, I understand about not fighting, but to pull up stakes and walk away from everything..."

He closed his mouth when a grimace of pain crossed Jonas's features. They quickly settled into their accustomed placid expression, but not before guilt knifed Jesse. The last thing he wanted was to cause his friend more pain.

"What if you sold Littlefield the part of the land he wants?" He had to force the words through clenched teeth, so strongly did he dislike the proposal he was about to suggest. "Let him have the water access. If you're forced to dig a well, it might as well be here as over at this other place. Even if only half the men who showed up last night pitch in, you could have a couple of wells dug in no time at all."

Interest flickered in Jonas's features, and Jesse warmed to the idea. "What about that field?" He pointed toward the open prairie to the south, beyond the road that led to Hays City. "Does anybody own that?"

The three Amish men exchanged questioning glances.

"I do not know." Jonas's voice held the faintest sign of hope.

"We can check on it in Hays City," Jesse said. "If it's unclaimed, you can move your boundaries. If it is, then you could buy it with the money you get from selling the water access to Littlefield. It's not a perfect plan, but you could keep your home, Jonas."

John leaned toward him. "Why do you think Mr. Littlefield will pay for what he has tried to take?"

"He might not. He's dirty. We all know his kind." Jesse shrugged. "But maybe he'd be happy to have a legitimate claim to the land. If you're dead set on keeping this peaceful, it's worth a try."

The interest faded from Jonas's face. "Bishop Miller has already spoken of this. He told me he intended to speak to Elizabeth Weaver today."

Jesse ran a hand across his stubbly chin, frustration threatening. Surely the bishop wouldn't—

"Katie! You must come."

The note of urgency in *Maummi* Switzer's voice echoed across the yard. The men turned toward the house. Katie, who had been kneeling on the ground with her hands in the dish pan, wasted no time in getting to her feet. *Maummi*'s searching gaze turned their way.

"Amos, you as well. It is Sarah."

Amos took off for the house at a run.

Jesse stayed back, uncertain of his role. Should he go too, or was this purely women's business?

FOURTEEN

Katie backed out of the bedroom, both hands full with the wash basin. No sooner had *Maummi* Switzer closed the door behind her than she was beset by a small, anxious group.

Amos planted himself in Katie's path. "Is she okay, my Sarah?"

The Beiler girls and little Karl hovered at his sides, fear stark on their pale faces. She struggled to come up with a truthful answer that would not alarm them more than necessary. No words came to mind. Best to speak the truth. "The baby is coming," she said.

Amos swallowed. "But it is too early."

She made no answer but a quick nod, her heart aching at the apprehension she saw plain on his face. Ducking her head, she darted sideways and made for the kitchen door.

Outside, she flung the soiled water into the grass and hurried toward the pump to rinse the rags. The air, still heavy with smoke, stung her nostrils. She had almost forgotten about the fire in the anxiety of the sickroom.

In the distance Jonas stood with his back to the house, his head bowed. Good. A continual prayer had run through Katie's mind since she entered the house and saw the blood pooling between Sarah's feet. They must all pray.

Another figure paced from the pile of smoldering wood toward the tree. Jesse. When he caught sight of her, he altered his path and walked in her direction. Discomfort pierced her, caused by the memory of their last conversation, but she paid it no heed. There were more pressing matters than Jesse's disturbing questions—questions she could not answer. Had she not thought the same thoughts in her lonely bed at night? Did she not long for a man's embrace and comfort—perhaps this cowboy's? Samuel would forever be in her heart, but he was gone. Did the Lord intend for her to live her life alone and barren? Yet to encourage Jesse would be inviting him to live a life without sons and daughters. She could not ask another man to suffer the same disappointment as her Samuel.

"Is Sarah in labor?"

"Yes, the baby comes." She grabbed the handle and began to pump. "It is before her time, and the baby is not yet ready."

Jesse's gaze dropped to the blood-soaked cloths in the basin. "Is she...will she be all right?" He brushed her hands away and took over pumping. Flashing him a grateful look, she turned to the task of rinsing the cloths beneath the spigot.

"I have only birthed one baby, and it was easy. Mrs. Wagler's third child." She glanced up at his face, relieved at the opportunity to confide her doubts. "This is not the same. There is too much blood, and it's too early. Even *Maummi* Switzer is worried."

"Do you want me to go for the midwife?"

Katie shook her head. "She passed on last winter."

The water from the cloths ran clear. She wrung out the excess and then rinsed the basin before filling it. When blood had flowed from Jesse's wounds, the doctor insisted on clean cloths and fresh water. He'd scrubbed his hands with lye soap, dipped them in carbolic acid, and made her do the same. Jesse had recovered without contracting the deadly fever that killed so many after wounds such as his.

Women died of fever too after childbirth, even when the birth was an easy one.

She looked up at Jesse. "Where is the whiskey I used to clean your wounds?"

"Gone." He met her gaze. "*Maummi* Switzer was afraid I might drink it."

So. No carbolic acid and no whiskey. They would have to make do with soap. She picked up the basin and hurried toward the house, speaking over her shoulder.

"Fill buckets with water, as many as you can find, and bring them to me inside."

Her voice came out brusque, and she sent a quick smile of apology back toward him. She didn't wait for his response.

The scene she found inside had not changed in the time she was out in the yard. Amos and the girls stood in the same place, staring at the closed door behind which Sarah labored. Katie brushed by them, speaking as she passed.

"In the bedroom at the top of the stairs you will find bed linens. Fetch them please. And the lye soap in the big chest in the kitchen, the one nearest the door." Balancing the basin with one hand against her stomach, she reached for the door latch. She turned to give Amos a meaningful stare. "Then you must go outside to wait. Sit in the shade to pray."

Rebellion flashed across his face, but she merely raised her eyebrows and let her gaze flicker toward his youngest daughter and son. Understanding dawned. The sounds of childbirth were often disturbing. Because his deceased wife had given birth three times, no doubt he knew that.

He gave a vigorous nod. "*Ja*. We will pray."

Katie didn't stay to see if they obeyed. She lifted the latch and entered the room.

The sickly sweet smell of blood filled the bedroom, even though the window had been open for hours. Sweat trickled down Katie's back, and she glanced at the limp curtains. Not a breeze stirred tonight. Where was the wind when they needed it?

A quiet moan escaped Sarah's cracked, white lips, and her grip on Katie's hand intensified. But it was feeble compared to earlier. In the long hours since her labor had begun, Sarah's strength was ebbing away, swept along with the blood that continued to flow from her body.

"'Tis all right to cry." Katie dipped the cloth in the water basin and dabbed it against her patient's pale forehead.

"Amish women don't cry." The hushed whisper was followed

by a weak chuckle. "At least not where anyone can hear. Ain't that right?"

"There are exceptions." Katie smiled, though Sarah's eyes remained shut. "This is one of them."

A very slight shake of her head. "I don't want to upset Amos. He's here, isn't he?" Her eyes cracked open wide enough to fix a worried look on Katie's face. "He's waiting outside, right?"

"Yes, he and the others are outside, praying for you and your baby."

"My baby." A sob choked her voice, and her eyes shut again. "Is he okay?"

Katie was spared answering when another paroxysm took control of Sarah. Fresh, dark blood gushed onto the already saturated bedsheet, and Katie resumed her silent prayer.

Almighty Healer, there is so much blood. Strengthen her by the power of Your blood, which was shed on the cross for our salvation. Let the babe be healthy.

She could not bear to consider that Sarah's child might be otherwise, though the possibilities were high. Based on the date of Sarah and Amos's wedding, this little one's arrival was at least six weeks early, maybe more. The swelling during the past two months gave cause for concern. But most alarming of all was Katie's near certainty that the child had not yet turned in the womb.

The door opened behind her, and Katie looked with relief to *Maummi* Switzer. The older woman backed into the room, a laden tray in her hands, and then kicked the door shut with her foot. "The others have eaten, and the younger ones are finally asleep. I have brought bread and cheese for you."

She set the tray on the floor in the corner and picked up a mug before moving to take Katie's place at the bedside. When Katie would have protested that she had no stomach for food, *Maummi*'s stern glare brooked no argument. Silently, she released Sarah's hand and stood, vacating her chair.

"Sarah, open your mouth." The elderly voice normally snapped with harsh tones, but now it was soft and full of compassion. "'Tis broth to keep you strong."

A weak chuckle issued from the parched lips. "Sometimes Amos still calls me Sassy. Not in front of the kids, though."

Maummi Switzer put a hand behind her tousled blond head and lifted, the rim of the mug held to her lips. "Drink, *Sassy*."

Katie smiled as she tore off a bite-sized chunk of bread. The soft yellow cheese spread easily with a knife and tasted sharp and delicious in her mouth. She was hungrier than she thought. How long had it been since she'd eaten a few bites of meat and an apple for supper? Several hours.

"Oh!" Sarah bolted upright in the bed, knocking the mug from *Maummi* Switzer's hand. It dropped to the floor, a puddle of broth spreading quickly across the boards. Panicked eyes fixed on Katie. "Somethin's happening."

Katie rushed to the bed and tossed aside the blanket that covered Sarah's lower half. A glance told her that the moment of birth was imminent.

"'Tis time." She hurriedly dunked her hands into the bucket of fresh water at the foot of the bed, scrubbing with vigor.

Maummi bustled to the stack of linens they had prepared and moved it within easy reach. Poor *Maummi* Switzer would need to restock her supply of sheets. Between Jesse's wounds and Sarah's childbirth, she would have none left.

Katie's prayer became a stream of pleas of which she was barely aware as she checked her patient. As she suspected, the babe had not turned as it should have. She caught *Maummi's* glance and conveyed her concern with a look. But when she spoke to Sarah, she was pleased that her voice betrayed none of her worry.

"Sarah, your baby is coming. When you feel the urge, you must push."

The woman collapsed against the fluffy pillow, a moan rising from her lips. "I'm so tired I can hardly breathe."

Katie could well imagine, after long labor and the amount of blood she had lost. The blood had stopped flowing, but only, she suspected, because the babe was blocking the way.

"I know, but you must be strong."

Sobs shook Sarah's swollen body, but she nodded. "I'll try." Her eyes widened. "Oh! Oh!"

Her stomach went rigid, and a tiny purple limb appeared. A foot. Katie swallowed against a suddenly dry throat. The child was coming feet first. She cast a second glance at *Maummi* Switzer, this one frantic. The woman returned her stare with a wide-eyed one of her own.

Biting back her panic, Katie turned her attention to the baby. Martha Hostetler had told her that the problem with a child born backward like this one came with the head. The widest part of an infant was its shoulders and head. If the feet and body came first, there was always a risk the head would be too large and the child would be stuck halfway born. In that case there was no possibility that the infant or the mother would survive. Wild, hysterical laughter threatened when Katie considered Amos's round, melon-shaped skull. If his babe was similarly shaped...

Another spasm took Sarah, and she nearly rose up off the bed. A guttural groan rumbled from low in her chest, animal like. The other foot appeared, and Katie grasped a tiny leg barely bigger around than her thumb. It gave a feeble kick in protest.

Come, little one. Do not be stubborn. Your mamm *and* daed *are eager to welcome you.*

The next convulsion came fast on the heels of the previous one. More of the child's body emerged, and Katie cupped her hands to support the infant's buttocks.

"The wee one is almost here," she said.

"I can't." Sobs choked Sarah's voice, and she collapsed backward. "I can't do it."

"*Du kannst es tun*," Maummi Switzer said.

"You can do it." Katie translated, though Sarah appeared to pay little heed. "You must. Your child's life depends on you."

Though she kept her eyes squeezed shut, Sarah nodded and made an effort to raise herself up, her elbows planted on the tick behind her. A flush suffused her face, and she grunted as she strained. Her deep groan became constant, pausing only when she gasped in a breath.

The baby's legs jerked, but no more of the little body emerged. Katie cast a frantic glance toward *Maummi* Switzer. What should she do? She wondered if she should try to pull the child, though Martha had stressed how dangerous such an action would be.

Wrinkled lips pursed into a tight bow, the elderly woman acted. Moving with a suddenness that surprised Katie, she threw herself across Sarah's body. Using her torso like a rolling pin, she pushed. Sarah's groan rose in pitch to become a shriek.

In the next instant Katie was holding a baby.

A feeble wail issued from tiny lips. The child's entire body fit in Katie's two hands. One palm cradled a skull the size of a large, ripe apple, covered with blond fuzz, and the other cupped the baby's body. Frail arms and legs waved in the air. Petite lips parted, and the wail gained volume. The infant's chest inflated with a breath, and the sound became a lusty cry.

Tears flooded Katie's eyes. The baby was tiny but, thankfully, looked and acted healthy.

"You have a girl, Sarah. A perfect little girl."

"A girl." The words fluttered on a breath not nearly as loud as the infant's cry. "Amos, we have a girl."

In the next instant her eyes rolled back and she lost consciousness. Katie saw that the blood flow had increased to a truly alarming level.

"Take the babe!"

She snapped the command at *Maummi* without wasting effort to temper her tone, and the older woman instantly obeyed. Acting on instinct, she snatched a clean bedsheet, ripped it in half, and then went to work trying to save Sarah's life.

Jesse jerked awake when his chin touched his chest. He glanced sideways on the porch to see if anyone had noticed. Jonas was dozing too, his head thrown back to rest against the whitewashed side of the house, but Amos sat with his eyes fixed on a distant place in the dark night. The song of crickets filled the smoke-scented air around them.

Jesse stretched. "How are you holding up?"

It appeared at first that Amos was so intent on his thoughts he hadn't heard the question. When he finally spoke, it was as though his voice came from some faraway place.

"She is a strong woman, my Sarah."

The doubt in his words tore at Jesse's heart. "Yes, she is. Spunky too."

A shadow smile flashed onto his face and faded as quickly. "My Alise also was a strong woman."

"Care to talk about her?"

"She died giving birth to Karl." The words were heavy with grief and worry.

"Sarah is not going to die." Jesse spoke with more conviction than he felt. The image of those bloody cloths was burned onto his mind's eye.

Lord, don't let her die. Amos is a good man, and he's already lost one wife.

The door opened, and Amos shot out of his chair like a bullet. Jonas woke, and he and Jesse hurried to stand on either side of their friend as *Maummi* Switzer pushed her way out backward, a small bundle in her arms.

"Your *dochder*, Amos Beiler." She placed the baby in Amos's ready arms.

Jesse craned his neck to peer at the opening in the blanket. "A what? Do we need to go for a doctor?"

"A daughter." Amos's eyes filled with tears as he gazed at the infant. "I have a beautiful daughter."

Jesse gave his friend a hearty slap on the back. "Congratulations."

Amos tore his gaze from the baby and lifted an anxious face to *Maummi* Switzer. "And my Sarah?"

The elderly woman's expression became grave. Jesse's heart wrenched inside his ribcage. *No. Not Sarah.*

Amos wavered on his feet, and his eyes closed against the news.

"She lives," *Maummi* Switzer hurried to say, her hands extended toward him as if to snatch the child should he should fall. "But she has lost much blood. Maybe too much. Katie has done what she can and Sarah is resting now."

"Can I go to her?" Amos's voice cracked on the words.

Her expression softened. "*Ja.* It will comfort her to have you near."

Amos wasted no time. Before Jesse could blink, the bundle was thrust into his arms and Amos disappeared into the house.

He gazed down at the sausage-wrapped infant while Jonas peered over his shoulder. A tiny face lay nestled in the soft folds of the blanket. The nose, no bigger than his little finger, looked like Amos's in miniature. Though the eyelids were shut tight, they were wide-set like Sarah's.

"Is it supposed to be so little?" he asked.

Maummi Switzer tilted her head, her gaze fixed on the baby. "None start out big, but *she* is smaller than most."

Rosebud lips pursed, and the little features scrunched. The tiny mouth opened, and the child started to cry.

"Here." Jesse thrust the bundle toward *Maummi* Switzer. "She's not comfortable with me."

Chuckling, she relieved him of the nearly weightless burden and tucked the child expertly into a crick in her arm. The crying stopped instantly.

Jonas glanced at the closed door and asked in a low voice, "And what of Sarah?"

The amusement vanished, and *Maummi*'s eyes filled with

sorrow. "She is weak. Katie has done what she can, but..." She shook her head.

Jesse turned away. Amos had already suffered such loss. It was not fair for him to lose more. Not fair for a baby to grow up motherless. And what of the older children? They had lost one mother and now might lose another. How well Jesse knew the pain of a mother's death.

The door opened again, and he almost feared turning around lest he see in Amos's face that she was gone.

"Where's my *daed*?" asked a young voice.

Jesse turned to find little Karl standing in the doorway, rubbing sleepy eyes with a fist.

"He is speaking with your *mamm*," Jonas answered kindly.

"Look." *Maummi* Switzer bent at the waist to show him the baby. "A new *schweschder* for you."

"I already have two sisters. I wanted a *bruder*." The child extended his neck to peer at the bundle. "But a *schweschder* is good too. May I have some milk?"

Jesse would have laughed, except Karl looked up at him, his expression curious. "Where is Butch?"

"He's in bed, isn't he?" They had put the boys together into the room where Butch had been sleeping, and the girls in the other room.

The child shook his head. "Not anymore. I woke up and he is not there."

Not there. A visit to the outhouse, perhaps? No, he would have had to cross the porch, where the men had been sitting for several hours. Jesse whirled, scanning the moonlit yard. In the distance the shadowy figure of Big Ed stood beside the makeshift pen he and Jonas had rigged for the goats. But where was Rex?

"I will search the house." Jonas headed for the door.

Jesse stopped him. "Don't waste your time. I think I know where he went."

He stretched his gaze across the dark wheatfield, toward Littlefield's place. A feeling of dread seeped between his ribs and crept toward his heart. What was that boy up to?

FIFTEEN

Jesse tightened his legs around Big Ed's barrel. The horse lived up to his name. He was half again as wide as Rex, which made Jesse feel as though he were straddling a bull. Though he was a mild-tempered beast, Big Ed was clearly uncomfortable carrying a man on his back, accustomed as he was to pulling a buggy, plow, or whatever other farm equipment Jonas used.

Jesse shifted his weight on the doubled-up blanket he'd thrown across the horse's back. His saddle had fallen victim to the fire. Big Ed skittered sideways, dancing like a nervous colt.

"It's okay, boy." Jesse rubbed his neck with vigor. "I don't like this any more than you do, but we're almost there."

A tangle of nerves twisted in his gut. What was Butch thinking? A stunt like this was so out of character for a timid kid like him. Jesse set his teeth. The fire had obviously upset him more than anyone realized. And no wonder, since savages had set fire to the wagon in which he'd hidden while they slaughtered his family. Jesse should have realized, should have checked on the boy after the others left. But with Sarah's baby coming early and worrying about Amos, he hadn't given Butch a second thought.

Up ahead lay the Littlefield place. The moon bathed everything in a clear, white light. Jesse slowed Big Ed and scanned the area, searching for any sign of movement. Nothing. No light glowed inside the main house or the ranch house. Where was that boy?

He sat up straight, cupped his hands around his mouth, and gave a low whistle. For a second nothing happened. Then a horse rounded the southernmost barn. Rex. But Butch was not on his back. He trotted toward Jesse, tossing his head.

"Hey, boy." Jesse slid off of Big Ed's back and rubbed Rex's neck. "Having a little nighttime adventure, are you? Where's Butch?"

"Is this what you're looking for?"

A harsh voice cut through the night. Jesse jerked upright, his gaze drawn to the man coming around the side of the ranch house. Woodard. And he wasn't alone. Butch was beside him. The man had hold of the back of the boy's shirt as they walked, and when they stopped fifty feet away, he gave a rough jerk. Jesse took a step forward, his hands clenching into fists.

"Let the boy go." He spoke in a calm voice, but he infused a note of warning into his tone.

"I can't do that." Woodard turned his head and spit, a habit that had gone beyond irritating. "I caught him sneaking around the barn intent on mischief. I can't let that go, can I?"

The door to the main house opened, and Littlefield exited.

He carried a lamp, and a circle of light traveled with him when he stepped onto the porch. "What's going on out here?" He held the lamp high, peering toward Jesse. "Who are you, and what are you doing, showing up at my house in the middle of the night?"

Jesse, who had been standing between Big Ed and Rex, stepped forward into full view. Recognition crept over Littlefield's face.

"Mr. Montgomery. I heard there was a big fire over your way. I hope your friends are safe." He chuckled.

Jesse returned his mock-pleasant smile with a grim stare. "I came for the boy."

"Boy?" The surprise on Littlefield's face was genuine. He glanced toward Woodard and caught sight of Butch for the first time.

"I caught him sneaking around, boss." Woodard gave Butch a shove, still holding tight to his shirt. Butch nearly lost his footing. "He was carrying this."

He lifted a lamp, and Jesse recognized it as being from the bedroom in Jonas's house. "It's full of oil, and he had a couple of matches in his pocket."

Though he kept his expression tightly under control, inwardly Jesse groaned. Butch's intentions were clear as could be. Littlefield had burned Jonas's barn, and the boy had decided to strike back in kind.

Judging by the expression on Littlefield's face, he'd come to the same conclusion. A smirk twisted his lips. "Well, now. That looks like more than a boyish prank to me. Looks like we stopped a serious case of vandalism before it happened."

"Lucky you," Jesse replied drily. "Some folks don't catch it until it's too late."

His comment was met with no surprise. Butch looked utterly miserable, and he had yet to lift his gaze from the ground in front of his boots.

"I heard about my neighbor's misfortune. What a relief that Mr. Woodard caught the culprit before he burned my barn down too."

Butch flared up. "I didn't set fire to Mr. Switzer's barn! *You* did, you horse's hiney!"

"Butch," Jesse said quietly.

Littlefield ignored the outburst and continued to address Jesse. "Perhaps we should send for our good friend Sheriff Wiley. I'm sure he has space for a vandal in his jail, especially such a small one."

Butch's shoulders slumped further. After his prior conversation with the sheriff, Jesse had no doubt Wiley would do whatever his "good friend" Mr. Littlefield asked. But he'd also seemed like a decent guy. Given proof he couldn't ignore, maybe Wiley would do the right thing.

He spoke as though the appeal of the idea just occurred to him. "Hey, that's not a bad idea. I'll bet Wiley will be interested to know that the coward who shot me in the back has turned up here again." He leveled a stare on Littlefield. "And no doubt he'll want to know of the boy's whereabouts last night. Butch snores like an old bull and kept me up half the night, so I can speak for his location. The sheriff might be more interested in why the boy felt the need to *retaliate*."

The implication that Littlefield was responsible for burning down Jonas's barn was clear. Jesse had the satisfaction of watching the man's lips go tight. Though the night made it hard to see eye to eye, he did not look away from the man's hard glare.

Finally, Littlefield spoke to Woodard. "Let him go."

Clearly, Woodard didn't like the idea. He drew himself up, ready for an argument. "But, boss, I caught him with—"

"I said let him go." The harsh command left no room for argument.

Disgusted, Woodard released Butch with a shove. The boy caught his balance before he went sprawling, and he crossed the distance toward Jesse with his boots dragging and his head down. When he arrived, Jesse didn't say a word but cupped his hands to heft Butch up onto Big Ed's back.

He turned to find Littlefield glaring at him. "It took a lot of effort to put up that fence. My boys didn't appreciate having all their hard work destroyed."

Jesse glanced toward the fuming Woodard. "A shame they misjudged the boundary. All we did was correct their mistake."

"Look here, Montgomery." Littlefield's voice was as hard as a rock. "I've filed a valid claim for my land."

"I'm not buying that. Jonas's claim is twenty years older than yours."

"Perhaps you should investigate before you take a stand."

Doubt nudged Jesse's mind. He sounded so sure of himself. Was something out of place with Jonas's claim? Or, more likely, had Littlefield bribed someone at the land management office into legitimizing a false claim?

Littlefield continued. "I have a thousand head of cattle coming from Texas next week. If that fence isn't put back in its proper place by then, I'll be forced to take action."

"What would that be?" Jesse asked. "Are you going to burn down his house next?"

"Just deliver the message to your Amish friend. I want my fence back in place before my cattle arrive."

With that, he turned and headed toward his house. Jesse started to call after him, to propose that he buy the land with the water access from Jonas, but couldn't make himself do it. Now was not the time. Given the man's rigid attitude, he'd laugh at a peaceful solution. Besides, his comment about having a valid claim needed to be checked out.

Woodard did not move even after his boss's door slammed shut. Jesse ignored the man, and whistled for Rex. He looked up at the horse's back which, though not as high as Big Ed's, was still an intimidating distance with a weak arm and no stirrup. He'd sure hate to make a fool of himself trying to mount his own horse, especially in front of a weasel like Woodard.

"All right, boy." He spoke in Rex's ear as he grabbed a handful of mane. "Just hold still."

With a couple of steps for momentum, he leaped off the ground and swung his leg up over Rex's back, at the same time grabbing the ridge of his neck with his right hand. Though his shoulder complained, he was pleased when he slid smoothly onto Rex's back. He was definitely getting stronger. Using his knees to guide Rex, he edged close enough to Big Ed to grab the lead rope he'd been using as makeshift reins and took off.

When they had ridden out of sight of the ranch house, he stopped and turned sideways to look Butch in the eye. "You want to tell me what that was all about?"

Butch kept his gaze fixed on the ground, but the moonlight was bright enough that Jesse saw the sullen droop to his mouth. He remained silent.

"Hey, look at me when I talk to you." Anger crept into his voice. "What were you doing, sneaking out of the house in the middle of the night and going up there? You could have been killed."

His head snapped up. "I'm not afraid."

The vehemence in his voice took Jesse by surprise. "I didn't say you were afraid."

"Well, everybody else seems to be. All those men last night saying how it's a shame about the barn, and that bishop telling Jonas he has to move." He shook his head. "None of them are going to stand up to Littlefield."

Jesse cocked his head. "You think they're not doing anything because they're afraid?"

"Well, aren't they?"

An image rose in Jesse's mind. Jonas's face, his struggle with anger obvious. And a couple of weeks ago, when he'd refused to talk to Littlefield, it had been because he was too angry. And last night, he'd seen the Amish men who came to help their friend, their expressions a blend of compassion and concern, not fear. Even Bishop Miller, whose anger had burned as fiercely as the barn, had displayed no fear.

"They're not afraid, son." He shook his head, surprised at the realization. "There isn't a coward in all of Apple Grove, at least not that I've seen. It takes more courage to control your anger than to lash out at somebody who's treating you unfairly. And a lot of strength."

"But they're going to let him get away with stealing." Butch jerked his head back toward Littlefield's house. "That's wrong."

"Stealing's wrong," Jesse agreed. "And so's burning someone's barn." He dipped his head and leveled a direct stare on the boy. "No matter what the reason."

Butch's gaze dropped away. "That's what I'm trying to tell you."

"Look at it like this. On the one side, you have Littlefield." Jesse held his hands out, palms up. "And on the other side, you have Jonas." He moved them up and down as though comparing the weight of one with the other. "Who would you rather be like?"

The boy's expression grew thoughtful as he looked from hand to hand. Then he lifted his eyes to Jesse's face. "I'd rather be like you."

The words cut right through Jesse's heart. And what was that gleaming in the young eyes fixed on his face? Admiration?

Lord, that's just plain wrong. He's a good boy. Don't let him turn out like me.

He spoke softly. "I'd rather be like Jonas."

Understanding passed between them, and though the reverence didn't dim from Butch's eyes, they both came away smiling.

"We'd better get on back." Jesse turned Rex toward the Switzer place. "The whole house was up when I left, and they're likely worried about us. You also have a disagreeable task in front of you."

Butch started. "What's that?"

Jesse awarded him a grimace. "You get to tell *Maummi* Switzer why she's missing a lamp from one of the bedrooms."

The boy groaned. With a laugh, Jesse tightened his legs and nudged Rex forward.

⁂

Katie awoke shortly after dawn, alerted by an inner nudge that her patient needed her. She jumped up from the chair and went to the bedside. Sarah stirred, her eyes shut tight but her lips moving in an alarmingly pale face.

"My baby."

The quiet voice woke *Maummi* Switzer, who had finally dropped off to sleep sometime after Katie. She leaped out of her chair and hurried across the floor to stand at the other side of the bed.

"She is here." Katie touched Sarah's arm, where they had laid the swaddled infant in hopes that the contact would give her strength.

Sarah's eyelids fluttered open. Surprised, she looked at the bundle in her arms, and then a beautiful smile curved her lips. "You said she. I have a girl. I thought I dreamed her."

"Not a dream." *Maummi* Switzer answered in a soft voice. "She is beautiful, though very tiny."

"Where is Amos?" Sarah's voice was barely audible.

"He is outside, helping Jonas milk his cows. I promised to call him if you woke." Katie picked up a cup from the bedside table. "But first drink this. It will make you stronger."

Did Sarah look slightly better this morning? Was there a touch of color in her pale cheeks that had not been there all night? It was hard to tell in the dim light of dawn. She curved her patient's unsteady fingers around the cup and motioned for the older woman to help Sarah lift it to her mouth. Whispering a prayer, she moved to the foot of the bed. Many times during the night she had replaced the cloths with which she had packed the womb, alarmed at the amount of blood that still continued to saturate them. It had been as though Sarah's life was draining away before her very eyes and she could do nothing to stop it.

A wave of relief wilted her tense muscles when she removed the packing. Sometime in the past few hours, the bleeding had stopped. She looked up into *Maummi* Switzer's anxious face and smiled. Though still very weak, perhaps Sarah would recover after all.

Thank You, Lord.

Sarah finished the tea and released the cup to *Maummi*. Jostled by her mother's movement, the baby squirmed inside the bundle and let out a weak cry that quickly gained in strength.

"What's wrong with her?" The anxious mother's frantic gaze flew to Katie's face.

"She is hungry," Katie answered. They had planned to send for Patricia Stolzfus, whose youngest was not yet weaned, first thing this morning. Perhaps now they would not need to.

Sarah turned a panicky look on the tiny babe. "I've never fed a baby before. I don't know what to do."

Maummi Switzer chuckled. "She knows."

While the elderly woman helped the young mother with her first nursing session, Katie slipped through the door to inform Amos that his wife was awake. When she stepped onto the porch, she found Jesse getting ready to jump up on the back of his horse. He searched her face.

"Is she…" From the dread in his tone, he feared the worst.

Katie answered with a relieved smile. "She is better."

"Thank the Lord" He glanced past the pile of ash and charred wood, where both Jonas and Amos were at work milking. "That's great news."

"You are going somewhere?"

He nodded. "I've got some business to take care of in Hays City." He stepped closer to her. "Actually, I feel we have some unfinished business to take care of between us."

Alarms sounded in Katie's mind, and she averted her eyes. "There is nothing left unsaid."

"I think there is."

He took a step toward her, and though she told herself she should move away, her feet appeared to be stuck fast to the ground.

"I want to apologize for my earlier words. I know it's a little soon, and you weren't expecting them. I wasn't expecting them either, but there they were and I suppose I'm standing by them."

"You suppose?"

His gaze met hers. "I'm standing by them. I can't imagine how hard it was for you when your husband died. I'm sure you loved him...fiercely." His voice dropped into a soft tone. "But a woman can love more than one person, can't she?"

He was so close the masculine scent of him invaded her senses, and his voice was like a purr in her ears. If she closed her eyes, she could imagine herself being swept into his arms.

"I..." Her throat held no moisture to give her voice strength. "I cannot."

"Don't see why not. Maybe not now, this day, but later, when things settle down a bit. I'll be going back to Luke's place. Figure I'll build a house nearby, raise a few head of cattle, and plant some crops. Life's not much different over there than it is here. You'd have Rebecca and Emma to keep you company." His pleading tone battered at her determination. "You care about me, Katie, and I figure if I stick around long enough that feeling will grow. If I became Amish—"

The sound of the new baby's cry echoed in her ears and gave strength to her resolve. Jesse deserved better than her. He deserved a wife who could help him build a home, and give him a family.

She stepped away and steeled herself before raising her eyes to look into his. "No. I told you last night. I will never marry again."

Turning quickly before he could stop her, she hurried away to tell Amos he could go to his wife's side.

SIXTEEN

The open prairie surrounded him as Jesse's gaze roved the landscape. This is where he felt most at home, alone with Rex and a couple of prairie dogs scurrying for cover. During his years on the cattle trail, he'd learned to find comfort in the solitude of being in the saddle for hours on end.

Today he had no saddle, thanks to Littlefield and his boys. He shifted his weight on Rex's back. After he visited the land management office in Hays City, he intended to find a tack shop and see how much he'd have to come up with for a saddle. He felt for the double eagle in his pocket. For twenty dollars he might be able to find a decent used one.

His thoughts turned to Jonas. The man seemed to draw the same kind of peace from working the land that Jesse used to find from the hours on the trail. How else could he handle the pressure? If only Jesse could find satisfaction from plowing a straight furrow.

Actually, when he'd worked alongside Luke, he did feel the gratification of watching something he'd planted with his own hands grow. That feeling must be even stronger when a man looked out over his own field.

Butch, now, he might one day make a good farmer. He had a way with animals, all kinds of them. Probably came from being quiet and mild mannered, like Jonas. That was as far from Jesse's nature as a kitten from a cougar. And yet...

He shifted again. Jonas wasn't really mild mannered. Over the last few weeks Jesse had watched him closely. What he'd told Butch last night was true. It took a lot more strength of character to control a fiery temper than to give it rein. More than Jesse possessed.

Katie's husband probably had that strength. No wonder she won't settle for somebody like me.

He didn't believe for a minute that she would never marry again. A woman like her had too much to give to be alone. Someday a man would come along who would stir the passion he sensed hovering behind that lovely and oh-so-calm facade. He'd have to be Amish, of course. After spending the last few weeks with the people of Apple Grove, the idea of becoming Amish wasn't nearly as far-fetched as he'd once thought. But it would never happen in Apple Grove, not with Bishop Miller calling the shots. He could not force himself to give that man control over him the way Jonas did. He'd lived too rowdy a life to ever agree to rules that made no sense.

But what if a leader was appointed by God? Could he follow the dictates of someone like, say, Jonas? Someone whose integrity could not be questioned?

Yeah. He thought he could. But what was the point, when Katie insisted she wouldn't have him even if he wore suspenders and grew his beard long?

A blur in the distance indicated his approach to Hays City. Shoving his glum thoughts aside, he urged Rex to a faster pace.

Though noon was still a long way off, the town was awake and stirring. Actually, some establishments never shut down. In times past that kind of constant activity appealed to him, but not anymore. There was a lot to be said for a good night's sleep and a fresh start in the morning.

He stopped in at a general store to inquire about the location of the land management office and was heading toward North Fort Street when he heard his name.

"Is that you, Montgomery? Well, I'll be a cross-eyed mule. It *is* you!"

He turned to find a man advancing on him, a wide smile on his familiar face.

"Morris! I don't believe it." Jesse pumped the man's hand and slapped him on the opposite shoulder. "I haven't seen you in, what's it been? Five years? Six?"

"At least that," Morris said. "Not since we rode for Carson on the Chisholm Trail. Hey, are you here for the Elway job?"

Jesse furrowed his brow. "What job?"

"You haven't heard? You know who Robert Elway is, right? He owns a huge spread and five thousand head down in Texas."

The name sounded familiar. Jesse might have ridden on a drive for him once, back in the old days. He nodded.

"Well, he's looking to lay claim to some land and bring some of the herd up here."

Like Littlefield. Jesse grimaced. "Yeah, I hear a lot of folks are doing that these days."

"Word is he's paying good money on account of it ain't as easy on the trail as it used to be. I'm on my way to talk to him. You ought to come with me."

Jesse's interest perked up. Another cattle drive? He thought he'd seen the last of the trail a few years back. "Where is he?"

"Right over there in Tommy Drum's Saloon. C'mon. I'll buy you a drink."

Morris headed across the wide, dirt-packed street. Jesse followed him toward a building with a pair of half-length wooden doors. The distant strains of piano music drifted through them and into the streets. As they neared, the pounding of Jesse's heart grew loud in his ears. He hadn't stepped foot inside a saloon in more than a year. A familiar hollow opened up in the center of his chest, a hollow that throbbed with an emptiness no amount of food could fill.

What could it hurt to go inside and talk to the man? Just because he entered a saloon didn't mean he had to order a drink, did it? And he'd jump at the chance to get on with another cattle drive. Finally, some real work, something besides busting sod on somebody else's farm. Resentment he didn't know existed suddenly blinded him. So he wasn't good enough for Katie. What made him think that he was good enough for any woman? Why deprive himself of the one thing in life that made him feel better?

Even as he pushed the swinging doors open, he knew he wasn't going in there to talk about a job on a cattle drive. The double eagle felt like a weight in his pocket. It might buy a decent saddle and it might not, but for sure it would stand him enough whiskey to fill that empty place deep in his chest.

His fingers touched the wood, and a thought slammed into his brain.

Lord, I don't want to do this. I need Your help.

Faces loomed in his mind's eye. Rebecca, who had tracked him down last year to discover he was a drunk, a wasted shadow of his former self. Luke and Emma, their gazes full of pity when he'd showed up without a cent to his name and no place to go. *Maummi* Switzer, glaring suspiciously as she snatched the whiskey bottle off the bedside table. Butch, his eyes gleaming with admiration as he announced, "I'd rather be like you."

And Katie...

Katie. She'd kept her eyes averted this morning, but when he had finally forced her to look at him, he'd seen sorrow lingering there. Sorrow that grabbed at his heart and squeezed like a fist. How he wished, *prayed,* he could replace her sorrow with joy.

Lord, do I have a chance? Could she ever love me?

One thing was certain. He would never convince her to give him a chance if he was on a cattle drive, where his old life would rise up from the ashes and pull him down again. No chance if he was a drunk.

He took his hand off the swinging door and stepped back.

Morris cocked his head. "What's wrong? Don't you want to talk to Elway?"

Jesse stared at him for a long moment and then shook his head. "No. That's not what I want."

He spun on his boot heel, suddenly eager to put as much distance between him and that saloon as possible.

"All right, then," Morris called after him. "Maybe I'll see you around."

"Maybe," he answered without turning.

A smile tugged at the corners of his mouth. The farther his boots took him from the saloon, the stronger his determination grew, until he turned the corner toward Fort Street, grinning like an idiot.

❦

The letters painted on the locked door read *United States Land Office.* Jesse paced the wooden walkway, stopping every so often to peek through the window in case someone came in from a rear entrance. Just when he'd decided to leave in search of a tack store, a man wearing a black suit and white shirt rounded the corner of the building, jingling a set of keys in his hand. He nodded a greeting toward Jesse as he stopped and unlocked the door. The cowboy followed him inside. After he hung his hat and coat on a stand, he extended a hand.

"Good morning, sir. Charles Reynolds."

Jesse shook it. "Jesse Montgomery."

"How can I help you, Mr. Montgomery?"

"I have questions about some property west of here, in Apple Grove."

"Ah. The Amish settlement."

Reynolds rounded a wide desk covered with neat stacks of paper and lowered himself into a chair, gesturing for Jesse to take the one opposite. Jesse removed his hat and, after sitting, set it on his crossed legs.

"That's right. One of my friends is having a dispute with a neighbor over the property lines."

"That's odd. Don't those Amish typically get along?"

"With each other, yes. This neighbor isn't Amish."

"Let me guess." He planted his elbows on the desk and steepled his fingers in front of his mouth. "Mr. Andrew Littlefield."

Jesse nodded. "That's right. You've heard of him?"

"Oh, yes. He's been in here several times in the past six months, filing various homestead claims."

Something in Reynolds's carefully even tone told Jesse he wasn't overly fond of Littlefield. A good sign for Jonas. "He ran a fence through the middle of my friend's land, cutting off his livestock's access to water."

The man shook his head. "I wish I could say this is the first time I've heard tell of such tactics. We're seeing more and more men like Littlefield coming up from the south, throwing their weight around and expecting people to stand back and give them whatever they want."

"He seems to think that this fence and a notice in the paper is all he needs to make him the rightful owner."

A silent laugh shook his shoulders. "Oh, he knows the law better than that. Don't let him fool you."

Something in the man's tone made Jesse cautious. "I confess I don't know the law myself. What's it involve?"

"A couple of things. First, a man files an application for one hundred sixty acres of surveyed government land." Before Jesse could ask, he nodded. "Yes, the area the Amish call Apple Grove was surveyed years ago. Then for the next five years, the homesteader has to live on the land and improve it by building on it and growing crops."

Jesse perked up in the chair. "Five years? Littlefield hasn't been here near that long."

Reynolds shook his head. "No, he hasn't. Unfortunately, there's another way, and it's quicker. Under the Homestead Act, a claimant can set up residency for six months and make trivial improvements, and then pay the government one dollar twenty-five cents per acre."

His hope deflated. "He's been here six months, has he?"

Reynolds looked sympathetic as he nodded. "He came in here last week and paid two thousand dollars on behalf of ten claimants."

Ten? Three, no doubt, were Woodard, Sawyer, and Lawson. The others must be widows from back East or others who could be as easily manipulated.

"But surely something can be done. We can't let him steal a man's land." Not to mention burning his barn, but Jesse didn't see how that would add to the argument.

"Look, I don't like the man. The first time he was in here, six months ago, he was barking orders as though he owned the place. Made me mad enough to spit fire. He had me check into your friend's claim back then."

"Jonas told me he filed his claim back when the Homestead Act was first enacted." From the serious look on Reynolds's face he knew the answer to his question before he asked it. "He made a mistake, didn't he?"

"Not a mistake, but an oversight. After his five years were over, he was supposed to file for his patent and pay a fifteen-dollar fee." The man shrugged. "He never did."

Fifteen dollars. Jonas had overlooked the payment and now he was going to lose his land. Jesse leaned forward, the fingers of both hands gripping the edges of the desk. "Are you telling me his claim isn't valid because of a *fifteen-dollar fee*?"

"I'm afraid so. Not only your friend, but none of the Amish have finalized their homestead claims. Back then this office hadn't been opened yet, so all the filings were done through the general land office in Washington, DC. Nobody locally was following up on the claims. It was up to the claimant to know the laws and follow them."

Of course the Amish wouldn't know that. They made a point of separating themselves from the *Englisch* and probably never bothered to research the requirements of the law beyond the basics.

"But when you discovered the mistake, why didn't you let them know?" His voice held a tone of accusation.

Reynolds drew himself up. "As an official of the government, I couldn't. Claims are confidential until finalized. Because the initial claims were made through Washington, I wasn't aware of the situation until six months ago. Once Mr. Littlefield completed an application, it wouldn't have been right to discuss land office business with anyone else."

Jesse snatched his hat off his lap and rose so abruptly the chair fell backward with a loud crash. Littlefield was going to take Jonas's land, and there was nothing he could do about it. There was also no possibility that Littlefield would pay Jonas for the land he wanted when he legally owned it himself. And what about Amos, John Beachy, and the others?

He didn't bother to filter the bitterness from his question. "Can the rest of the people in Apple Grove come in and pay the filing fee before someone runs them off their property too?"

Reynolds dipped his head. "Of course. Anyone who has filed the appropriate claim, waited the proscribed time period, met the improvement requirements, and paid the fifteen-dollar fee can file for their patent." The man fixed a sympathetic gaze on Jesse's face. "Mr. Montgomery, believe me. I respect the Amish. I don't appreciate a man like Littlefield coming in here and setting up his own kingdom as though he is a dictator. It was all I could do not to throw his *two thousand dollars* back in his face when he slapped it down on my desk last week. But he turned around and marched out of here before I could say anything."

The intensity in Reynolds' eyes grew sharp. Jesse heaved a breath and blew out some of his frustration with it. He ran a hand through his hair before setting his hat firmly on his head. "I'm sorry. It wasn't your fault."

"No, it wasn't. The man paid his *two thousand dollars* and didn't want to listen to anything I might have to say."

His emphasis on the amount for the second time drew Jesse's attention. Reynolds' lips were pressed tightly together, but his eyes held an unspoken message.

"He paid two thousand dollars?" Jesse repeated the amount to see the man's reaction.

A slight nod, and the intensity in his gaze increased. "That's right. Twenty one-hundred-dollar bills, right here on my desk." He slapped the surface with a palm. "Ten claims at two hundred dollars each." Again that intense look.

What was he trying to say? "Ten claims. Two hundred dollars." Jesse did the calculation. Ten times two hundred was two thousand, all right. If he had that kind of money he'd...

Realization dawned, and Jesse's jaw dropped as Reynolds' unspoken message became clear. He took a step toward the desk.

"Don't you mean two thousand for the ten claims, plus a hundred and fifty for ten filing fees?"

Reynolds leaned back in his chair, silent but with a wide smile on his face.

Excitement bubbled up in Jesse's throat, and he released it with a laugh. He'd just been handed the way to beat Littlefield at his own game. "Mr. Reynolds, shouldn't Littlefield be told that his claim isn't finished yet?"

"Yes, he should. Funny thing about that, though." He spread his hands wide to indicate the piles of paper on his desk. "I've been so busy I haven't been able to spare a minute to send a message out that way."

"So, if someone else who has met all the requirements for that land were to come in here and pay that fee, like my friend Jonas Switzer, you're saying his claim would be officially filed first?"

"Mr. Switzer or his agent." He looked meaningfully at Jesse. "An agent being anybody who is acting on his behalf."

With a grin as wide as Texas, Jesse reached in his pocket and pulled out his twenty-dollar gold piece. He slapped it down on the desk. "Mr. Reynolds, I'm here on behalf of Mr. Jonas Switzer. I'd like to file for the patent on his land."

Reynolds returned the grin with one of his own. "Let me grab the appropriate form and we'll get that done, Mr. Montgomery."

SEVENTEEN

As Jonas finished plowing the last row in his new cornfield, he saw Amos picking his way through the tall grass toward him. The man's light step and his smile lifted a weight off of Jonas's heart.

"She is well, your Sarah?" he called as Amos neared.

"Not well, but better." He came to a halt in front of Big Ed and absently reached up to rub the horse's forelock.

"And the child? She is healthy?"

A light lit in his face. "Ja. So small, but strong like her mother." He became serious. "Katie says they cannot yet go home but must stay here for a week, perhaps two. I know you have troubles of your own and would not overburden you at such a time, but..."

Jonas dismissed his concern with a wave. "It is no burden at any time to provide shelter for those in need."

No doubt Amos would visit daily, but he must return home

to tend his farm. Jonas came around the side of the plow to stand near his friend. A decision of import had been pressing against his mind in recent weeks, and he needed godly input.

He halted beside Big Ed's head and reached up to flick a chunk of dried mud from his mane. "I would ask your wisdom concerning an important matter."

A knowing expression crept over Amos's face. "Is it concerning the matter of Weaver's farm?"

Jonas watched his friend closely as he spoke. "I have decided I will not move there."

Amos did not express surprise but merely nodded. "You will follow Jesse's plan and claim the land to the south of your house?"

"*Neh*. I have spent many hours in prayer and reached a decision." He clasped his hands behind his back and gazed northward, where his former cornfield lay neatly plowed and ready for planting. If he had known it would become a field for cows, he would have left last year's stubble in the ground. "I will leave Apple Grove."

Amos's eyes widened. "And move to Troyer?"

Here was where Jonas's plans faltered. "I do not know where I will move."

"Troyer is a long way from here," Amos said carefully. "It would be hard to live so far from everyone you know and love."

Therein lay the difficulty with which he had struggled. For twenty years he had made his home among the families of Apple Grove. Through hardship and trials, such as when his beloved Caroline died, or when his girls chose to become *Englisch* instead of Amish, or like two nights ago, when his barn burned, his Amish brothers and sisters had stood by him and come to his aid. He did have family in Troyer, a sister and nieces and nephews, but because six long days of travel lay between them, he had not seen them in years. He and *Mader* could make a home there, but if they did they would more than likely not see Emma or Rebecca or their families again.

He glanced at Amos and then back to the distance. "A shame there is no Amish community nearer." From the corner of his eye, he saw that his friend watched him closely. "I have wondered if perhaps the Lord might be pleased to start one."

Amos's chest inflated with a sharp intake of breath. "I have wondered the same."

Surprised, Jonas turned to face him. "You?"

"My Alise was a godly woman and a good wife. Together we worked hard to build our home and our farm." He turned so that he faced the house where his new wife and daughter lay. "It is difficult for a woman to step into the place of another. Perhaps it is time to leave the old life behind and build a new one."

Though his words were true, Jonas sensed there was more behind Amos's decision, so he waited.

After a long pause, Amos turned a sideways smile in his direction. "At least, that is the reason I will give the bishop."

Such a sense of joy flooded Jonas's heart that his laughter rang out over the neat furrows of rich soil. Not only did Amos's agreement relieve him of the burden of acting alone, but his words confirmed the heaviness that the Lord had placed in his heart.

"It is hard work to build a new farm," Amos said, his smile reflecting Jonas's joy. "And even harder work to establish an Amish district."

"*Ja*," Jonas agreed. "When we founded Apple Grove, ten

families shared the burden. With only two, the burden will be even heavier." He straightened and spoke from the confidence that was even then growing in his soul. "With the Lord's help, we can do it."

"I may be mistaken, but I think there will be more than two sharing this burden."

Jonas looked sharply at him. Had Amos heard whisperings to which he had not been privy?

"No one *speaks* against our bishop, but there is much that can be learned from watching a man's eyes." Amos shrugged a shoulder. "I watch."

Curiosity itched in Jonas's mind, but he did not ask. Speaking about another man when he cannot speak for himself was gossip. "The Lord must appoint a new bishop and preachers. It will be good to have more than two to choose from."

Perhaps, if a few other families joined them in the new district, Jonas would be spared the burden of the Lord's calling.

A flicker of passion ignited in Amos's close-set eyes. "I have long felt the desire to serve the Lord more deeply. Perhaps He will answer my prayers."

Jonas looked at his friend through new eyes. Amos had considered becoming a bishop or a preacher? Most men dreaded the call to leadership and the lifetime burdens that came with it. But when the Lord chose, a man answered. That was the Amish way.

In a rare display of affection, Jonas clapped Amos on the shoulder. "I will pray that the lot falls to you, my friend."

Spurred by excitement at the news he bore, Jesse urged Rex into a gallop as he approached Jonas's place. The road fell away beneath him as a welcome wind blew into his face. He breathed deeply, savoring the wholesome scents of prairie grasses and rich soil so different from the stink of a cattle drive. His heart felt lighter than it had in years, relieved of a burden that had descended on him long ago when he was a boy and learned that his mother's death had left him alone in the world. Today he'd faced the urge to drink and won. Not because of anybody who might be watching with a disapproving frown or a pitying look. No, he'd done it on his own.

Well, okay, Lord. You had something to do with it, didn't You? Thank You.

He took off his hat, urged Rex to a faster speed, and let the clean Kansas wind bathe him of the stench of whiskey once and for all.

When he rode into Jonas's yard, he found Amos hitching up his buggy. If he was going home, that meant he wasn't worried about Sarah anymore. He stopped Rex nearby and hopped to the ground. Butch came running up to take the reins.

"Do me a favor, would you?" Jesse reached beneath the horse and released the cinch on his new saddle. "Give him a good, long drink and then brush him down. And here." He lifted the saddle off Rex's back and thrust it toward the boy. "Put that over on the porch for me. It needs a good oiling."

"You sure oiling will help?" Butch's eyebrows drew together as he inspected the saddle. "I'd say it needs to be thrown away."

Jesse heaved a laugh. "You're probably right, but that was the best I could find for five bucks."

Butch hurried off with the secondhand saddle—or third or fourth, more likely—and Jesse turned to where Jonas and Amos were almost finished hitching up the buggy.

"Jonas, I have good news! The best." He didn't hold back a wide grin. "Your troubles with Littlefield are over."

Instead of the joy Jesse expected, Jonas merely smiled and gave a nod. "*Ja,* they are. The land is his."

"No, it isn't. He may think it is, but he's dead wrong."

He described his trip to the land office and what he'd discovered.

"So the land is yours fair and square. I paid your fee, and the title is filed with the United States government." He cast an apologetic look at Amos. "I would have paid yours too, Amos, except I didn't have enough money. You should get over there and do it right away."

The two exchanged a quiet glance, not nearly as excited as Jesse expected. Well, *excitement* might have been too much to expect from these sedate two, but at least they could show a bit of gratitude. After all, he'd just saved their farms.

"*Danki,* Jesse," Jonas finally said. "You are a good friend."

His voice contained a notable lack of enthusiasm. Jesse's gaze traveled from one to the other. "You two are up to something. Mind sharing it with your good friend?"

Another swapped glance, and Amos nodded. Jonas looked back at Jesse.

"We have decided to leave Apple Grove."

His jaw dropped. Surely his ears were playing a trick on him. "You're leaving the Amish?"

"No, no." Jonas rushed to deny the accusation. "We will start a new community."

The reason dawned on Jesse. "You mean one where you can write your own rules?"

Amos looked at Jonas before answering slowly. "We are Amish, Jesse. We will continue to practice Amish tenets, and we will live by the *Ordnung* the Lord dictates. But we will seek His wisdom concerning every decree."

A slow smile took possession of Jesse's lips. If anybody could hear from the Lord and lead people the way He directed, it was these two. In fact, he'd trust either of them more than Bishop Miller.

"So you see that my need for this farm no longer exists." Jonas waved a hand toward the creek that was the source of the conflict. "Let Mr. Littlefield have it with my blessing."

"No!" The protest rose from a deep sense of injustice. Littlefield shouldn't be allowed to profit from his bullying tactics.

He would have gone on to try to convince them, but the door to the house opened and Katie came out, flanked by the Beiler children. Their gazes met, and she paused before descending the porch steps. An aching lump settled in Jesse's throat at the sight of her. A lovelier woman had never existed. She averted her eyes.

"We are ready," called the oldest as they crossed the grass. "*Mamm* and Katherine are sleeping."

"Katherine?" Jesse raised a questioning brow in Amos's direction.

"*Ja*, that is the little one's name." He beamed at Katie. "Katherine Marta Beiler, after the two who saved her *mader*'s life."

The two younger children climbed up into the buggy, though the oldest daughter waited for her papa to lift her up. When Jonas helped Katie climb onto the front bench, Jesse realized she was leaving too.

"You're going home?"

She gave a quick nod. "Amos will take me on his way. Sarah is weak, but she will recover with rest and food."

"And tea?" Jesse teased.

The smile that flashed onto her face warmed him. "And tea."

Amos settled on the bench beside her and picked up the reins before speaking to Jonas. "Tomorrow evening, then?"

"Ja."

With a flick of the reins and a cluck of his tongue, Amos urged the horse forward. Jesse stood beside Jonas and watched until they turned onto the road. Some of his newfound joy disappeared with that buggy. He'd hoped to speak privately with Katie and tell her of his victory at the saloon.

"He's coming back tomorrow to visit Sarah?"

Jonas nodded. "And to meet for prayer about the new community."

Jesse turned to face him. "Speaking of that, it doesn't make sense to walk away from your farm, Jonas."

"What makes sense is not always what is right. I am convicted that the move is right." He laid a fisted hand over his chest. "I feel it here."

"That's fine, but don't let Littlefield get away with stealing from you. Wherever you go, you're going to have to file a new claim and set up a new farm. How are you going to pay for that?"

A troubled crease appeared between his eyes but cleared after a moment. "The Lord will provide. I must follow my convictions and not resist when someone would take what is mine." He turned a kind smile on Jesse. "You do not understand because you are not Amish."

Jesse watched his friend's back as he walked away. With a feeling akin to wonder, he realized Jonas was wrong. He did understand. The man standing before him possessed a strength he admired more than he could say. Did he draw that strength from his faith? And if so, could Jesse one day have a measure of that force, that conviction, that let him turn his back while a scoundrel like Littlefield robbed him?

Maybe. But Jesse was not Amish. Not yet.

"Hey, Butch!"

The boy stood beside the watering trough where Rex was drinking his fill. He looked up at Jesse's shout.

"Never mind about brushing him. I have a call to pay first."

He found Littlefield outside, overseeing work on yet another fence. This one was round, like a training corral for horses, and sturdier than the makeshift barrier he'd erected on Jonas's farm. The man caught sight of him at a distance, and by the time Jesse halted Rex in front of him, he was flanked by Woodard and Lawson. Sawyer and another man continued their work on the fence, though they both kept cautious eyes on him.

Littlefield held a lit cigar, which he raised to his lips before speaking. "Mr. Montgomery, you seem to be spending a lot of time here lately. You're not looking for a job, are you?"

Jesse controlled a bark of laughter that threatened at the idea that *Maummi* Switzer would call *narrisch*. What a crazy notion. "No, but thanks for thinking of me." He continued before Littlefield could deny that his comment was an offer. "I came to talk about property boundaries."

"That again?" The man took a puff from the cigar and blew a stream of smoke. "Unless you're here to tell me that your Amish friend has moved my fence back to its proper place, I don't think there's anything more to be said on the subject."

"Actually, I paid a visit to the land management office over in Hays City this morning."

"Did you now?" Littlefield's smile deepened. "I'm eager to hear what you learned there."

Lawson's chest heaved with a silent laugh, and Woodard's lips crooked sideways. Yesterday the man's smirk would have gone right through Jesse, and he would have been tempted to punch that ugly face. But today he felt...if not exactly kindly toward the man, at least satisfied to let his words do the punching.

"Yeah, I had a good talk with a Mr. Reynolds down there. Nice fella, and he knows a lot too. Explained all the details about the Homestead Act to me." Jesse pushed the brim of his hat back on his forehead. "I already knew about filing claims and building and planting and such. But I wasn't aware that a man could hurry along the process by paying the government for his land."

Littlefield puffed on his cigar again, his expression arrogant. "A man needs to understand the law if he wants to work it to his advantage. You might instruct your friend on that count."

"Oh, yeah. I agree." Jesse shifted in his saddle. "Jonas did everything he was supposed to. He filed his claim, built a house and a barn, planted crops, and marked his land with a furrow. What he didn't do was go back five years later and file the final petition to get his title. A pity he didn't understand. A man's ignorance can hurt him."

Woodard snickered, but the smile had faded from Littlefield's face. The snake's eyes narrowed with suspicion, as though he knew Jesse was about to level him with a blow.

"Yep. Poor Jonas almost lost everything because of an oversight and fifteen measly dollars. Good thing I went down to check on it before it was too late."

"What?" All amusement was now gone from the man's voice.

"Oh, yeah. Turns out there's a fifteen-dollar filing fee that goes along with the petition for the title. Didn't you know that? I had a twenty-dollar gold piece in my pocket to buy a new saddle with, seeing how mine got burned up in the fire." He turned a look toward Woodard. "But I put it to better use. Now my friend's claim is secure."

"That's impossible!" Littlefield's snarl snapped with anger. "I paid two hundred dollars for this land, and it includes the watering hole."

"See, that's where you're wrong. Reynolds tried to tell you about the fifteen dollars, but apparently you were in too big a hurry to listen. Jonas is the rightful owner of that watering hole, and I have a note from the government to prove it." He patted his vest pocket.

Woodard and Lawson had lost their smirks and stood watching their boss with caution. A deep red flush suffused Littlefield's face and the muscles in his jaw bulged. If Jesse had been standing in front of him instead of in the saddle, he would have been bracing for the man to take a swing at him.

"I do have some good news for you, though. My friend is

thinking about pulling up stakes and settling elsewhere. Doesn't like the stink in these parts. He might consider selling his place if the price was right."

"I will not *buy* that land." The words were ground out between gritted teeth. "It's already mine."

Jesse shrugged. "Well, suit yourself. We were going to give you first shot at it, but there's another buyer waiting." That was the most carefully worded statement he'd ever made. Not a lie. He didn't claim that anyone else had expressed an interest in Jonas's farm, though if Littlefield drew that conclusion, so much the better.

The man's eyes narrowed to slits. "Another buyer?"

"Actually, you might know him. He has a big spread down in Texas like you do. Name's Robert Elway. As chance would have it, he's in Hays City right now, buying up land and putting together a crew to move his herd up this way." Jesse removed any guile from his smile. "You two will make good neighbors since you have so much in common."

The flush deepened to purple, and a vein throbbed in Littlefield's forehead. "How much do you want?"

"Me?" Jesse put a flat hand on his chest. "It's not my land. But my friend might listen to an offer if I bring it. 'Course, I'll have to think of his welfare and make sure he gets a fair price."

"I'll give him two dollars and fifty cents for the twenty-acre strip that includes the creek. That's twice what it's worth."

No doubt Jonas would be happy with the terms, but Jesse shook his head. "He's not interested in parceling out his farm. You buy the whole one hundred sixty acres or I'll offer it to Elway."

He leaned forward, one arm resting on the saddle horn. "And, by the way, I think the price of land is about to go up in these parts."

Littlefield looked as though he might have an apoplectic fit. He crushed the cigar in his fist and then threw it on the ground and pulverized it beneath his heel, a stream of curses flying from his mouth. Even though Jesse had spent most of his life in the presence of cowboys, gamblers, and drinkers, he'd never heard some of the words Littlefield uttered. Woodard and Lawson each stepped backward, out of arm's reach, and the two working on the corral cast anxious glances his way. Jesse arranged his features into an imitation of Jonas's placid expression and waited for the man to finish.

Finally, Littlefield regained a semblance of calm, though fury still showed in his rigid stance and clenched fists. "Five dollars an acre and not a cent more."

With an effort, Jesse kept his expression calm. He'd been hoping for three. When he could be sure his tone would stay even, he said, "I think he'll consider that offer favorably. I'll let you know."

The cattle baron whirled and stalked away. He stomped up the steps and into the house. The door slammed shut behind him.

When he was gone, his men exchanged stunned expressions. They had probably never seen their boss bested. Jesse was tempted to taunt them with a victorious smirk, but for some reason he couldn't see the pleasure in it. What would arrogance get him, except a reputation like Littlefield's? Instead, he bobbed his head in a brief nod toward Lawson and Woodard.

When he tugged at the reins to turn Rex, he caught Sawyer watching him. Was that fear in his face? Jesse could set Sheriff

Wiley on him, but what purpose would that serve? They would string him up for shooting a man in the back. Jesse had seen enough killing in his lifetime.

He touched a finger to his hat in a gesture of farewell and had the satisfaction of seeing Sawyer's jaw drop before he kicked Rex into a gallop.

Now that one confrontation was out of the way, he might as well take care of the second before he headed back to the Switzers' for the night.

When Jesse rode up to the Miller place, a little girl he recognized from the church meeting ran from a chicken coop to gape at him, a basket half full of eggs clutched in her hands. He smiled a greeting but didn't stop, instead steering Rex toward the figure he spotted in a distant field.

The bishop heard his approach and straightened from his inspection of a row of bean plants. Jesse halted Rex on the grassy strip of land between one field and the next, and then he swung out of the saddle. Instead of coming toward him, Bishop Miller stood waiting while Jesse walked carefully between straight lines of six-inch plants, his expression stern.

"Hello, sir." Jesse greeted him when he drew near enough for conversation.

His answer was silence accompanied by a slight nod.

"I wanted to share something I learned today." He related his conversation with Reynolds, concluding with, "So I figure you might want to let people know they need to get down to the land office as soon as they can."

He avoided mentioning Jonas or the deal he'd struck with Little-field. Let Jonas handle his business with the bishop.

"*Danki.*"

For someone who'd had a mouthful to say the other night, he was quiet today. Jesse waited for him to say something else, but the man merely continued to stare at him.

"All right, then." He waved at the plants. "I'll leave you to it." He turned to go.

The bishop cleared his throat. "I would speak with you on a different matter."

Here it comes.

He turned back and, though he knew the answer, asked, "What would that be?"

Thin, tight lips parted enough to squeeze out a comment. "Our Katie is Amish."

Jesse almost laughed. Like that was big news? Instead of a sarcastic response, he controlled his tone. "Yes, sir. I know."

The man's rigid spine stiffened even more. "I have seen you watch her, but your eyes behold what you cannot have. She is not for you."

Jesse wanted to argue, to challenge the man's right to control Katie's life, but what would be the point? Katie herself had said the same thing.

Swallowing his words, Jesse merely nodded before turning away.

Katie isn't for you. Get used to it, Montgomery.

❦

When Jesse returned to the Switzers', he found Jonas closing the goats into their makeshift pen for the night. This, at least, was one discussion he would enjoy.

Hearing his friend's approach, Jonas turned and waited. He wore the same placid expression Jesse had learned to identify as his trademark. Were there new depths of peace lurking in those kind eyes tonight? The decision to leave Apple Grove must have been weighing on the man, and now that the burden was lifted, his entire countenance was more relaxed.

When he drew near, Jonas spoke first. "Was Mr. Littlefield happy with my decision to give him my farm?"

Jesse pulled up short. "How'd you know I was heading over to Littlefield's place?"

Jonas actually laughed. "Your ways are not as mysterious as you seem to think, my *Englisch* friend."

"I guess not." Jesse joined in with a chuckle. "I wouldn't say Littlefield was exactly *happy* when I left, but it was a good visit. He agreed to our terms."

The man paused in the act of looping the twine barrier around a post. "Our terms?"

"That's right. Once I explained how you'd decided to sell your land, he—"

"But I do not intend to sell my farm. I told you I would give it as a gift."

Jesse held up a hand. "I know what you said, and I admire you for wanting to find a peaceful way out, but like I've been trying to tell you all along, men like Littlefield don't understand peaceful ways. So I talked to him in his own language."

Apprehensive lines appeared on Jonas's forehead beneath his round hat. "What language is that?"

Jesse almost said "Intimidation" but decided on a better word. "Business. Littlefield and I reached a business agreement. He's prepared to buy your land, all of it, for five dollars an acre."

Jonas's jaw dropped open wide enough to toss an apple inside.

"But...but..." He snatched the straw hat from his head and scrubbed at the sparse hair beneath it. "That's eight hundred dollars!"

"Yep. That's what it comes out to." Jesse held up a hand. "And before you say something stupid, like you won't take the money, think a minute. You and Amos are going to have a lot of expenses when you make this move. You'll have houses to build and land to lay claim to and barns to raise. Plus, you'll probably have to buy supplies to help you over the first year or so till you get your fields plowed and crops going."

"*Ja*, what you say is true."

But despite his agreement, hesitancy still weighed heavy in his voice. Jesse had saved the most convincing argument for last. "And if you decide you don't need all eight hundred dollars, you can always make a donation to your new Amish district. Once the church gets going, I have a feeling other Amish folks will want to come too. You'll be able to put the money to good use."

"A district has many needs." The struggle twisting Jonas's features faded, replaced by a slow smile. "Perhaps this money is the Lord's way of blessing our plans."

Jesse answered with a grin of his own. "I've been thinking the same thing."

Grateful tears sparkled in the eyes Jonas lifted. In a rare display of emotion, he gripped Jesse's shoulder—the good one—and squeezed. "*Gott* has used you to bless me beyond what I deserve, my friend. *Danki.* I am grateful to Him and to you."

God used a broken-down cowpoke like *him?* The thought was so foreign Jesse couldn't grasp it. Embarrassed, he lowered his eyes and scuffed at the dirt with a boot heel. "I'm glad I could help. I owe you and Miz Switzer a lot."

"You owe us nothing. Friends help friends." A playful tone entered his words and lightened the moment. "Even *Englisch* friends."

Jesse returned his grin. At that moment the door to the house opened and *Maummi* Switzer's voice carried across the distance, calling them in to supper. With a lighter heart than he'd had all day, Jesse fell in step beside his friend.

EIGHTEEN

When the eighth Amish buggy arrived on Sunday afternoon, Jesse and Butch had to start a second row in which to park them. Jonas and Amos stood in front of the house to greet those who arrived and to help the women climb down. Both wore stunned expressions. Earlier in the day Jonas had confessed that he expected three or maybe four families to show up for their discussion about starting a new community.

"Here comes another one." Butch took the horse's lead from Zacharias Schrock and led him past the row of buggies toward the makeshift corral they had erected that afternoon.

Zacharias straightened from his inspection of one of the wheel spokes. "That is Levi Beachy."

Katie's brother? Jesse turned and watched as Levi's buggy rolled to a stop in front of the house, and Amos helped the young woman seated on the front bench to the ground. When her footing was secure, he turned to help the girl on the second bench.

Katie.

She joined the other woman, and together the two of them headed for the house. Before she stepped onto the porch, she turned. His throat constricted as he watched her scan the fields. Was there a lovelier woman anywhere in the world? Then her gaze came to rest on him. He couldn't be sure because of the distance, but he thought he saw a smile, and his pulse stuttered. Then she disappeared inside.

Jesse hadn't planned on attending the meeting. It wasn't his business, after all. He was an outsider. But if Katie was going to be there, maybe he'd change his mind.

When the twelfth family had arrived and their horses and buggies were tended, the meeting began. Jonas's house was big enough to accommodate a large crowd, as it apparently did when his turn came to host church meetings, but tonight there were no backless benches to sit on because no one had anticipated a gathering big enough to require them. Jesse was amused to see that the attendees still arranged themselves as they did for church, with the men on one side of the room and the women on the other. Every chair in the house had been brought in and offered to the women in order of age. The men and younger women either stood along the wall or sat on the floor.

Jesse did not enter, but hovered in the doorway, an observer only. He scanned the room for Katie but did not see her. That's when he noticed that the door to *Maummi* Switzer's bedroom was cracked open, no doubt so she and Sarah could listen to the proceedings.

Most of the conversation unfolded exactly as Jesse expected. Jonas began by announcing his decision to sell his farm and move away from Apple Grove. Then Amos spoke, his voice steady as he described how the Lord had urged him, independently of Jonas, to also consider moving away. The men and women listened, many of them nodding as though in agreement.

Not a single word of accusation against Bishop Miller or anyone else in Apple Grove was uttered, with one exception. When discussion was invited, a young man whose name Jesse did not know got to his feet.

"What explanation will be given to Bishop Miller?" He glanced around the room, and went on in a sharp tone. "I think he should be told what his actions have wrought."

Amos cleared his throat before he spoke. "My decision came from the Lord, not from the actions of any man." He fixed an almost tender look on the young man. "We are commanded to respect authority, not to speak against our brothers and sisters. I will not participate in any discussion that is not governed by that edict. That is not why we are here."

There were nods all around, and Jesse saw several approving glances exchanged. He looked at Amos, a new respect blossoming inside him. Once he'd thought the man staid and dull. How wrong could he have been?

"Where will we settle?" asked one of the women. "We will not go west, into the territory of the wild savages, will we?"

Jonas gave the answer. "We will pray to the Lord for guidance."

He glanced at Amos, who nodded for him to continue. "There is a place only two hours from here, east of Hays City, where the land is fertile and plentiful. A small *Englisch* church was built there not long ago, but there is little besides that."

Jesse straightened, his attention snagged. Was he talking about Colin's church? Of course he was. It was the perfect place for an Amish community, with plenty of land stretching out in all directions. And if he were a betting man, he would put money on which piece of land Jonas would claim. His new home would be within sight of Emma's and Rebecca's.

"Is that not the church of your *Englisch* son-in-law?" The man who asked had introduced himself as Aaron Wagler when Jesse helped him park his buggy.

"The same." Jonas looked the man straight in the eye. "I will not deny that I will be happy if the Lord allows us to settle near my daughters. But if He sends us elsewhere, I will go."

Amos, who had been standing off to the side, stepped up beside him. "We will send a delegation to see the land and to pray to the Lord for guidance."

The suggestion was met with approving nods all around.

"Who will go?" *Maummi* Switzer turned in her chair to look at the others. "When we came here to Apple Grove, we sent our bishop to see the land we were to buy."

"Then we must ask the Lord to appoint new leadership." Zacharias looked around the room. "Is it the intent of all here to go?"

The sound of shuffling feet drew attention to Levi Beachy. "I do not know. I must pray first and then speak with my father and... others." He sent an inquiring glance across the room to the young woman who had arrived with him and Katie.

"A wise answer." Jonas smiled at the young man. "And because you are not married, your name will not be included in the lot regardless."

Zacharias nodded. "Eight married men. We have no song-books, but have we eight of any books?"

From his place leaning against the doorjamb, Jesse watched as the people shuffled around, searching through their belongings. *Maummi* Switzer brushed past him and disappeared up the stairs. They were going to pick a new bishop right now? And what was with the books? "I have one." Zacharias's wife, who was seated on the second row, pulled a worn book from her bag. "*Die Bibel.*"

Sarah's voice came from the sickroom. "I have a Bible too. Katie, here. Take this to them."

Heads turned as the bedroom door cracked open a bit farther and Katie emerged carrying a book that resembled the other, only newer. Then *Maummi*'s footsteps sounded on the stairs, and she came into the room, a stack of books in her arms. Two were Bibles, and the others were various sizes. "I found these in the chest from Emma's room, left from her school days. Always a reader, our Emma."

When they had assembled eight books, Zacharias carried them to the front of the room and handed them to Amos.

"Deacon Beiler, you are the only one among us who has born the yoke of leadership. I believe yours should be the hand to ready the lot."

With a grave nod, Amos took the stack. *Maummi* Switzer, who had gone to a writing table in the corner, set a spool of spun wool and a slip of paper on top of the books. Everyone watched as Amos crossed the length of the room with a measured step. When he passed by Jesse as he exited, his lips moved in prayer.

Silence fell in the room. Most heads were bowed, though

Jesse caught a few anxious gazes exchanged between the men, or between a man and his wife. The atmosphere became heavy, pensive. Even Jonas, who had turned toward the wall, his hands clasped behind his back and his head bowed, maintained the rigid posture of one who dreaded what was about to come.

Sarah's piercing voice cut the silence. "What's going on out there? I can't stand being in here where I can't see anything."

A few answering chuckles did little to ease the tension. From his position in the doorway, Jesse could see Amos in the kitchen. He laid out the books before him on the work surface, and then he picked one up. From the thickness, Jesse guessed that it was one of the Bibles, though he couldn't see which one. Amos slid the piece of paper inside, closed it, and then tied the book with a piece of spun wool. That done, he tied wool around the rest of the books as well. Then he stacked them and carried them back to the room. When he had handed the load to Zacharias, he retired to a place in the far corner where he bowed his head and closed his eyes.

Zacharias carried the books to the writing table and laid them out, one at a time, on the desk. "May the Lord let the lot fall where He wills."

The first man to approach the table was Jonas. Jesse watched closely as his hand hovered over the surface and then selected one of the books. He held the book at arm's length, as though he dreaded touching it, and untied the wool. When he fanned the pages and revealed no slip of paper, a relieved smile lit his face. With a light step, he returned to his place beside Amos.

One by one the men followed his lead. Jesse noted with interest that their expressions ranged from worry to dread to, in a few cases, resignation. Aaron Wagler selected one of the Bibles, and

Jesse held his breath as he fanned the pages, looking for the paper that would change his life until the day he died. It was not there, and he smiled broadly. The next Bible was chosen by Leo Stolzfus, but again, the paper was not tucked within its pages.

When there were two books left on the table, both Bibles, Zacharias made his selection. Holding his book he turned to Amos, who had kept his eyes closed during the entire process. As though aware of the man's regard, Amos raised his head. His expression did not change as he took note of the Bible in Zacharias's hands and the other one on the table.

Zacharias slid the wool off of the cover. The silence in the room deepened as every eye focused on his hands. He opened the book, fanned the pages...

And came up empty.

Just to be certain, he held the book at arm's length upside down and fanned the pages again. No paper fluttered to the floor.

Amos, his expression as unreadable as ever, left the corner and approached the table. The tension in the air stretched like a tight wire as he picked up the book, his movements slow and reverent. He untied the string and opened the pages.

There, tucked into the center of the Bible, was the slip of paper.

A collective sigh rose from every throat. A smile spread across Amos's face as he once again bowed his head and closed his eyes, his lips moving in prayer. This time, Jesse felt sure, it was a prayer of thanksgiving.

Maummi Switzer turned in her chair in the front row to face the room. "Our new bishop is Amos Beiler!"

"Waaaaaahooooooo!" The cheer from the sickroom drew chuckles from some and smiles from everyone.

Something stirred in Jesse's chest. He had no doubt that the Lord had directed the selection process. Amos would make a fine bishop. He would administer his duties with wisdom and much prayer. A leader to be respected and admired. The urge inside Jesse's ribcage increased until it became a pressing need to act. This was what he'd been waiting for, what he'd been searching for his whole life. The peace he needed wasn't found from long hours in the saddle. It wasn't found at the bottom of a whiskey bottle. It was here, among men and women who loved the Lord and listened for His direction. Finally, after years of looking, he'd found his home.

Almost before he knew he intended to move, his feet propelled him into the room. The quiet whispers fell silent as everyone fixed their attention on him. He didn't stop until he stood at the front, looking into Amos's eyes.

"Congratulations, Bishop Beiler." He straightened to his full height, his spine erect. "I'd like to be your first convert."

Amos's close-set eyes widened, and behind him he heard *Maummi* Switzer's swift intake of breath. He grinned at that, glad to have gotten one over on her. Behind Amos, Jonas wore a grin that could light up half of Kansas.

When he turned, he was greeted by the delighted smiles of his new family. But his eyes were drawn to the back of the room, to one lovely pair of eyes fixed on him. Katie had thrown the sick-room door open and stood with her gaze riveted on him, both hands clutching her throat. The joy that had filled Jesse's heart a moment ago fled when he realized that the tears in her eyes were not joyful. Pain etched deep lines on her face. One hand rose to clamp over her mouth, as if to stifle a sob, and then she fled the room. The sound of the door slamming shut behind her echoed throughout the house.

Katie burst through the front door and ran past the group of children who played in the grass waiting for their parents to leave the meeting. She did not stop, not even when Butch called after her. She stumbled and nearly fell, but still she ran, until her feet trod on a carpet of wilted apple blossoms. Throwing herself against the slender trunk of a tree, she finally allowed the tears to flow.

It was not fair! Yes, Jesse had told her he would consider becoming Amish, but she did not believe him. Turning him down was easy when she had her faith to fall back on, but that excuse had been taken from her. Now she was left with nothing but the truth. She was barren, worthless, a woman with nothing to offer. She had already spoiled one man's dreams, had caused the end of an entire family line. And the man she loved was becoming Amish.

The pounding of feet behind her took her by surprise. Jesse. She should have known he would follow her.

"Go away." Tears choked her, and the words came out strangled. "I want to be alone."

"No, you don't." He came to a halt behind her. "You don't want to be alone any more than I do."

A bitter laugh slipped unbidden from her mouth. "What do you know of me? Nothing."

"I know enough." His voice fell softly on her ears, and he stood so close his breath warmed the back of her neck. "I know everything I need to know about you. The way you sip your tea with your little finger held high. The way you put extra butter on your bread when you think nobody's looking. I know you like cream on your berries, and the smell of your fingers after you handle tomato plants."

Her tears slowed. How did he know those things? The times when she thought him asleep, he must have been watching her through the window while she worked in the garden.

"I know you pray for those you look after because I've seen your eyes close and your lips move. Your hands are tender and careful when you're caring for a wound, but firm when they need to be." His voice grew softer, almost a purr in his throat. "And I know you love children. You should see the way your eyes shine when you hold little Katherine. You need babies of your own, Katie. And a husband to help you care for them."

Pain shafted through her. She turned to find him even closer than she realized. If she leaned forward, their bodies would touch. Instead, she shrank against the tree trunk.

"That is the one thing I cannot have." Sobs threatened to close her throat, but she swallowed them back.

His head cocked sideways as his eyes pried into hers. "What do you mean?"

"Five years of marriage and no babies. Month after month we prayed, but either God did not hear or He chose to ignore our prayers." The rough bark pressed into her back, and she leaned harder into it, welcoming the discomfort. "I am barren, Jesse. That is why I can never marry again."

There. The words were spoken. Now all that was left was for

him to turn away, mumbling an excuse as he fled. She closed her eyes, unwilling to see the disappointment in his face.

"Is that why you won't marry me?"

His question did not sound disappointed so much as curious. Cautiously, she cracked open an eye. His head was cocked sideways, and his lips had twisted into a bemused line that wrenched at her heart. That same smile had set her stomach to fluttering so many times.

"You deserve to have a family." Though she had to rip the words from deep in a heavy heart, she forced herself to voice them. "A wife *and* children."

The piercing gaze that searched her face softened. In the next instant she found herself pulled forward, encircled by his arms.

"Katie, Katie." The whisper that tickled her ear held the hint of a chuckle. "If the only way I can have children is with someone else, I don't want them. It wouldn't be fair to marry another when you are the only woman I love."

The warmth of his body, the strength of the arms that embraced her, and the heady, masculine scent that clung to him invaded her senses. Her spinning thoughts threatened to pull her into a whirlwind at which Jesse was the center.

She shook her head in an attempt to clear it. "But you would be such a good *fader*."

"Well, I don't know about that, but I do know you will make a good mother." Warm, soft lips nuzzled her ear. "And I know a boy who needs a family. You won't even have to change his dirty linens, though you might need to force him into a tub for a good scrubbing every week or so."

Butch. A feeling akin to amazement flickered to life deep in her soul. Butch did need a family, and she loved him already. Together she and Jesse could provide the home he so desperately needed. What joy it would give her to teach him the pathway to true peace.

She couldn't think, not with Jesse's breath warm against her cheek and his arms around her waist, pulling her closer. Jesse, who had announced his intention to become Amish moments ago. Jesse, who wanted to marry her, even though he knew she was barren.

Jesse. The man she loved.

"Marry me, Katie. Let's build a life together."

Her arms rose and her fingers brushed across the shoulders she had tended. She buried them in the soft curls at the base of his skull and pulled him down to her. The last of her reserves fled in the moment his lips touched hers.

EPILOGUE

White Church, Kansas
Thanksgiving 1886

Jesse scratched at his beard, still not easy with hair on his face after six months of growth. On the other hand, some outward signs of Amish life had been easy to adapt to. He slipped his thumbs beneath his braces and rocked on his shoes, aware that he was imitating a gesture of Jonas's. Suspenders were a definite improvement over belts, and the broadfall trousers a far sight more comfortable than the tight denim britches of a cowboy. But he would never get used to this round hat. No matter how hard he argued, Bishop Beiler refused to consider changing the *Ordnung* to allow for the oblong shape of a man's head.

"Hey, Amish man. Get over here and help."

Jesse answered Luke's good-natured jibe with a grin and

crossed the churchyard to help unload benches from Bishop Beiler's wagon. He grabbed one end while Luke took the other, and together they carried the bench toward the place where they had set up boards on barrels to form tables for the bountiful feast the women had worked for days to prepare.

When the bench was set in place, they headed side by side back to the wagon for another.

"I haven't seen much of you since the wedding." Luke speared him with a teasing grin. "That new farm must be keeping you busy."

Jesse refused to rise to his bait. Truth was, he didn't feel much like visiting lately. He and Katie and Butch were happy with their long days of work on the farm and their peaceful nights together in their cozy new home.

"The road runs both ways between your place and mine. Anytime you feel like visiting, come on over and we can talk while you help me milk the cows."

Luke's only reply was a laugh as they hefted the next bench.

The last in a string of buggies and wagons deposited its female passengers at the house and headed for the open field where Butch and Noah Stolzfus were corralling the horses after they had been unharnessed. Jesse almost tripped over a trio of smaller boys who dashed beneath the bench he carried, one in Amish garb and two in *Englisch* shirts and britches.

"Hey, I think that was my son." Luke frowned after the boys as they disappeared around the corner of the white church building. "He's supposed to be helping his mother in the house."

"Let him go," advised Jesse. "That house is full to bursting already, and too many people are around for them to get into much trouble without somebody seeing."

It was true. Everyone in White Church had turned out for today's Thanksgiving dinner. Everywhere he looked, Amish and *Englisch* men stood talking, and women formed a continuous line from Colin and Rebecca's big house to the already loaded make-shift tables. The scent of pies and roasting meat filled the air, and the happy laughter of children rang across the fields.

They set the last bench in place and straightened, watching the bustle that surrounded them. Jesse realized his friend was staring at him, his mouth crooked into a quirky grin.

"What?"

"I was thinking about our cattle drive days and what a rowdy cowpoke you were." Luke shook his head. "If somebody would have told me you'd end up Amish, I would have laughed them off the trail. If there was ever a hopeless case back then, it was you."

Jesse joined in with a chuckle. It was true. Of all the possible futures he'd envisioned, becoming Amish had never occurred to him. And yet here he was, enjoying a life he never thought possible, and a peace he thought would forever be beyond his reach.

The last six months had held more changes for him than many men endured in years. He'd helped Amos, Jonas, and the others leave Apple Grove and set up a dozen new farms here in White Church, as they had decided to call their new community. He'd completed nine classes, conducted by Bishop Beiler, Zacharias, and Jonas, over a course of several months. There he had learned the tenets of the faith, the customs and habits of his new community, and had studied the Confession until he could quote it in his sleep.

The day of his baptism was forever etched in his mind. He'd knelt before Bishop Beiler in front of the community. The bishop's cupped hands rested on Jesse's bowed head. Jonas poured water from a pitcher into the bishop's hands, and though Jesse knew it was nothing but plain spring water, he would swear until the day he died that the trickle that flowed over his head and dripped down his face washed away the last shred of rebellion from his soul. When he rose to receive the holy kiss, he felt like a new man.

But that was nothing compared to the day, three weeks later, when he and Katie stood together before the same community to be joined forever as husband and wife.

Jesse's gaze strayed across the churchyard, his eyes drawn unerringly to the loveliest Amish woman in the gathering. As though she felt his regard, Katie looked up from her work of arranging overflowing bowls and trays on the table. Their eyes met, and the bustle of their surroundings fell away. For a moment they renewed the intimacy of their love, and the secret she had whispered into his ear in the dark of night only a week ago. Come spring, the Lord would bless them with a gift more precious than any they had ever dared to hope for. Katie was not barren; Samuel had been. Jesse and Katie would welcome a child, a baby of their own, born of their love for each other.

What would Bishop Miller think when he heard the news? He'd received the announcement of the intended departure of eight families from the Apple Grove district silently, his expression stoic. The word from their friends who had remained said the man's harsh attitude had softened somewhat, though grief still rested heavily on him. Would this little one harden his heart again, or would Jesse and Katie's child be a harbinger of peace for the bitterness that had wrapped around the man's heart like a shroud? That was Jesse's prayer.

He realized Luke was still watching him, waiting for a response. Laughing, Jesse clapped his friend on the shoulder. "One thing I've discovered, buddy. The Lord is partial to hopeless cases. I'm proof of that."

The church bell rang, calling everyone to the tables. Amish and *Englisch* alike gathered around the feast. Bishop Beiler and Sarah stood alongside Colin and Rebecca, whose little Isaac was already half again as big as baby Katherine. Luke and Emma corralled their pair while Jonas stood nearby beaming at his grandchildren. *Maummi* Switzer hovered over the food with a ready hand, daring any bugs to draw near. All of his neighbors were there, their faces beaming with thanksgiving.

Jesse joined Katie, standing as close to her as propriety allowed. The smile she turned on him reached inside his chest, straight to his soul. The truth of his words to Luke echoed in his ears and resonated deep inside him.

If God could bring peace to this restless cowboy's heart, nobody was beyond His reach.

AUTHORS' NOTE

We hope you enjoyed *A Cowboy at Heart*, our third book about the Amish of Apple Grove. As soon as we wrote Book 1, *The Heart's Frontier*, we knew we would eventually tell Jesse's story. He was such a rowdy but lovable cowboy. We couldn't wait to see who would tame his restless heart. In the first book he teased Luke about falling for one of those "Aim-ish" gals, so we chuckled when Jesse fell in love with an Amish woman himself.

Though this story is a work of fiction, we always like including a bit of actual history. The 1880s were a fascinating time in the American West. As the days of the great cattle drives came to an end, the economy underwent drastic changes. The demand for beef did not decrease, and cattle barons could be ruthless in their acquisition of land with easy access to the railroads. The circumstance in which Jonas Switzer finds himself in *A Cowboy at Heart* wasn't at all uncommon during that period.

Medicine was also changing during that time. As Dr. Sorensen explains to *Maummi* and Katie, an English doctor named Joseph Lister had discovered the role microorganisms played in infection a few years earlier. The concept of antisepsis before and during surgery had become common in Europe in the 1880s, but the practice took a while to become popular among American doctors. Most thought the whole idea was hogwash.

Those who have read the previous Apple Grove books will notice that *A Cowboy at Heart* isn't as humorous as the others. The themes in this story are serious ones—alcoholism, barrenness, inconsolable grief at the loss of loved ones, and the soul-searching that comes from standing your spiritual ground in the face of adversity. We are both certain that God can soothe every hurt, heal every injury, and strengthen every heart to endure even the toughest times with faith intact.

We'd love to hear from you. Let us know what you thought of our book by visiting www.LoriCopeland andVirginiaSmith.com.

Lori and Virginia

A Special Treat for You!

Though we love all the characters in the Amish of
Apple Grove series, one person touched our hearts
in a special way from the first moment he appeared.
Jonas Switzer, Emma and Rebecca's wise and loving
papa, is a man of sterling integrity, quiet strength, and
deep faith. We loved spending time with him throughout the three books and thought it would be fun to
peek into the past to see what he was like as a younger
man. And, of course, we wanted to meet the woman
who captured his heart and gave him two wonderful
daughters. We hope you enjoy this glimpse into the
early life of Jonas Switzer.

Lori and Virginia

A HOME IN THE WEST

**A short story from the
Amish of Apple Grove Series**

*Berlin, Ohio
April 1858*

When you finish here, Jonas, will you hitch up the wagon and help the women load it? They are nearly ready."

Jonas Switzer kept his forehead firmly planted against the cow's side, his eyes fixed on the rising level of milk in the bucket in front of his stool. Frustration flared like a flame in the center of his chest. Help the women? There was real farm work to be done this day, corn to be planted in the rich, fertile soil that lay ready to receive it. At nineteen years old his back was strong and his hand steady at the plow. But where was he during the plowing? In the barn milking the cows and in the house helping the women.

I am better with the plow than either Peter or Melvin.

The thought, though entirely true, brought a stab of guilt. Pride was one of the worst sins and despised of the Lord. Besides, Peter's and Melvin's lack of skill was the very reason Helmuth Byler insisted that his sons handle the work. After all, one day they would take over the running of this farm, whereas Jonas was little more than a hired hand.

Only when he had mastered his emotions and was sure no trace of bitterness lingered on his face did he raise his head and look at the man standing in the open doorway of the barn.

"*Ja*, I will help the women."

Though he was sure his voice betrayed nothing but calm acceptance, sympathy softened Helmuth's kind features. Jonas thought he might speak, and he paused in his milking. But after a moment Helmuth merely said, "*Danki*," and left the barn.

With a sigh Jonas returned to his task. Milk flowed into the pail in two steady streams, the rhythmic swishing sounds a comforting accompaniment to the quiet serenity of the barn. In the next stall, Betsy's teeth chomped sweet straw as the mare waited to be hitched to the wagon to haul the women and their cheeses and jams to the market in Berlin.

As the pail slowly filled, guilt continued to plague Jonas. Surely his feelings of discontent were displeasing to *Gott*. They certainly were to *Mader*, who missed no opportunity to remind him that they had a home thanks only to the generosity of the Amish district of Berlin, and especially to Helmuth and Elizabeth Byler. When Jonas's *Englisch* father died, the Bylers had taken in *Mader* and her two young children, Gerda and Jonas. The Amish community had even built a small house on the Byler farm where they might live together as a family.

At a church meeting a few years ago, Jonas overheard Helmuth tell one of the men that when Peter was old enough to take over the farm, the Switzers' house would become a *dawdi haus* for him and his wife. The realization had slapped at Jonas like an open hand in the face. Of course he had known that *Mader* and Gerda and he didn't own the farm on which they lived, but for the first time he realized that the house they called home wouldn't remain theirs forever. As the man of the family, the task fell to him to provide for his *mader* and *schweschder*.

At that moment a dream had been birthed in Jonas. He would not always live by the charity of others. One day he would build his own house, plow his own fields, and milk his own cows.

Gott, *let it be so.*

Of course, a man couldn't build a home alone. He needed a wife by his side. And Jonas knew which woman he would choose.

An expanding warmth crept over him as the image of Caroline Hersberger rose in his mind. The loveliest girl in Berlin, all the young men agreed. Whenever her name arose, a moment of silence fell among them, and Jonas had recognized in the eyes of many of his friends the same wistful longing he felt. The thought doused his hopes like a bucket of creek water. What had he to offer when Caroline could choose her husband from at least a dozen eager young men, eldest sons with the promise of prosperous farms that would one day be theirs? Jonas squeezed with renewed force, and the cow turned her head to fix a reproachful brown eye on him.

But Jonas had something to offer that those others did not. He had a plan. No doubt *Mader* would call it a *narrisch* notion, but he would not give it up. And he hoped that the adventurous spark he'd seen on the occasions when he was bold enough to meet Caroline's eye meant his plan might hold some appeal for her as well. He intended to find out, and soon. At tomorrow night's singing.

Of course, she might laugh at him.

He set his jaw. That was a risk he was prepared to take. He was nearly twenty years old. It was high time he got a start on a life of his own.

A movement to his right drew his attention. A gray barn cat, one of his favorites, edged through the open doorway and paced sedately toward him. The animal approached bravely, ignoring the cow, and came to a stop two feet away. He sat, wrapped his tail around his body, and fixed an expectant look on Jonas.

Chuckling, Jonas resisted the urge to stroke the tomcat's fur. This one would not stand for caresses like some of the other cats in residence at the Byler farm. Jonas knew what he wanted.

"Open up, greedy one."

The cat's mouth stretched wide, and Jonas aimed a stream in his direction. Practice had made his aim perfect, and the cat lapped milk from the air.

"There. That's enough for you. Go catch one of those mice I saw lurking around the corn crib this morning."

Satisfied with his treat, the cat wandered off with the same unhurried pace, his tail held high. With a touch of envy, Jonas watched him go. If only he could manage to appear as unconcerned tomorrow when he spoke with Caroline.

Jonas thought the singing would never end. The Lapps' barn was filled with young men and women seated on benches, their combined voices rising to the upper rafters where the lantern light could not reach. Just when he thought they had sung every song in all of existence, someone would toss out the title of another and the singing would begin again. The only thing that made the evening bearable was the fact that he'd selected a seat where he had an unobstructed view of Caroline's profile. A tendril of soft brown hair had escaped the confines of her *kapp*, and as she sang it waved against the long slender line of her neck.

Finally the last song was sung. Now began the fun part of the evening, the part they all looked forward to. The singers rose, and Jonas pitched in to help the other young men move the benches out of the barn. Groups formed, clusters of girls who giggled together and cast quick glances toward the boys under the watchful eyes of the parents who hovered nearby. Jonas's own *mader* stood near the doorway, ladling out apple cider. He avoided her and sidled toward a corner of the barn where a pair of his friends stood.

Melvin welcomed him with a playful elbow in the ribs. "Our Jonas has hopes for the evening. He borrowed my *fader*'s buggy."

Jonas's face warmed when Eli Shrock fixed a knowing gaze on him. There was only one reason for a young man to beg use of a buggy on the evening of a singing.

"Who's the girl?" asked Eli with a grin. "Mary Litwiller, perhaps? I saw you eyeing her in church last week."

"I did not," Jonas replied with some heat. He had not realized his actions had drawn notice, though misinterpreted. Mary had been seated beside Caroline.

"'Tis a *gut* thing." Eli lowered his voice. "I heard that Jacob Burkholder hopes to take Mary home this evening."

Jonas scanned the group until he caught sight of Jacob, who stood in close conversation with three others near the food table. He kept glancing across the room with quick, jerky motions, looking nervous as a cat. The only time a young man could be alone with a girl was if she agreed to let him take her home after a singing. The subject of who carried whom home was noted and widely discussed for weeks.

"Matthew Kennel has his *fader*'s buggy tonight as well." Melvin's eyebrows arched as he leaned forward and spoke in a lowered voice. "I heard he plans to ask Caroline Hersberger."

A rocklike lump landed with force in the pit of Jonas's stomach. For a moment the room wavered. He jerked his head around, trying to locate Matthew. There. Standing near the door and speaking intently with John Miller. Was Matthew even now giving John instructions to approach Caroline on his behalf? There was no time to lose.

He turned back to his friends, his throat suddenly tight. If only he could approach Caroline himself, but that was not the way things were done. A friend must speak to her for him. No doubt it was better that way, for he might fumble his words when face-to-face with a lovely girl like her. But that meant confessing his feelings to his friends and risk their teasing from this point forward.

"I...I..." His voice failed. The pair looked at him curiously. He swallowed and tried again. "Would one of you speak for me?"

"Speak to who?" asked Eli.

"To...Caroline." To his embarrassment, her name came out barely more than in a whisper.

"You wish to take Caroline home?" Amusement colored Eli's voice, and he landed a hearty slap on Jonas's back. "What a surprise this is."

A smile tweaked Melvin's lips. "Not to me. I have seen you gazing after her like a love-struck puppy."

Normally Jonas would have reacted to his jibe, but just then John turned away from Matthew and began making his way across the barn. He was headed directly toward Caroline.

Jonas grabbed Melvin by the arm. "You must hurry. Ask her for me."

He gave a shove, and Melvin nearly stumbled. He righted himself and, with an indulgent smile, straightened his coat before striding across the floor with a long-legged gait. Sweat broke out on Jonas's upper lip as he watched Melvin and John arrive at the same time. Caroline stopped talking to her friends and turned polite attention on them. John spoke first, and disappointment sank into Jonas's stomach. But before she answered him, Melvin spoke. His hands gestured in the air. A moment later Caroline's head rose. A jolt shot through Jonas when her gaze met his across the distance. What answer lay in those lovely eyes?

Melvin returned with a swagger in his step. "Thanks entirely to my persuasiveness, she accepted you."

Eli chortled and gave him a congratulatory shove.

"She did?" A curious sensation set a ringing loose in Jonas's ears.

"It was a close thing. She seemed favorable to Matthew at first, but when I explained how you have been pining after her for weeks, and if she refused she would be accountable for your death when you wasted away from sorrow, she changed her mind."

For one horrified moment Jonas thought his friend was serious. Then he caught sight of Melvin's grin.

"I merely explained that you had gone to pains to borrow the buggy and stow quilts inside to protect against the chill." He lowered his head and speared Jonas with a look. "You have quilts?"

Jonas nodded. "*Ja.*"

"*Das gut.*" Melvin leaned forward and spoke with a smile. "I believe she favors you, my friend."

Jonas risked another glance. Caroline caught his eye. At her smile, his head went light.

"Are you warm enough?" Jonas kept his head facing forward, pleased that his voice betrayed none of the nervousness that caused his insides to tremble.

"Plenty warm." From the corner of his eye he watched her run a hand over the quilt that covered her lap. "'Tis a beauteous work. Your *mader's*?"

"*Ja.*"

"I like quilting. I find my mind is peaceful when my fingers are busy." Still stroking the fabric, she fell silent.

The moon illuminated the packed-dirt road they followed with a steady white light, a million stars lending their glow to overcome the blackness of the sky. The air held a touch of chill left over from the winter just past, turning their breath into puffs of cloud that dissipated almost instantly.

Jonas cast about in his mind for something to say. Long had he hoped for time alone with Caroline, but now that he was here with her, his tongue felt awkward.

The silence threatened to become uncomfortable. He burst out with the first thing his mind grasped on. "I begin the classes next week."

He had made the decision over the winter to complete the training that would prepare him for baptism into the Amish church. The classes would be held on church Sundays over the next four and a half months. By fall he would be ready to make the commitment to a peaceful and Plain life as dictated by the teachings of Christ and the *Ordnung*.

Caroline shifted on the bench to turn a smile on him. "I begin the classes next week as well. Come fall, we will be baptized together, Jonas."

A pleasant thought, and especially because it seemed to please her. Jonas sat a little taller.

"What will you do after?" she asked. "Will you continue to help Mr. Byler on his farm?"

"*Neh,*" Jonas said quickly, unwilling to have her think he had no ambition to be more than a farmhand. He smiled to soften the hastiness of his reply. "I have plans for a farm of my own. I'm *gut* with the land and with livestock as well." He snapped his mouth shut. Did his words sound boastful?

"I know you are, Jonas."

She spoke in a soft, almost admiring tone that set his pulse to racing. He risked a sideways glance at her. The look she fixed on him held a hint of the warmth he'd hoped for. Her gaze stirred courage in him, and he made a decision. Before he could change his mind, he pulled on the reins and brought the buggy to a halt. Surprise showed on her face, but she didn't object.

Jonas turned so that he could face her fully. "May I tell you of my plans, Caroline?"

"I would like to hear them," came her soft reply.

"One day I will leave Ohio." When her eyebrows arched in surprise, he hurried to continue. "Last fall an *Englisch* man on his way home to Boston stayed with us overnight. He told us of a law that will someday be made where farms in the West will be free for the claiming."

"Free?" Doubt colored her words.

Jonas nodded. "Truly. The West is vast, miles and miles long. Many *Englisch* men have already gone, and there have been fights over the boundaries." Her eyebrows crept upward, and Jonas shrugged. "It is their way. But the *Englisch* government wants to put an end to the disputes by regulating the way land is claimed. They will make a law that allows a man to build a home and farm first, and then pay afterward when the land becomes profitable."

"And you believe this *Englischer*'s words?"

"I hope his words are true. I pray they are so."

Though doubt creased her forehead, Jonas glimpsed a spark of excitement in her eyes. Encouraged, he leaned forward. "Imagine, Caroline. A new Amish district could be established. We could own the farm that lies farthest to the west of any in the whole country."

"We?"

Jonas looked away, heat flooding his face. Did he say "we"? The word had slipped out unguarded on a wave of enthusiasm. He fumbled for a quick explanation. "The...the new community, I mean."

While he willed the chilly night air to cool his burning cheeks, her fingers plucked at a loose stitch on the quilt covering her lap. "On occasion I have thought of leaving Ohio myself," she said in an offhand voice.

He widened his eyes. "You?"

"*Ja*." Her lips twitched with almost a smile. "My plans are not so lofty as yours. I thought of joining my *mader*'s family in Pennsylvania, perhaps. My Aunt Emma has written that I am welcome."

Something in her manner, in the way an appealing dimple hovered in one smooth cheek, caused a tickle to start in Jonas's stomach. "Pennsylvania is a *gut* place, I hear."

Her eyes held his for a moment before sliding sideways shyly. "But already crowded with Amish. Or so my Aunt Emma writes."

He leaped on that. "New farms may be harder to come by, and not so big. Whereas in the West..."

"The West does have a lot to offer," she conceded. White teeth appeared to nibble at her lower lip. "Especially if you go there, Jonas."

Were his ears betraying him? Had Caroline Hersberger, the prettiest girl in all of Ohio, just expressed an interested in *him*?

Daring greatly, he reached out and took the hand that rested on the quilt. When she entwined her fingers in his, the tickle in Jonas's stomach expanded to his chest.

"It would not be an easy life. The challenges will be many, and the work hard."

Her head tilted sideways as she considered. "My *grossmudder* has a saying. Silver only shines with hard work." Soft lips twitched again with humor. "Nobody wants dull silver."

His thoughts whirling, Jonas could hardly believe his good fortune. Though he had never known Caroline to be coy, surely she was toying with him now. He had to be sure, had to hear the words spoken from her lips. "Are you saying...Do you mean you would consider..." He cleared his throat. "You will help me start a farm in the West?"

A soft chuckle, and then she answered in a playful tone. "Is that a proposal of marriage or an offer of employment?"

Emboldened by her teasing manner, Jonas squared his shoulders. From childhood had he loved Caroline. There would never be another woman for him, not ever. Though he had not planned to voice his intentions tonight, his heart was full to the bursting point. With a certainty that could not be doubted, he knew this moment had been created by *Gott* alone.

He enfolded her hand in a warm cocoon between both of his. "Caroline Hersberger, it would be the honor of my life if you will agree to be my wife."

Above him the stars seemed to burn brighter in the sky and cast their twinkling light to reflect in Caroline's eyes. Eyes that softened as they gazed at him. "*Ja*, Jonas Switzer. I will."

Joy broke over him, and he could not stop a smile from stretching across his face. "You will not be sorry." He made his words a vow. "The life we build together will be *gut*. I promise it will be a *gut* life! We will have sons—many strong strapping sons to work the land and build their heritage."

"And perhaps daughters?"

"*Ja*—perhaps," he agreed. "But sons for certain!"

She raised a hand and placed it against his clean-shaven cheek. After they married he would grow a beard in the tradition of the Amish, but for now he reveled in the soft touch of her fingers on his skin. "I will raise your sons and daughters and make you a happy home, Jonas." Her grin broke free, and she turned the full force of it upon him. "A home in the West."

With slow, deliberate movements, Jonas leaned toward her. How often had he dreamed of this moment, when he could take Caroline in his arms and declare his love? Delicate eyelids closed as she lifted her face to his. Their lips touched, and a prayer of thanksgiving welled up from his overflowing heart.

Danki, Gott. *Danki for my Caroline.*

- *Exclusive Book Previews*
- *Authentic Amish Recipes*
- *Q & A with Your Favorite Authors*
- *Free Downloads*
- *Author Interviews & Extras*

*A*MISHREADER.COM

FOLLOW US:

facebook twitter

Visit **AmishReader.com** today
and download your free copy of

LEFT HOMELESS

a short story by Jerry Eicher

To learn more about Harvest House books and
to read sample chapters, log on to our website:

www.harvesthousepublishers.com

HARVEST HOUSE PUBLISHERS
EUGENE, OREGON